LASSOED
in
Texas

MARY CONNEALY

Gingham
Mountain

BARBOUR
PUBLISHING

Other books by Mary Connealy

Lassoed in Texas series:
Petticoat Ranch
Calico Canyon

Alaska Brides (a romance collection)

Published by Barbour Publishing, Inc., P.O. Box 719, Uhrichsville, Ohio 44683
www.barbourbooks.com

Our mission is to publish and distribute inspirational products offering exceptional value and biblical encouragement to the masses.

 Member of the
Evangelical Christian
Publishers Association

Printed in the United States of America.

Gingham Mountain is dedicated to my mom, Dorothy Moore. She and my father, Jack Moore, raised me and seven other children in a two-bedroom home. I love all my brothers and sisters (Ruth, Nila, Don, Lois, Dwight, Linda, and Jackson Jr.) and am proud to be related to them.

Two bedrooms was a bit of an exaggeration though. It was actually a *one-bedroom* home with a fold-out couch in the dining room. When my sixth sibling, Dwight, was born, my parents added on to our house—but they also quit using the teeny attic as a bedroom until Don moved up there a few years later. So the *almost* two-bedroom home became a (brace yourself for the excitement) *three-bedroom* home.

Though we lacked in material things, we never lacked in love. My mother's greatest gifts were her beautiful ability to love us and the gracious life of faith she lived in God.

"Pure religion and undefiled before God and the Father is this, to visit the fatherless and widows in their affliction, and to keep himself unspotted from the world."
JAMES 1:27

ONE

Sour Springs, Texas, 1870

Martha had an iron rod where most people had a backbone.

Grant smiled as he pulled his team to a stop in front of the train station in Sour Springs, Texas.

She also had a heart of gold—even if the old bat wouldn't admit it. She was going to be thrilled to see him and scold him the whole time.

"It's time to get back on the train." Martha Norris, ever the disciplinarian, had a voice that could back down a starving Texas wildcat, let alone a bunch of orphaned kids. It carried all the way across the street as Grant jumped from his wagon and trotted toward the depot. He'd almost missed them. He could see the worry on Martha's face.

Wound up tight from rushing to town, Grant knew he was late. But now that he was here, he relaxed. It took all of his willpower not to laugh at Martha, the old softy.

He hurried toward them. If it had only been Martha he would have laughed, but there was nothing funny about the two children with her. They were leftovers.

A little girl, shivering in the biting cold, her thin shoulders hunched against the wind, turned back toward the train. Martha, her shoulders slumped with sadness at what lay ahead for these children, rested one

7

of her competent hands on the child's back.

Grant noticed the girl limping. That explained why she hadn't been adopted. No one wanted a handicapped child. As if limping put a child so far outside of normal she didn't need love and a home. Controlling the slow burn in his gut, Grant saw the engineer top off the train's water tank. They'd be pulling out of the station in a matter of minutes.

"Isn't this the last stop, Mrs. Norris?" A blond-headed boy stood, stony-faced, angry, scared.

"Yes, Charlie, it is."

His new son's name was Charlie. Grant picked up his pace.

Martha sighed. "We don't have any more meetings planned."

"So, we have to go back to New York?" Charlie, shivering and thin but hardy compared to the girl, scowled as he stood on the snow-covered platform, six feet of wood separating the train from the station house.

Grant had never heard such a defeated question.

The little girl's chin dropped and her shoulders trembled.

What was he thinking? He heard defeat from unwanted children all the time.

Charlie slipped his threadbare coat off his shoulders even though the wind cut like a knife through Grant's worn-out buckskin jacket.

Grant's throat threatened to swell shut with tears as he watched that boy sacrifice the bit of warmth he got from that old coat.

Stepping behind Martha, Charlie wrapped his coat around the girl. She shuddered and practically burrowed into the coat as if it held the heat of a fireplace, even as she shook her head and frowned at Charlie.

"Just take the stupid thing." Charlie glared at the girl.

After studying him a long moment, the little girl, her eyes wide and sad, kept the coat.

Mrs. Norris stayed his hands. "That's very generous, Charlie, but you can't go without a coat."

"I don't want it. I'm gonna throw it under the train if she don't keep it." The boy's voice was sharp and combative. A bad attitude. That could keep a boy from finding a home.

Grant hurried faster across the frozen ruts of Sour Springs Main Street toward the train platform and almost made it. A tight grip on his arm stopped him. Surprised, he turned and saw that irksome woman who'd been hounding him ever since she'd moved to town. What was her name? Grant'd made a point of not paying attention to her. She usually yammered about having his shirts sewn in her shop.

"Grant, it's so nice to see you."

It took all his considerable patience to not jerk free. Shirt Lady was unusually tall, slender, and no one could deny she was pretty, but she had a grip like a mule skinner, and Grant was afraid he'd have a fight on his hands to get his arm back.

Grant touched the brim of his battered Stetson with his free hand. "Howdy, Miss. I'm afraid I'm in a hurry today."

A movement caught his eye, and he turned to look at his wagon across the street. Through the whipping wind he could see little, but Grant was sure someone had come alongside his wagon. He wished it were true so he could palm this persistent pest off on an unsuspecting neighbor.

Shirt Lady's grip tightened until it almost hurt through his coat. She leaned close, far closer than was proper to Grant's way of thinking.

"Why don't you come over to my place and warm yourself before you head back to the ranch. I've made pie, and it's a lonely kind of day." She fluttered her lashes until Grant worried she'd gotten dirt in her eye. He considered sending her to Doc Morgan for medical care.

The train chugged and reminded Grant he was almost out of time. "Can't stop now, miss." What *was* her name? How many times had she spoken to him? A dozen if it was three. "There are some orphans left on the platform, and they need a home. I've got to see to 'em."

Something flashed in her eyes for a second before she controlled it. He knew that look. She didn't like orphans. Well, then what was she doing talking to him? He came with a passel of 'em. Grant shook himself free.

"We'll talk another time then."

Sorely afraid they would, Grant tugged on his hat brim again and ran. His boots echoed on the depot stairs. He reached the top step just as Martha turned to the sound of his clomping. She was listening for him even when she shouldn't be.

Grant couldn't stand the sight of the boy's thin shoulders covered only by the coarse fabric of his dirty brown shirt. Grant pulled his gloves off, noticing as he did that the tips of his fingers showed through holes in all ten fingers.

"I'll take 'em, Martha." How was he supposed to live with himself if he didn't? Grant's spurs clinked as he came forward. He realized in his dash to get to town he'd worn his spurs even though he brought the buckboard. Filthy from working the cattle all morning, most of his hair had fallen loose from the thong he used to tie it back. More than likely he smelled like his horse. A razor hadn't touched his face since last Sunday morning.

Never one to spend money on himself when his young'uns had needs—or might at any time—his coat hung in tatters, and his woolen union suit showed through a rip in his knee.

Martha ran her eyes up and down him and shook her head, suppressing a smile. "Grant, you look a fright."

A slender young woman rose to her feet from where she sat at the depot. Her movements drew Grant's eyes away from the forlorn children. From the look of the snow piling up on the young woman's head, she'd been sitting here in the cold ever since the train had pulled in, which would have been the better part of an hour ago. She must have expected someone to meet her, but no one had.

When she stepped toward him, Grant spared her a longer glance because she was a pretty little thing, even though her dark brown hair hung in bedraggled strings from beneath her black bonnet and twisted into tangled curls around her chin. Her face was so dirty the blue of her eyes shined almost like the heart of a flame in a sooty lantern.

Grant stared at her for a moment. He recognized something in her eyes. If she'd been a child and looked at him with those eyes, he'd have taken her home and raised her.

Then the children drew his attention away from the tired, young lady.

Martha Norris shook her head. "You can't handle any more, Grant. We'll find someone, I promise. I won't quit until I do."

"I know that's the honest truth." Grant knew Martha had to protest; good sense dictated it. But she'd hand the young'uns over. "And God bless you for it. But this is the end of the line for the orphan train. You can't do anything until you get back to New York. I'm not going to let these children take that ride."

"Actually, Libby joined us after we'd left New York. It was a little irregular, but it's obvious the child needs a home." Martha kept looking at him, shaking her head.

"Irregular how?" He tucked his tattered gloves behind his belt buckle.

"She stowed away." Martha glanced at Libby. "It was the strangest thing. I never go back to the baggage car, but one of the children tore a hole in his pants. My sewing kit is always in the satchel I carry with me. I was sure I had it, but it was nowhere to be found. So I knew I'd most likely left it with my baggage. I went back to fetch it so I could mend the seam and found her hiding in amongst the trunks."

Grant was reaching for the buttons on his coat, but he froze. "Are you sure she isn't running away from home?" His stomach twisted when he thought of a couple of his children who had run off over the years. He'd been in a panic until he'd found them. "She might have parents somewhere, worried to death about her."

"She had a note in her pocket explaining everything. I feel certain she's an orphan. And I don't know how long she was back there. She could have been riding with us across several states. I sent telegraphs to every station immediately, and I'm planning on leaving a note at each stop on my way back, but I hold out no hope that a family is searching for her." Martha sighed as if she wanted to fall asleep on her feet.

Grant realized it wasn't just the children who had a long ride ahead of them. One corner of Grant's lips turned up. "Quit looking at me like that, Martha, or I'll be thinking I have to adopt you so *you* don't have to face the trip."

Martha, fifty if she was a day, laughed. "I ought to take you up on that. You need someone to come out there and take your ranch in hand. Without a wife, who's going to cook for all these children?"

"You've been out. You know how we run things. Everybody chips in." The snow was getting heavier, and the wind blew a large helping of it down Grant's neck. Grant ignored the cold in the manner of men who fought the elements for their living and won. He went back to unbuttoning his coat, then shrugged it off and dropped it on the boy's shoulders. It hung most of the way to the ground.

Charlie tried to give the coat back. "I don't want your coat, mister."

Taking a long look at Charlie's defiant expression, Grant fairly growled. "Keep it."

Charlie held his gaze for a moment before he looked away. "Thank you."

Grant gave his Stetson a quick dip to salute the boy's manners. Snow sprang into the air as the brim of his hat snapped down and up. He watched it be swept up and around by the whipping wind then filter down around his face, becoming part of the blizzard that was getting stronger and meaner every moment.

Martha nodded. "If they limited the number of children one man could take, you'd be over it for sure."

Grant controlled a shudder of cold as he pulled on his gloves. "Well, thank heavens there's no limit. The oldest boy and the two older girls are just a year or so away from being out on their own. One of them's even got a beau. I really need three more to take their places, but I'll settle for two."

Martha looked from one exhausted, filthy child to the other then looked back at Grant. "The ride back would be terribly hard on them."

Grant crouched down in front of the children, sorry for the clink of his spurs that had a harsh sound and might frighten the little girl. Hoping his smile softened his grizzled appearance enough to keep the little girl from running scared, he said, "Well, what kind of man would I be if I stood by watching while something was terribly hard on you two? How'd you like to come out and live on my ranch? I've got other kids there, and you'll fit right in to our family."

"They're *not* going to fit, Grant," Martha pointed out through chattering teeth. "Your house is overflowing now."

Grant had to admit she was right. "What difference does it make if we're a little crowded, Martha? We'll find room."

The engineer swung out on the top step of the nearest car, hanging onto a handle in the open door of the huffing locomotive. "All aboard!"

The little girl looked fearfully between the train and Grant.

Looking at the way the little girl clung to Martha's hand, Grant knew she didn't want to go off with a strange man almost as much as she didn't want to get back on that train.

"I'll go with you." The little boy narrowed his eyes as he moved to stand like a cranky guardian angel beside the girl.

Grant saw no hesitation in the scowling little boy, only concern for the girl. No fear. No second thoughts. He didn't even look tired compared to the girl and Martha. He had intelligent blue eyes with the slyness a lot of orphans had. Not every child he'd adopted had made the adjustment without trouble. A lot of them took all of Grant's prayers and patience. Grant smiled to himself. He had an unlimited supply of prayers, and the prayers helped him hang onto the patience.

Grant shivered under the lash of the blowing snow.

The boy shrugged out of the coat. "Take your coat back. The cold don't bother me none."

Grant stood upright and gently tugged the huge garment back

around the boy's neck and began buttoning it. "The cold don't bother me none, neither. You'll make a good cowboy, son. We learn to keep going no matter what the weather." He wished he had another coat because the girl still looked miserable. Truth be told, he wouldn't have minded one for himself.

Martha leaned close to Grant's ear on the side away from the children. "Grant, you need to know that Libby hasn't spoken a word since we found her. There was a note in her pocket that said she's mute. She's got a limp, too. It looks to me like she had a badly broken ankle some years ago that didn't heal right. I'll understand if you—"

Grant pulled away from Martha's whispers as his eyebrows slammed together. Martha fell silent and gave him a faintly alarmed look. He tried to calm down before he spoke, matching her whisper. "You're not going to insult me by suggesting I'd leave a child behind because she has a few problems, are you?"

Martha studied him, and then her expression relaxed. Once more she whispered, "No, Grant. But you did need to be told. The only reason I know her name is because it was on the note. Libby pulled it out of her coat pocket as if she'd done it a thousand times, so chances are this isn't a new problem, which probably means it's permanent."

Grant nodded his head with one taut jerk. "Obliged for the information then. Sorry I got testy." Grant did his best to make it sound sincere, but it hurt, cut him right to the quick, for Martha to say such a thing to him after all these years.

"No, I'm sorry I doubted you." Martha rested one hand on his upper arm. "I shouldn't have, not even for a second."

Martha eased back and spoke normally again. "We think Libby's around six." She swung Libby's little hand back and forth, giving the girl an encouraging smile.

All Grant's temper melted away as he looked at the child. "Hello, Libby." Crouching back down to the little girl's eye level, he gave the shivering tyke all of his attention.

Too tiny for six and too thin for any age, she had long dark hair caught in a single bedraggled braid and blue eyes awash in fear and wishes. Her nose and cheeks were chapped and red. Her lips trembled. Grant hoped it was from the cold and not from looking at the nasty man who wanted to take her away.

"I think you'll like living on my ranch. I've got the biggest backyard to play in you ever saw. Why, the Rocking C has a mountain rising right up out of the back door. You can collect eggs from the chickens. I've got some other kids and they'll be your brothers and sisters, and we've got horses you can ride."

Libby's eyes widened with interest, but she never spoke. Well, he'd had 'em shy before.

"I can see you'll like that. I'll start giving you riding lessons as soon as the snow lets up." Grant ran his hand over his grizzled face. "I should have shaved and made myself more presentable for you young'uns. I reckon I'm a scary sight. But the cattle were acting up this morning. There's a storm coming, and it makes 'em skittish. By the time I could get away, I was afraid I'd miss the train."

Grant took Libby's little hand, careful not to move suddenly and frighten her, and rubbed her fingers on his whiskery face.

She snatched her hand away, but she grinned.

The smile transformed Libby's face. She had eyes that had seen too much and square shoulders that had borne a lifetime of trouble. Grant vowed to himself that he'd devote himself to making her smile.

"I'll shave it off before I give you your first good night kiss."

The smile faded, and Libby looked at him with such longing Grant's heart turned over with a father's love for his new daughter. She'd gotten to him even faster than they usually did.

Martha reached past Libby to rest her hand on the boy's shoulder. "And Charlie is eleven."

Grant pivoted a bit on his toes and looked at Charlie again. A good-looking boy, but so skinny he looked like he'd blow over in a hard wind. Grant could fix that. The boy had flyaway blond hair that needed a wash and a trim. It was the hostility in his eyes that explained why he hadn't found a home. Grant had seen that look before many times, including in a mirror.

As if he spoke to another man, Grant said, "Charlie, welcome to the family."

Charlie shrugged as if being adopted meant nothing to him. "Are we supposed to call you pa?"

"That'd be just fine." Grant looked back at the little girl. "Does that suit you, Libby?"

Libby didn't take her lonesome eyes off Grant, but she pressed herself against Martha's leg as if she wanted to disappear into Martha's long wool coat.

The engineer shouted, "All aboard!" The train whistle sounded. A blast of steam shot across the platform a few feet ahead of them.

Libby jumped and let out a little squeak of surprise. Grant noted that the little girl's voice worked, so most likely she didn't talk for reasons of her own, not because of an injury. He wondered if she'd seen something so terrible she couldn't bear to speak of it.

The boy reached his hand out for Libby. "We've been together for a long time, Libby. We can go together to the ranch. I'll take care of you."

Libby looked at Charlie as if he were a knight in shining armor. After some hesitation, she released her death grip on Martha and caught Charlie's hand with both of hers.

"Did I hear you correctly?" A sharp voice asked from over Grant's shoulder. "Are you allowing this man to adopt these children?"

Startled, Grant stood, turned, and bumped against a soft, cranky woman. He almost knocked her onto her backside—the lady who'd been waiting at the depot. He grabbed her or she'd have fallen on the slippery wood. Grant steadied her, warm and alive in his hands.

TWO

"Excuse me." He said it even though it was all her fault he bumped into her. She'd obviously been eavesdropping. He'd thought she was pretty before. Now she just looked snippy.

The woman looked past Grant like he was dirt under her feet and said to Martha, "You can't put these children into a home without a mother."

"Don't worry, Miss...Miss..." Martha came to stand like a bulwark beside Grant.

He appreciated her siding with him, especially when common sense would tell anyone that, in the normal course of things, this busybody was right.

"I'm Hannah...uh...Cartwright. Surely there are laws against a man simply sweeping up children to take them home for laborers. If there aren't, there should be."

"Laborers?" Grant went from annoyed to furious in one fell swoop.

He had the sudden desire to wipe the superior expression off Hannah Cartwright's face. "This isn't any business of yours."

"Now, Miss Cartwright, that's not—"

The train whistle blasted again, drowning out Martha's words even though her lips kept moving.

"It's very much my business if children are being exploited."

"Exploited?" Grant erupted, but then he caught hold of his temper.

He didn't calm down for the prissy female. He did it for the children. They didn't need to start out their life watching their new pa throw a pitched fit at a young woman, no matter how bad-mannered and misinformed that woman might be.

With exaggerated politeness, he said, "You don't know what you're talking about, so I'll forgive your rudeness."

He turned to Libby and Charlie. "Let's go. We need to get back to the ranch in time for the noon meal."

Libby backed away from him a step and peeked up at the nagging woman behind him. Out of the corner of his eye he saw Miss Priss take a step forward—to keep an eagle eye on him, no doubt.

"Why don't the children stay with me until we can find a suitable home for them?" Her voice had a nice quality to it, all smooth and sweet. At the same time, it rubbed on him like a rasp, burning him until he felt all raw and tender inside. He wished for just one second she'd use it for something besides giving him a hard time.

"Oh no, that would never do," Martha said. "We can't let an unmarried woman have a child. That's out of the question."

"Why is it out of the question for a single woman but not a single man?"

Grant glanced over his shoulder. "You really want to adopt these children?"

Dismay crossed Miss Cartwright's face, as if she'd spoken without thinking. Grant decided the look was fear that she'd be saddled with two kids when all she wanted was to be a troublemaker.

"Well, a single man probably would be out of the question most of the time," Martha said in her brisk, stern voice that concealed a heart as big as Texas. "I know orphanages sometimes place their children with bachelors or spinsters, but I've never approved of it. Children need a family, a mother and a father. Grant is a special case. We make an exception for him."

The pest pushed past Grant to face Martha directly. "Mrs. Norris, you know I've been on the train with you for a while now. I've taken a liking to the children. I don't want them. . .that is. . .can't they. . ." The lady frowned at Martha, her blue eyes shining in the swirling snow, her dirty face going pink under the grime. "Can I at least talk to the children before you decide? I want to make sure they really want to go with him. They might be so tired from the train that they're desperate. And they might still find families elsewhere if we—"

"Miss Cartwright, please," Martha cut her off. "This is the last town we have appointments in. No, if they don't find a home at this stop, Charlie and Libby will have to ride all the way back to New York. The children will be better off with Grant."

Grant and Martha exchanged a look. He reached for the children's hands and felt a small but firm grip on his arm. Exasperated, he wheeled around and faced Miss Cartwright.

"I'm not allowing you to leave with these children. I know how this works. You take them out to your ranch, virtually stack them in inadequate space, and press them into being little more than slaves. I'm not going to allow—"

Libby made a little sound that sounded like pure fear. She started crying, dry sobs escaping her otherwise silent lips. She hurled herself into Charlie's arms, and Charlie staggered backward a step but held on and looked angry, his eyes darting between Grant and Miss Cartwright.

Grant gave Miss Cartwright a furious look, which she returned in full measure, shooting flaming arrows from her blue eyes that liked to stab him to death on the spot.

The whistle blasted and the train began inching out of the station.

Grant turned away from the nag, feeling like a spinning top going round and round from Martha to Hannah to the children. Speaking louder to be heard over the chugging engine, he said, "Hurry up, Martha. You're going to miss your train."

"Grant, I don't want to leave this woman with the impression that—"

Grant caught Martha's arm and firmly guided her to the platform, leaving the children and the irritating meddler behind. "If you miss your train there won't be another one along for days. You've no doubt got appointments scheduled for the return trip and you'll have to cancel them. We'll be fine. I'll handle that little pest back there."

Martha smiled at him through the soot on her face. "Now Grant, be nice."

"Nice?" Grant yelled as the train started moving faster. "I'll be nicer'n she deserves."

Martha quit protesting and hurried toward the nearest car. She jumped on board like the seasoned traveler she was and turned to yell over her shoulder. "I'll send the paperwork for the adoptions through the mail just like always."

Grant waved good-bye and turned to see Miss Cartwright fuming. He wondered how mad she had to be before she'd melt all that snow off her bonnet. Her temper didn't bother him much. What upset him was Libby's fear as she clung to Charlie.

Grant strode over to the children and, ignoring the cranky little woman who stood there looking at him like he was 180 pounds of stinking polecat, he hunkered down again. With a gentle chuck under Libby's chin, he said, "Don't worry about what she said about slaves. She is shaping up to be a very silly woman who doesn't know what she's talking about. My home is a nice place."

"Mr. Grant"—Hannah's hand closed on his shoulder so tight he wished for his coat back for protection from her fingernails—"how dare you call me names?"

Grant stood up, stretching to his full six feet as he turned, making it a point to look down on her. "You call me a slave owner."

Trying to keep his voice down so the children couldn't hear every word, he narrowed his eyes at her and spoke through his clenched teeth. "You frighten these innocent children who are already going through such a tough time."

He leaned closer. "You insult me with every word that comes out of your mouth." Their noses almost touched. "And then you have the nerve to take offense when *I call you silly?*"

With a snort he didn't even try to make sound friendly, he said, "I'd think, tossing out insults the way you do, you'd have grown a hide as thick as a buffalo by now." He leaned even closer. "I'd think you'd've been called silly a thousand times in your life and be used to it."

He spoke through gritted teeth. "I'd think the only single, solitary chance you have of getting through a day without someone calling you silly is if the world plumb goes and turns flat and the rest of us fall off the edge."

Grant glared at her for a long moment. She glared right back. He had one tiny flash of admiration for her guts. She might insult the stuffing out of him, but she didn't back down when she thought she was right. Too bad she was wrong.

Sick of the staring match, he turned back to the children. "You'll have some chores to do, but there'll be a lot of time for fun."

Libby stared at him. The only sound she made was her teeth chattering.

Grant saw the hurt in the little girl. He knew having a mother was the dearest dream of every orphaned child's heart. A father came in a poor second. But a poor second still beat having nothing, which was what Libby had now. He rested a hand on her too-thin arm and answered the question he knew she wanted to ask. "No, little one, there's no ma. But I've got a couple of nearly grown daughters who will love you like you were their very own. I think you'll like 'em."

Libby watched him in silence for a moment then stared forlornly after the rapidly disappearing train. She looked at Miss Cartwright again, and Grant decided the two must have struck up a friendship on the trip because so much passed between them with that look. At last Libby squared her tiny shoulders, as he could tell she'd done a thousand times before in a life that didn't offer much good news.

That was the best Grant could hope for—for now.

"Mr. Grant," Hannah repeated.

He stood. He needed a few more moments to reassure the boy, but he had to get this nagging woman off his back. "What is it, Hannah?"

"Well, first of all"—her eyes flashed like summer lightning—"it's Miss Cartwright to you."

Grant noticed they were very pretty blue eyes. Too bad they were attached to a snippy woman who seemed bent on freezing him to death or nagging him to death, whichever came last, because he had no doubt, if he froze here, solid in his boots, Hannah would go on snipping at him long after he'd turned to an icicle.

Grant crossed his arms over his chest. He knew it made him look stubborn, which he wasn't. He was a reasonable man. But the truth was he was cold. He tried to look casual about it. Charlie hadn't wanted to take his coat in the first place. It wasn't right to suffer visibly right in front of the boy. "All right, Miss Cartwright, what awful thing do you want to accuse me of now?"

Hannah seemed prepared to launch into a list of his shortcomings. Grant braced himself for a blizzard of cold, critical words to go with the weather.

Libby tugged on Grant's arm. He turned to her and waited to see what she wanted to tell him. All she did was tug and squirm around, doing a little dance Grant had seen thousands of times before.

Bending close to her, he whispered, "There's an outhouse behind the depot. Let's go. Then we'll head on out to the ranch and get you two out of this cold weather."

Libby nodded frantically and hopped around a bit.

"Come on, Charlie." Grant swooped Libby up in his arms.

"Now wait just a minute, Mr. Grant." Hannah jammed her fists onto her waist.

Grant noticed she wasn't wearing gloves and her teeth were chattering from the cold, just like Libby's. She was skin and bones, too, and her coat was worn paper thin. He had a moment of compassion for the little pest. She didn't deserve the compassion, but Grant knew she had to be suffering.

Libby looked back at Hannah.

Deciding he was right about Libby and her friendship with Hannah, Grant, spurs clinking, headed for the edge of the platform. He glanced over his shoulder. "It isn't *Mr.* Grant. It's just Grant."

"Well, what *is* your last name?" The woman kept nagging even as he left her behind.

Grant wondered who was supposed to come get her. "I don't have a last name."

"No last name?" She seemed frozen with shock, but Grant considered the possibility that she was actually frozen. The temperature was dropping as fast as the snow.

Grant and the children started down the clattering wooden steps of the train station. "Libby, what's your last name?"

Libby shrugged then clung to his shoulders as they bounced down the stairs.

"Charlie, what's yours?"

"I don't have one." Charlie waved good-bye to Hannah.

"Me neither." Grant glanced back at Hannah as he got to the ground. "It's just one of the facts of being an orphan, often as not. I did finally get adopted when I was almost grown, but after my folks died, I decided I'd live my life without one so I'd never forget what it feels like to need a family. I don't expect you to understand, Hannah Cartwright. No one can who isn't an orphan."

He jerked his chin down in a terse nod at Hannah that said good-bye more clearly than words. He disappeared around the corner, leaving her with her mouth hanging open.

THREE

It cut like a razor to be left standing in the bitter January cold wondering what her last name might be.

The wind whipped Hannah, lashing her like Parrish's belt. She understood exactly what it felt like to be an orphan. And she knew exactly what Libby and Charlie faced now that they'd fallen into Grant's clutches. Fists clenched, she wanted to scream at the unfairness that forced her and Libby to pretend that they didn't know each other. They were sisters, of the heart if not the flesh. They belonged together.

Hannah stared into the cruel blizzard winds, fighting tears that would only freeze on her cheeks if she let them fall. Libby—she had to save Libby. She'd never considered the possibility that Libby would be adopted. No family stepped forward to accept a child who wasn't perfect.

No one had wanted her in Omaha when they'd stowed away on the orphan train the first time. Of course no one would want her now. So why had that awful man taken her?

Had Libby limped in front of Grant? Libby had walked off the train, so of course she'd limped. But he hadn't been here yet. Maybe he hadn't noticed. Or maybe the work he had in mind for her might be done by a girl with one badly broken foot. Maybe, once he got her home, he'd realize what he'd done and throw her out, maybe this very night in the middle of a blizzard.

Libby had been thrown out before. She'd been around three, living in a Chicago alley, fighting the rats for bits of food, when one of the boys who made up Hannah's ragtag family had found her and brought her home to the abandoned shed they slept in.

Hannah and Libby had been sisters for nearly four years now, and Hannah had yet to hear Libby speak a word.

There were no limits to how cruel people could be. Someone had thrown Libby away as if she were trash. The scars on Hannah's back attested to the lengths to which her own adoptive father had gone to wrest obedience from his daughters.

The instant Grant knew Libby wasn't perfect he'd get rid of her. Throw her out or keep her for hard labor, starving and beating her. Either was a disaster for frail, little Libby.

She rushed after Grant, but she stopped, almost skidding off the slippery station platform. The snow slashed at her face and the wind howled around her as she tried to decide what to do.

Hannah had to stop Grant. But what could she do alone against him? It was more than obvious that he had no intention of letting her stop him. Making off with two more indentured servants put speed in his step.

She thought of how awful he looked, like an outlaw. Long stringy hair and a smell that Hannah thought belonged to an animal and not a man. Eyes flashing gold at her like a hungry eagle swooping down to snatch away youngsters and carry them off to his nest. Captivating eyes that sent a shiver through her when she thought of how they shined out of his grimy, whiskered face.

The shiver wasn't exactly fear though. It wasn't normal that she hadn't feared Grant. Her fearful reaction to men was something she'd been fighting all her life, at least since Parrish.

Her shoulders squared and she lifted her head as she remembered confronting Grant. Never for a moment had she considered cringing or dropping her eyes. Why wouldn't Grant have that effect on her, when he was so much like Parrish?

A feeling of power firmed her jaw. She'd been taking one daring chance after another in the last few years. Maybe she'd finally built herself a backbone.

She couldn't defeat him physically, but she and Grace had outsmarted Parrish. And Grant struck Hannah as none-too-bright. She'd have to outthink him.

She rushed back to her satchel. It held her and Libby's few possessions in the world. Then she marched herself straight across the wide Sour Springs street, stepped up on the boardwalk, and went into a building with the words STROBEN'S MERCANTILE painted on the front window.

Shuddering from the delicious warmth and the smell of food, she ignored her frozen fingertips and empty stomach and dodged around bolts of cloth and barrels of nails toward the whipcord lean woman standing behind the counter.

Another woman, unusually tall, painfully thin, and nearer Hannah's age, stood in the corner of the store feeling a bolt of cloth. She looked up when Hannah charged in, but Hannah barely spared a glance.

Pointing back toward the street, Hannah said, "A man just took two orphans off a train and is planning to take them home. He has no mother for them. I tried to stop him, but he ignored me. I need help. He said his name is Grant."

The shopper drew Hannah's attention when she jerked her head around. Setting the fabric down, she turned toward Hannah, opening her mouth as if to ask a question. Then her teeth clicked and she went back to browsing.

The lady behind the counter looked up from a scrap of paper in her hand and stopped in the middle of setting a jar of molasses into a wooden box. "Lord'a mercy, that Grant. Another two kids?" She started laughing, loud braying laughs that would have set a donkey's heart into an envious spin.

"It's not funny." A noise from the street snagged Hannah's attention and she spun around. Through the storefront window, she saw Grant driving out of town in a rattletrap wagon, with Libby barely visible, sitting squished between Grant and Charlie on the seat.

Hannah ran to the door just as Grant disappeared into the swirling snow. With a cry of anguish, she ran back to the lady in the back of the store. "He's leaving. We have to stop him."

"Harold." The lady turned away from Hannah and hollered into the back of the store, "Grant took two more kids out to the Rockin' C."

Laughter came from the back room.

Desperation making her furious, Hannah snapped, "If you won't help me then direct me to the sheriff."

Turning to Hannah with narrowed eyes, the storekeeper smoothed her neat gray braid, curled into a bun at the base of her skull. Her woolen dress was as faded as Hannah's and patched at the elbows, but the work was done with a skill Hannah admired. A couple of missing teeth, a beak of a nose, and round, wire-rimmed glasses gave the lady a no-nonsense appearance, and Hannah thought at first she'd made the woman angry.

Then the woman started laughing. "The sheriff don't have no call to go chase Grant down. Ned and Grant are friends. Ned's not going out in this storm just to meet two more of Grant's young'uns. Ah, Grant and that crowd of his. Just thinkin' of it fair tickles me to death."

Hannah turned to storm out of the store, aware that she'd done more storming around in the last few minutes than she'd done in her entire, meek life.

Before she could move another step, the woman asked, "Hey, who are you anyhow?"

Hannah stopped, not sure where she was storming to anyway. "I'm Hannah. . .Cartwright." She stumbled over the name she'd made up so she could get general delivery mail from Grace. She'd never used it much, avoiding people for the most part except for Libby, and Libby certainly never spoke Hannah's last name.

"What are you doing in Sour Springs?"

"I. . .I am. . ." Hannah drew a blank. There was one thing that was the truth. She was staying until she could save Libby and all the other children Grant had absconded with. And she couldn't afford to stay because she had no money. "I'm looking for work."

The storekeeper jumped as if she'd been poked with a hatpin. "Really, can you read and cipher? Because we need a new schoolteacher."

The storekeeper pointed a thumb at the other woman, now moved on from the dress goods to a stack of canned vegetables. "We offered Prudence the job, but she's come to town to take up as a seamstress. Not a lot of sewing around these parts. But she's bent on it, aren't you?"

Prudence nodded her head.

"It's a respectable enough business for a woman, I reckon, but you're apt to starve. Still, that's your business and no one else's."

Prudence's silent response reminded Hannah of Libby. She had to save Libby.

Hannah gave a friendly nod of hello to Prudence then opened her mouth to admit she'd never spent a day inside a classroom. She caught herself. That wasn't the question. "Yes, I can read and cipher."

"Harold," the storekeeper bellowed into the back of the building, "get out here."

A huge, unkempt man ambled out from the back room, wearing a union suit that might have been white years ago and a pair of brown broadcloth pants with the suspenders dangling at his sides.

"We got a young lady here, huntin' work. She'd make a fine school-marm, I'd say."

Wiping his hands on a dingy cloth as he plodded in, Harold said, "Great, we weren't going to be able to open up on Monday, since the last teacher ran off." He caught sight of Hannah and tilted his head to stare at her as if he was reading her mind, hunting for intelligence.

Hannah knew this might well be the only job in this tiny town. And she had to feed herself until she could get Libby back. "I have some experience teaching."

She didn't go into details—that she'd taught her little sisters after

Parrish went to bed at night. Then she'd taught the street children who had teamed up with her after she'd escaped Parrish's iron grip.

Harold headed for the front of the store. "I'll get the parson and Quincy Harrison. We can vote on it right now."

Harold grabbed his coat off a bent nail by the front door as he left the store, letting in a swirl of snow and frigid wind. He pulled the door closed firmly with a crack of wood and a rattle of its window.

Hannah turned to the storekeeper. "Uh. . .Mrs. . . .uh. . ."

"I'm Mabel Stroben and that's my husband Harold. Call me Mabel. Do you have a place to stay? A room goes with the job. It's the room above the diner."

Hannah had no place to stay and only a few coins left in her pocket. "A room would be wonderful."

"Great, then it's settled, all except getting you hired."

That sounded like a really big "except" to Hannah.

The door squeaked like a tormented soul when Harold came back. He shed his coat, dusting snow all over the room. Before he'd hung up his coat, a man wearing a parson's collar and another man, dressed a lot like Harold but half as wide, came in.

Mabel pointed at Hannah. "Here she is."

"Well, that's just fine. I'm Parson Babbitt." The parson turned kind eyes on Hannah. "Let's sit down here and have a nice chat."

There were chairs pulled up around a potbelly stove in the front corner of the store, opposite that lone shopper.

Hannah knew this wasn't going to work. She had no idea what being a teacher required. She was fairly certain she had the ability to teach, but she had no schooling or experience and she wasn't about to lie. She relaxed as she gave up this pipe dream. She'd only had a couple of minutes to consider the idea anyway. It's not like she had her heart set on it. She took a seat and folded her hands neatly in her lap.

Prudence was now leafing through a book of fairy tales.

Hannah had learned to be suspicious to stay alive, and she had the distinct impression the woman was eavesdropping. But why? Maybe she had children and wanted to know if there'd be a school. Except, no, Mabel said they'd offered Prudence the teaching job and no married woman would be allowed to work.

The parson settled on her left; the other man sat on her right. Harold perched his bulk on a chair on past the parson and. . .the chairs were gone. Mabel moved down the counter that stretched the length of the small store and leaned on it to listen.

"I'm Quincy Harrison. I'm president of the school board. The parson and Harold are the other board members."

"Hello, Mr. Harrison, Parson Babbitt." She smiled calmly, completely sure this farce would soon be over. Her insides were gnawed with worry over Libby, but she had no worry about getting hired. They'd say, "No thanks"; then she'd go rent a horse and chase down her little sister, hide out somewhere with Libby in this dinky town, and stowaway on the next train coming through.

But what about the other children? Hannah had to save them, too. She would listen for a few minutes then decide what to do next.

Quincy Harrison said, "Can you read and cipher?"

Hannah nodded. "Yes, very well in fact."

"Do you want the job?" the parson asked.

"Yes, I'd like it very much." No lies necessary yet.

"It's settled then." Harold stood up. "You're hired."

Hannah's jaw dropped open. This was the interview? "Uh. . .don't you want me to take some tests? Show you what I know?" Hannah could pass those tests, she had little doubt.

"No need." Quincy stood next. "If it turns out you can't read or cipher, reckon we'll just fire you." He headed toward the door.

"Wait for me, Quince. We'd best stick together in this weather."

Hannah was distracted from needing to save Libby and that sweet little boy for just a second. She had a job. As a teacher, of all amazing things.

"Did you leave your things over at the station, Miss?" Harold started to pull his coat on.

The door slammed as the two men went out.

"Yes. . .I mean no." How did she explain to this man that she didn't have any *things* except her satchel. "Everything's been taken care of already."

Since everything she owned in the world was on her back or in her satchel, that was true. She went back to what was important, possibly life and death. "What about that man? We can't just stand by while he steals two children."

"Steals children? Grant?" Mabel started laughing as she headed back toward the center of the counter.

A bit slower to react, Harold started in, too. "I think I'll box up some of the extra pumpkins in the cellar. They aren't gonna make it to spring anyhow." Harold seemed to accept Hannah's statement that her things were dealt with.

Mabel nodded. "He's got a sight of mouths to feed."

Hannah remembered about the girls Grant had told Libby would love her. "How many children has he made off with like this?"

"Don't rightly know." Mabel looked at the ceiling as if only God could count fast enough and high enough to keep track. "Over the years. . . maybe twenty or twenty-five. Some of 'em're done growed up and gone nowadays."

"There's half a dozen or so of the older ones married and living around Sour Springs, and that many again scattered to the wind." Harold grabbed his heavy coat off the nail where he'd tossed it a few short seconds earlier. Hannah's whole life had changed in less time than it took the snow on Harold's coat to melt. "I'd say he's only got five or six out there."

"Four, I think," Mabel said with an unfocused look that made Hannah wonder if Mabel could read and cipher herself. Of course, Mabel wasn't the new schoolteacher. "Until today. Now he's up to six."

"Twenty or twenty-five?" Hannah exclaimed. "*Twenty-five children?*"

At his very worst, Parrish had kept six. All crammed into one room while he had a nice bedroom all his own. The children were stacked into one set of bunk beds, three on the bottom, three on top, with no more regard than if he'd been stacking cordwood.

"All together, give or take," Harold said, satisfied with the estimate. "Not all at one time. Lordy, that'd be a passel of mouths to feed, eh, Mabel?"

Hannah pictured a hovel filled with underfed children gnawing on raw pumpkin while they were forced to work from dawn until dusk to make money for the man with no last name. She also realized that the town accepted this wretched state of affairs and she'd get no help—at least not from these two.

She should have enlisted the parson's help. It didn't matter. The parson had to know and had done nothing to stop it. If they wouldn't help her save those children, she'd do it herself. "Someone has to put a stop to this. Why, the man is no better than a slave master."

Mabel didn't seem capable of being riled. "Now, Miss Cartwright, it's not that'a way with Grant. Don't go getting your feathers all in a ruffle. Just let us explain how things work here in Sour Springs, and you'll see that you just need to be reasonable."

Hannah balled up her fists. "I have no intention of being reasonable!"

Mabel blinked.

That'd come out wrong. Hannah heard the door open and close and glanced back to see the other shopper leave without buying anything.

She looked back. From the set looks on Mabel's and Harold's faces, they were supportive of the miserable way Grant treated his children. Well, maybe some people could live their lives like this, but she wasn't one of them.

Rather than waste another second arguing with these two, she decided to handle this situation herself. She had a few meager pennies left. She'd see where she could hire a carriage, ask directions, and take care of Mr. . . . Grant herself.

FOUR

She turned to Harold. "I'd appreciate it very much if you could direct me to my room."

"I'll guide you over, miss. It's the room over the diner."

Hannah sniffed in disgust as she turned to walk out. As she left the store, she heard Mabel say to herself, "Steals children. . .Grant? Imagine." Then Mabel started laughing all over again.

Pulling on his coat as he walked, Harold led Hannah through the cutting snow, down the wooden sidewalk, toward the town's only diner. Harold led her down an alley that seemed to catch all the wind and shove it through at top speed. He rounded the back of the diner, went through a door and up a narrow flight of creaking steps.

Hannah clutched her satchel and followed.

It was exactly what she expected, but at the same time she was dismayed at the cramped space. A single room not more than ten-feet-by-ten-feet, with a sloped roof that made the place even smaller. A narrow cot, a row of nails on which to hang her clothes, and a rickety stand with a chipped white pottery washbasin and pitcher. The only heat radiated off a stovepipe that came up through the floor from the diner below. "Do all the teachers stay in this room?"

"The last four have. We've had a sight of trouble keeping a teacher in this town though. The women tend to up and get married or run off for one reason or another. I remember one that got kidnapped,

I think. Or no, maybe she ran off with a tinker. Or was that two different teachers? It's hard to keep track."

Kidnapped? Who got kidnapped? Hannah thought of Grace, teaching in a small town in far west Texas. Could she have met such a fate? That would explain why the letters quit coming. Hannah wondered if she'd ever see her sister again.

Harold crossed his arms and screwed up his face as if thinking were painful. "Or did she get kidnapped by a tinker then marry him? I can't rightly remember. And I think we had one once that turned to horse thievin'. Bad business that one was. They all kinda fuzz together in my head." Harold shrugged as if willing to make up a story if he couldn't remember the truth.

"Mabel and I have seven boys, but they're all grown now, so even though I'm on the school board, we don't have much to do with the school. We've been known to run through three or four teachers a year."

This town obviously chewed teachers up and spit them out. It occurred to Hannah that she could be the next in a long line.

Afraid more thinking might make Harold's brain explode, Hannah said, "We can discuss the other teachers later." She moved to the door, thinking to shoo him and his body lice out.

"Oh, little advice, miss. Think long and hard a'fore you go walin' on any of the kids. Some of the town folk don't take kindly to it."

Hannah stiffened. "I don't intend to *wale* on any child, for heaven's sake. I'd never strike a child."

"Now don't go making promises you can't keep. The Brewsters've moved on, but their like've come through town before 'n more'n likely'll come again. Need a good thrashin' real regular, those young'uns did."

"No youngster needs a *thrashing*. Children need love and under-standing. Now really, I must ask you to leave. I've got things to do."

Harold must have been long on mouth and short on ears because he apparently didn't hear her and kept talking. "No figurin' people near as I kin figure. But the likes of the Brewsters'll be back. Two boys and a girl. The lot of them Brewsters could stand a good thrashin' to my way of thinkin'."

Hannah bristled up until she could have shot porcupine quills at Harold. *Thrash a child indeed.* Why, she'd be no better than Parrish.

She had to get Harold out of here so she could go save Libby.

Swamped with stubbornness she didn't know she was capable of, Hannah decided then and there she'd neither thrash a child, nor steal a horse, nor let herself be kidnapped, nor marry any man. She'd had her fill of men, first Parrish and now that awful child-stealing Mr. . . . .Grant. She planned to have no man in her life ever. In fact, squaring her shoulders, she vowed right then and there she'd start a new tradition and stay at the school forever—unless she had to steal Libby away from her new father and save the other children out there and run. She tried to imagine twenty-five children stowed away on a train. Or was it six or four? She'd heard several numbers. Hannah got a headache just thinking of all she had to do.

As Harold finally ran out of chatter and turned to leave, Hannah, now sworn to her job for the rest of her life, asked, "Who do I talk to about the school? I want to know all of my pupils' names, and I hope to visit them in their homes before the start of the winter school term." Grace had written that a teacher must visit, and Grace was the best teacher Hannah had ever known. Although, honesty forced Hannah to admit that Grace was the only teacher Hannah had ever known.

"No time for that. School starts Monday."

Already she was failing. "Well then, I'll visit after school starts."

"Try asking Louellen downstairs. Running the diner the way she does, I reckon she knows about everything that goes on around here. I know there are a dozen children in town and maybe that many again in the surrounding ranches. Oh, and Grant's young'uns? That's another dozen." Harold broke down and laughed until he had to wipe his eyes.

Hannah's jaw clenched as she waited the man out.

Tucking his handkerchief back in his pocket, Harold shook his head. "He doesn't usually send 'em in 'cuz he hasn't liked the teachers we have. So don't count them. They'll be here for a few days most likely, and then he'll just take 'em home and school 'em hisself like always. Were I you I wouldn't even let 'em sit at a desk. They'll be gone afore you need to bother."

"He don't. . ." Hannah stumbled then corrected her grammar. Honestly, she'd only been here an hour and she already sounded like Harold. "He doesn't send his children to school? Well, we'll see about that. Could you direct me to his ranch?"

That question seemed to amuse Harold because he began chuckling and shaking his head. Of course Hannah was beginning to believe that a rabid wolf would amuse Harold so she didn't put much stock in what struck him as funny.

"Gonna get after Grant, miss?"

Hannah crossed her arms while she waited for directions.

"That I'd like to see."

"Directions?" Hannah tapped her toe.

"You can hire a horse at the livery stable or the blacksmith shop. But Ian O'Reilly is the blacksmith, and I think he's gone for the day, so don't waste your time goin' there. He wouldn't like you scolding Grant anyway, because he's one of Grant's kids."

"The blacksmith? How old is he?"

Harold shrugged. "About Grant's age, I 'spect."

"Mr. . . .Grant adopted children *his own age*?"

"To get to the Rocking C, go straight out'a town west for about five miles. The woods clear out for a spell, then there's a thicket of bright red sumac and huckleberries that's been cut back so's a trail'll go through it. Take that trail and go south a spell. The woods'll start up again and the bluffs'll rise up on both sides. Gets might rugged. Grant has an old wagon wheel by his place, with a piece of bent iron hooked on it in the shape of a C. Turn east and that trail'll take you right up to the cabin."

Hannah tried desperately to remember everything he'd said. West five miles. Trail through a thicket. South between some bluffs. Wagon wheel. East.

Harold gave her a jaunty wave and went out. He was back the next second. "There's a shorter way, but it's kinda confusing."

Hannah shuddered at the thought of directions more confusing than the ones she'd already been given. "No, thank you."

He said good-bye and exited her room. He came back in. "Turnin' into a mighty mean day, miss. Not fit for a ride by my way'a reckonin'. If you can wait till tomorrow, Grant'll be in to Sunday services so you could ride back out with him."

When Harold said Grant would bring the children to church, Hannah doubted herself for the first time. That spoke well of the man. Parrish had certainly never let her or the other children attend church. But she couldn't overcome her first impression of Libby and Charlie being taken off into a dangerous situation. And if her instincts were right, she didn't think it could wait until tomorrow.

"I believe I'll go on out myself." How well she remembered her first night in Parrish's clutches. She wanted to save those children before Grant had time to frighten them into submission.

Harold shrugged.

Hannah had heard this was the way things worked in the West. People minded their own business. Indignantly she thought that was the very reason Grant had been allowed to abscond with so many children.

Harold went out, then he came right back. "If'n you get lost just start heading south. You'll run into the spring. Sour Springs we call it. Named the town for it. Stinks like a herd of polecats. Can't miss it. Upstream'll lead you right smack into town." He tipped his hat and left.

Hannah sighed in relief to have the bad news bearer gone.

He popped his head back around the corner. "Oh, and don't touch the sumac. It's poisonous." He left again.

Hannah stared dolefully at the empty doorway where the man

bobbed in and out like a sneaky prairie dog.

He rounded her door again. "But the sumac'll be buried by snow more'n likely, so forget about it."

He'd told her to turn at the sumac. If it was buried, how was she supposed to use it as a landmark? She waited for the voice of doom to return so she could ask him. He appeared to have given it all to her at last. She pulled her worn-out coat tight around her and headed for the stable before she could second guess herself.

A mountain of a man forked hay into feed bunks for a half dozen horses. He introduced himself as Zeb Morris. He was as hairy as his horses, nearly as big, and he smelled none too much better. Hannah knew that even though she stayed well away.

"Hey, missy. Heard you're the new schoolmarm." Zeb grinned, showing more teeth missing than present.

Word did get around in this town.

"Welcome to Sour Springs. My pappy founded this settlement."

Sour Springs was named after a spring? Or the way his father smelled? Then she thought of a town that would ignore the plight of orphans and wanted to sneer at his pride. Instead she said politely, "I'd like to rent a carriage for the rest of the afternoon."

The man looked doubtfully out the wide open door. "No day for pleasure ridin', miss. I wouldn't stray six feet from town if'n I didn't have to."

"Well, I have to. So, if you'll please do as I ask?"

The man hesitated. Then, just as Harold had done, he let her go about her own business. "Don't rent carriages, only saddle horses."

That wasn't what Hannah wanted at all, but her fear for the children overruled her fear for her own safety. "That will be fine."

She rented a horse that seemed as unhappy to go to work as it was swaybacked, but Hannah had grown up in the Wild West, or the next thing to it—Chicago. So she'd ridden a horse a time or two. Actually she thought carefully and decided exactly a time, not two. Well, there was no help for it. The children needed her.

She was tempted to ask for directions again from the man who rented her the horse, but she thought she had Harold's advice memorized and didn't want to muddy the waters.

Zeb saddled the horse. He—Zeb, not the horse—got far too close for her nose's comfort when he boosted her on its back. Then he led her out the door.

Taking up the reins, she kicked the horse and the horse kicked back. Since she sat on top of the beast, it didn't hurt her but it bounced her around some. Finally, with a slap on the backside from the hostler, she got the beast moving at a snail's pace in the right direction.

She hadn't ridden five minutes on the lazy, uncooperative creature before she admitted to being hopelessly lost. The skittish horse twisted around and pranced sideways. If there'd ever been any trail, it'd been well and truly buried under the snow. Once she'd left the meager shelter of town, the wind whipped harder until the snowstorm became a full-fledged blizzard.

Looking desperately, she searched for the prints of her own horse in the snow to make sure she hadn't left the trail. The snow around her was trampled down in all directions by the nervous horse, and his prints were filling in fast. She gave the animal its head, hoping it would start for the barn, but the horse just let its head sag as if it didn't have enough energy to move another step.

Hannah kicked the horse, and it moved a few steps forward then stopped again. Her heart pounded as the snow drove itself through her thin coat. Fighting down panic, Hannah realized she'd become hopelessly lost in a Texas blizzard. She should have left Libby to Mr. . . . Grant for one night, because now Hannah would freeze to death in a blizzard and not be around to save her from her nightmarish fate.

FIVE

Libby snuggled up on Grant's left knee and, with a smile, rested her head on his shoulder.

Grant eased his toes closer to the fire with a blissful sigh and opened the book.

Benny scrambled onto Grant's right knee. Charlie sat on the floor with his back leaning against the stones that edged the fireplace. Joshua leaned on the other side of the fire playing "Silent Night" softly on his mouth harp. Christmas was just over, and the whole family still felt the glow of the holy season.

Sadie and Marilyn sat at the table doing the studies Grant had set for them, but he wondered if the girls were really reading. Josh's playing was too sweet to ignore. He could coax music out of that harmonica that could break a man's heart or make him laugh out loud.

When the music ended, Grant opened his well-worn copy of *Oliver Twist*. He produced it every time a new child came into the house. Grant had found it helped start the new young'uns talking about where they'd come from.

Of course Charlie had that hostile look. Children with that look rarely talked about their lives before they came to Grant's home. And Libby wasn't likely to start in talking. But they could at least hear that a book had been written about some of what they'd been through. It was Grant's way of letting them know he understood, and they weren't alone.

Grant looked up from the book before he began. "Dinner was good, girls. Thanks for having it hot and ready when I got in from chores."

Marilyn, his oldest daughter, her blond hair curly and fine as a cobweb, nodded. "You're welcome, Pa."

Sadie grinned, her white teeth shining against her ebony black skin. "We all cooked together whilst you, Joshua, and Charlie worked with the cattle. We had the easy part of this storm."

"Knowing we'd have a hot meal kept us going." Grant pulled Libby closer, his arm around her, holding the book.

Six-year-old Benny, supposedly near Libby's age but about twice her size, snuggled closer, his head resting on Grant's shoulder. He glanced up through the shaggy hair that had flopped onto his forehead. "Want me to hold the book, Pa?"

"Thanks, Benny. I just remembered I hadn't said a proper thank you to the girls." He let the book settle in his youngest son's hands. Grant wasn't the only one in this family who needed a haircut. "Let's get started reading."

Grant looked around the tiny room. Yes, it was a tight squeeze for them all, three bedrooms—if those tiny spaces could be called bedrooms—for seven people. And yes, he'd be sleeping on the kitchen floor for a while. But he'd done that many times to make space. The kitchen was warm, and he didn't mind being cramped.

He loved this tiny house, these children. He loved his whole life. God had given him the family he'd dreamed of while he shivered in the New York City alleys. Here they sat with full bellies thanks to the girls' dab hand with a skillet, a warm, crackling fire, and a roof over their heads no one could take away from them.

He gave Libby a gentle hug, and she looked up and smiled her quiet smile. That smile meant more to Grant than if a million dollars had rained down on his head. He had everything in the world that mattered. He was a happy, contented man.

His contentment was broken by the memory of that snippy woman at the train station. All she'd accused him of, all her insults. The smile faded from his face for just a second. Why would she come to mind now? It's like she meant to ruin his night.

Maybe it was because she looked cold and hungry.

And why had she gotten off the train and let it leave her behind? What business had brought her to Sour Springs? She must have family here. Grant hoped she finished her visit lickety-split and got back on her way before he ever had to see her again. How dare the little meddler accuse him of mistreating his children?

He could picture her right now, sulking, judging him and his orphaned children while she sat somewhere warm and fed and comfortable.

Driven snow slit at her skin like a million tiny knives. The wind lashed her.

Disoriented, Hannah thought of the times she'd been lashed by Parrish, his belt punishing her for something or nothing.

God, no, don't let Parrish get me. Protect me.

How often had she prayed that prayer as a child? How many nights had she been jerked awake by nightmares and been punished for screaming out in her sleep? How often had Hannah clung to God, even when Parrish came and God let the worst happen?

As the storm assaulted her, Hannah thought of how Parrish dragged her out of the bedroom she shared with her sisters. How Grace tried to turn Parrish's anger away from Hannah. Sometimes it would work. More often Parrish would laugh at Grace and slap her aside, then whip Hannah until she collapsed.

Now, in the wind, Hannah heard her father's sadistic laughter ringing in her ears.

And then Grace had done the unthinkable. She'd fought back. She'd had Parrish arrested. Drawing Parrish's fury on herself, Grace had run like a mother bird faking a broken wing. . .with Parrish in pursuit. Hannah had taken the other children and hidden away in Chicago's streets until Grace could send for her.

Despite Grace forbidding it—Grace had a deep horror of adoption—Hannah had found homes for the four little sisters left in her care. And then, before Hannah had set out to join Grace in Mosqueros, Texas, she'd found more children.

Trevor, who tried to rob Hannah and ended up sharing what he'd already stolen. Nolan, who crept into the shed she and Trevor lived in and defiantly slipped up to their tiny bit of heat, expecting to be thrown out but willing to face danger to escape the killing cold of another winter night. Other children had come and gone and Hannah had found them homes, all but Libby with her broken body, silent lips, and heartbreaking, beseeching eyes.

Now Libby was gone. Grace was gone. Hannah, alone, shouted into the teeth of the blizzard, "God, they're all gone."

The horse jerked forward, startled by Hannah's screams.

Hannah broke down and wept into the bitter, driving, merciless wind. Shuddering with sobs, holding her arm up to shield her face, Hannah blinked and, as if God himself had pulled back the veil of driven snow, she saw a blurred object. She clung to her horse's reins with one hand and dropped her shielding arm to clutch the collar of her coat. Peering into the storm, trying to make out the shape, a strange peace settled over her.

As she calmed, she realized it was a building she'd passed just moments ago on the edge of town. She could find her way back. She could save herself.

But what about Libby? Who would save her?

Hannah knew she could do nothing tonight. Wiping the already freezing tears from her face, she headed quickly back toward Sour Springs, leaving Libby to her fate for one night. But Hannah promised it would be one night only!

She left the horse with the smug hostler, who kindly returned her two bits, only saying, "I told you so," six or seven times. Then Hannah trudged through drifts to her room.

As she battled the storm, she saw that all the businesses were closed and shuttered. It was late enough in the afternoon that the sun had set and there'd be no customers in this weather.

Then as she passed a building near the mercantile, she saw one lone light flickering in a window. Through thin curtains, Hannah saw a tall, reed-thin shape pass the light. Prudence, maybe, the seamstress she'd met in the general store. Hannah paused, drawn by the light and life of that building, even as she knew she didn't dare pause on the way to her own dark room.

As she watched, a second shape moved in the same direction as Prudence. A man, a giant of a man, bigger even than Harold, was in Prudence's room with her. They'd offered Prudence the job as school-marm, hadn't they? Only a single woman would be offered that job. And Mabel had definitely said Prudence was new in town. So what man was with her on this bitter cold evening?

True, it wasn't very late, just after suppertime most likely. But people would want to get home and tuck themselves in safe for the night. The aching of Hannah's feet prodded her onward. She had almost no feeling in them as she hurried home.

The diner was closed but the back door was unlocked, and Hannah got to her room without trouble. She spent the rest of the bitter night clutching her worn coat and the single thin blanket she'd pulled off the narrow cot around her. Leaning into the stovepipe with its meager warmth, she trembled with cold in the wretched room and thought of the glowing letters she'd gotten from Grace about her comfortable situation in Mosqueros. Hannah, with no food and no dry clothes, shivered and her stomach growled.

Hannah wrapped her arms around herself, missing all of her sisters. If Libby were here, the two of them would snuggle in bed, share their warmth, and survive the night by being strong for each other. They'd done it many times in Chicago and Omaha and other places.

Hannah vowed to God, as she stared into the ceiling of her black room, that she'd save Libby. She'd save all those children Grant had taken. Then she'd show this town there was such a thing as a teacher who stuck, no matter the provocation.

Barely twenty, she felt like she'd been old since the day she was born. She was so tired of always having to be strong, beyond tired of all work and no play. Grim experience told her what Libby and Charlie were going through tonight and she wept. From the deepest part of her heart, she cried out to God through her tears.

Forgive me for failing them and subjecting them to that hard, miserable life.

S I X

"L et's go sledding!"

Grant was jerked out of a restless sleep when Benny tripped over his stomach.

Benny fell with a terrible clatter against the kitchen table, hitting so hard he should have broken every bone in his body. The six-year-old bounced back to his feet and grinned down at Grant, who lay on his bedroll on the kitchen floor. "Can we get the sleds out, Pa? Can we, huh? Can we, please?"

Benny'd been on the orphan train when it turned around here three years ago. He'd ridden all the way from New York with Martha and never been adopted because he was too young. Three when Grant got him, Benny was the closest to a baby Grant had ever taken, and Grant couldn't have loved him any more if he'd been his own flesh and blood.

Trying to shake off a lousy night's sleep, he massaged his head to clear it. Grant rubbed a hand over his face. No bristles. *Oh yeah, I shaved last night.* Why had he shaved? Normally he'd do that Sunday morning not Saturday night. For that matter, what was he doing sleeping on the floor?

Grant sat up straight. *I adopted two more kids yesterday.*

Benny didn't wait for an answer. He dashed to the little window beside the front door and pressed his nose against the frosty pane. "This is the bestest snow I've ever seen." Benny glanced over his shoulder and gave Grant a sly look. "I mean, this is the worstest snow I've ever seen. We can't get through it to church. No way! It'd be"—Benny paused for dramatic effect—"dangerous!"

Grant grinned at Benny. Then he laughed out loud.

The other children came pouring out of their rooms wearing their heavy nightgowns or union suits—depending on whether they were girls or boys. Even the older girls rushed to the window and crowded around fighting for a square inch of glass.

Libby was right behind them, still as silent as a tomb. He wondered what it was the little girl couldn't say.

Marilyn turned and scooped Libby up in her arms so the little one could see the snow outside. Their two heads together, Libby's dark and Marilyn's fair, the expressions of joy and excitement matched until they looked almost like sisters.

Before they'd covered the window with their rampaging herd of bodies, Grant had seen that the sun wasn't even up yet. Only the faintest light glowed in the eastern sky. Grant couldn't resist saying, "If the mountain pass is snowed in, we can still make it through the valley."

Grant heard Benny groan, which made Grant grin all the more. "I think there's time for a couple of quick trips up and down the hill before church."

There was a collective gasp of joy, and the children vanished out of the room so quickly Grant might have thought he'd dreamed the whole thing if Benny hadn't stepped on his stomach again in the stampede.

If he let them go, he'd be stuck with all the morning chores. But in New York City, where Grant had grown up, there had been plenty of snow but never time for sledding. And here in Texas, it got cold, but the snow didn't come this deep very often, and it never lasted for long. He wasn't going to deny the children this pleasure.

Thinking of the fight on his hands to get the young'uns ready for church, he heaved himself up off the floor and groaned. He was getting too old to sleep on a hardwood floor. He quit his groaning to smile at himself. He was twenty-six. Not too old for anything. Although, raising twenty children on his own, starting from the time he was seventeen, might have made him an old man before his time.

He got to his feet and laid more wood on the fire before he did another thing. Then he adjusted his suspenders onto his shoulders and pulled on his boots over the thick socks he'd worn to bed. With a couple of quick scrapes of his fingers, he gathered his hair at his nape then tied it back with a leather thong to keep it out of his eyes, wondering if one of the older girls would mind whacking some of his mane off for him. Pulling on his buckskin coat, he grabbed the bucket to go for water.

Benny beat him to the door, shouting with glee and running for the barn and the ragtag sleds Grant had collected over the years.

By the time Grant hauled back the first bucket of water, all six kids were long gone sledding. He poured water into a pot for coffee and a basin for washing. He hustled to milk both cows, gather eggs, and make sure the livestock in his barnyard had gotten through the blizzard in one piece. Hefting an armload of firewood inside, he stoked the stove then reached for the boiling coffeepot to pour himself a cup before he went to wrangle with the children about coming back in to get ready for church.

Then something snapped. He poured his untouched coffee back in, shoved the pot to a cooler spot so it wouldn't burn. . .and ran.

He got to the bottom of the sledding hill just as Marilyn and Libby sailed down the slope on the little toboggan. They upended the sled in a snowdrift and came rolling out of the snow, giggling hysterically.

Grant shouted, "*My turn!*"

The kids started shrieking and jumping up and down, yelling encouragement to him.

Grant grabbed the rope of Marilyn's sleek wooden toboggan, one that Grant had built himself last winter, and plunked Libby down on it. He trudged up the hill, giving his newest daughter a ride.

Joshua passed him on a runner sled going down. Benny, Charlie, and Sadie were next on the big toboggan.

He got to the top only a few paces ahead of Joshua.

"I'm faster'n you, Pa," Joshua taunted in his deep, adult voice. His black skin shone with melting snow, and icicles hung off his woolen cap. "I was way behind you when I went down."

Grant laughed at his seventeen-year-old son. "I gave Libby a ride. You made Benny walk. All the difference."

Joshua shoved Benny sideways, and the little boy plopped over into the snow. Benny came up hurling snowballs, and Joshua whooped and ran.

Grant turned Libby around to face downhill. "Let's get out of here, Lib, before we get attacked!"

Libby laughed out loud, and Grant's joy was so great to hear this solemn little girl laughing he wanted to dance. He jumped onto the back of the sled, tucking his long legs around her, and pushed off. Just as he started moving, he felt something heavy hit his back, and he glanced behind to see Benny tackling him. Grant pulled Benny over his shoulder while the boy laughed and wrestled. Libby started giggling again.

Grant glanced sideways to see Charlie riding in front of Sadie and Marilyn, laughing. Charlie's laughter meant the world to Grant. He knew the boy would be a tough nut to crack. Hostile and suspicious, Grant understood that the boy expected every moment in this house to be his last. He didn't trust anyone. All of the new brothers and sisters hadn't gone down well. He had especially hated sharing his tiny loft room with Benny.

And now Charlie laughed and played. Grant's heart danced even if he was too buried under kids to do it for real.

The sled soared down the hill, completely out of control because Benny had a boot in Grant's face. The wreck came as it always did against the drifts that had formed at the base of the slope.

By the time Grant got the snow wiped out of his eyes, all six of his children were scattered around beside him, buried at all different depths. All of them laughing like loons.

Grant knew he was pushing his luck, but he couldn't make them quit yet. "Once more down the hill."

All the laughing stopped and the complaining began.

"Pa," Benny wailed, "it's already warming up."

Charlie kicked at a clump of snow in front of him. "It'll be gone by the time church is over."

"Two more times down the hill," Grant amended. "If we hurry!"

He caught the sled rope and planted Libby back on the sled and raced Joshua, pulling Benny, to the top of the hill. Charlie was right beside him. The girls beat the rest of them to the top and jeered at Grant for being slow.

The kids nagged him into four more times down the hill. Then they had to skip breakfast and head for church with their coats still wet and their hair straggling around their faces. Grant knew they were all a mess, but laughing was something none of them had known how to do when they'd first come to him. Enjoying family life was as much a kind of worship to an orphan as sitting in the Lord's house.

"The gap is filled up to the canyon rim."

Daniel's announcement nearly broke Grace's ear drums as he slammed the door open to their cabin. To knock the snow off his broad shoulders, he shook himself like a wet dog.

"Daniel!" Grace held up both hands to ward off the flying snow. She risked a peek through her fingertips and saw him grinning at her.

"No school till spring! The canyon's snowed shut for sure." Mark launched himself at Luke and the two of them slammed to the floor. "I thought it'd never happen. I thought we'd be stuck schoolin' all winter."

Grace closed her eyes so she wouldn't see the breaking bones and blood. She peeked again. Of course no one broke. A Texas cyclone couldn't play this rough, and yet the boys stayed in one piece more often than not.

A cry out of the bedroom pulled Grace's attention away from the riot in front of her.

"I'll get him. Your little brother's up, boys!" Daniel ran toward the room with all five boys charging after him. Daniel beat the crowd through, but the boys clogged in the doorway and fought each other to be second.

"*Be gentle with him!*" Grace used to be soft-spoken, but no one seemed to hear her. Now she hollered, and they still ignored her for the most part. But at least they now ignored her because they were rude, not because of any failure on her part to let them know what she wanted. So she could blame them fully when they didn't mind her.

Daniel appeared from the bedroom with Matt, still droopy-eyed from an unusual afternoon nap. The boy wasn't inclined to unnecessary sleep. None of the men in this family were.

Her three-year-old son was bald as an egg, but Daniel said all of his sons started out that way. He claimed it was real convenient to have no hair on a baby because it made mopping the food off their heads easier. Grace had found that to be the honest truth.

Abe and Ike shoved through the door next. They'd shot up in the last year. Fourteen years old now, soon to turn fifteen, they were within inches of Daniel's height but not nearly as broad. Their shoulders and chests hadn't filled out yet, and they had a gaunt, hungry look, no matter how much food Grace poured down them.

The boys were eating the herd down so fast, one of these days Grace expected to see the cattle making a break for it.

Abe and Ike did the work of men, but they still played like kittens. Big kittens. One hundred-fifty-pound kittens who would sooner knock the furniture over than go around it.

Mark, Luke, and John, the nine-year-old triplets, came in next. Luke tripped Mark because Mark dodged in front of him to get out of the baby's bedroom. Mark smacked into his older brothers. As long as they were within reach, Mark made a point of knocking them sideways as he fell. The two of them turned and attacked. John, a step behind Luke, jumped on the pile of wriggling, screaming boys.

Daniel ignored the ruckus, as did Grace to the extent she was able. They met in front of the fireplace, and Daniel handed little Matthew over. Grace settled into the rocking chair Daniel and the boys had built. Matthew lasted all of ten seconds on her lap, then he yelled and squirmed until she let go. He launched himself at his brothers. His high-pitched screams were deafening, so his brothers howled all the louder and proceeded to grab Matt and toss him in the air between each other. It was the baby's favorite game.

Grace covered her eyes.

"What's the matter, honey?" Daniel leaned down, resting one hand on the back of her rocker while he pressed his forehead to hers.

She loved it when he touched her. She loved the way he smelled. On the rare occasion when she could get a sweet word out of the big lummox, she almost melted into a puddle at his feet. She breathed him in.

Luke fell over the kitchen table and broke one of the legs off.

Daniel yelled, "*You boys go outside and fight!*"

Grace, her ears ringing, looked up at her grinning husband as the boys stormed through the outside door. She could tell that he was already planning to repair the table. He was good at it, thanks to all the practice.

Thanks to the moment of silence, Grace could concentrate, and she realized what Daniel had said. "The gap's snowed shut?" And oddly, her throat seemed to swell shut at the news. "We're trapped here until spring again?"

"Yep, but it held off a long time this year. We got in to Mosqueros for Christmas. But I'm tired of the run to town for school. Glad to be shut of it for the year. And it don't matter none. We have supplies for the winter. I stocked up good and early. Plus, I married me our own private teacher." Daniel grinned at her then took a step away toward the table.

Grace caught his arm, choking on the idea of being trapped for months. "You're *sure* it's all the way snowed shut. Have you ever tried to shovel a path through? Just wide enough to walk out?"

"Naw, it's packed in tight, fifty feet deep. No gettin' out. I s'pose we could get an early thaw, but that don't usually happen. You know how slow that gap is to melt. Spring will have been here for a long time before we can get out."

Grace's finger sank deep into Daniel's sleeve. "Daniel, I think we're going to have to get out of here once or twice this winter. You got a lot done on that high pass, didn't you? We can get out of here once in a while, can't we?"

"We could, but why should we?"

Something hit the front door so hard one of the hinges snapped. Grace saw Ike and Luke through the splintered wood before they fell to the ground.

"Because I get a little. . .oh"—her fingers tore little holes in the fabric—"restless, I guess, not seeing another woman all winter. If we could just go to the McClellens every month or so. . ."

Daniel went over and lifted the door back into place.

"I'd go alone," she offered. "I could just jump on a horse and ride up to the pass. I'd let the horse go and he'd come right home. Then I'd walk to Adam and Tillie's. It can't be more than five miles. I'd be fine on my own."

"You can't get over that pass alone."

"Sure I can." Grace felt her throat shutting tight, not unlike the gap. "Scaling that last cliff isn't so hard."

"What do you mean it isn't so hard?" Daniel set what was left of the table upright using the broken-off leg to prop it then came back to her side. "Even after all the work we done, we have to hang on by our fingernails. John fell almost a hundred feet when he went over the edge last summer."

Grace decided the sleeve hadn't gotten his attention nearly enough. She grabbed Daniel's skin beneath the cloth, picturing her hand on his neck. That wasn't like her. "But he rolled most of the way. It's not like it's a dead drop. He had hardly a scratch. And besides, he was wrestling with Abe. I wouldn't be reckless like the boys are."

Normally the winters didn't bother her all that much. But for some reason, right now, it was driving her to panic. Her fingers sank into a hunk of Daniel's skin. And speaking of claws. . . "I would just claw my way up and out. I'd be glad to go alone if you didn't want to come along."

Mark screamed like he was being stabbed to death.

Grace flinched. "In fact, I'd *insist* on going alone. I'd go see Sophie. I might stay for a day or two, just once a month."

Grace heard someone roll off the roof, shrieking like a banshee.

"Once or twice a month, for two or three days each time." Grace gave him her most fetching smile. The one that often got her what she wanted, or rather got her Daniel, which was often what she wanted. "You could manage without me."

Daniel leaned down and kissed the tip of her nose. "No, we couldn't, honey. What would we eat?"

"You could have steak and eggs and biscuits and potatoes and milk?"

He caught her hand and removed her fingers from his skin. "It's good, but it has an extra sweetness when it's made by your pretty little hands."

Grace heard more racket on the roof. Her pretty little hand formed a fist. A puff of soot whomped out of the fireplace and the flames danced wildly. She waited to see if one of the boys would fall through.

"Oh." Daniel slapped his forehead then reached for the back pocket of his broadcloth pants. "There was another letter for you in Mosqueros. I forgot. I've been carrying it around for a few days. It's from your sister who writes from time to time."

"What?" Grace launched herself to her feet. "Hannah wrote and you forgot to tell me?"

Daniel held the letter out then backed away as if a Texas cougar had just popped into the kitchen.

Grace snatched it out of his hand, tore it open, and read. "She's in Texas." She read more, faster. She'd reread it a thousand times, savoring every word, but right now she just wanted to make sure her sister was alive and well.

Grace looked up, her heart racing. "She's just a short train ride away." Well, most of the whole state, but still, only one state. . .a large one, granted.

"That's nice, honey." Daniel turned his attention back to the table.

"Daniel, she says she's working. She can't come the rest of the way. But we could go."

A vicious, half-wild longhorn stormed past the window, bellowing in terror. Three blond heads zipped right along behind it, as if they were after dinner on the hoof. Yes, her boys could scare a longhorn to death.

A break from that might be nice. For Grace. In fact, the more she thought of it, the more she decided the rest of the family didn't need to go at all. "I think, maybe, if I don't get out of here a few times, I might. . . uh. . .kind of. . .go crazy." Grace was surprised to realize how much she meant it. She furrowed her brow as she tried to figure out why hearing about that sealed-up gap was making her feel so trapped.

"You'll be fine, honey. Best to avoid the cliff. Winter doesn't last long." Daniel patted her like he was taming a fractious horse and smiled. "Three or four months, tops."

"But this would be such a great chance to go see Hannah. Visit my sister. You know how worried I've been about her. She's written several times, but she's told me she's never gotten but one letter from me in all these years." She heard herself wheedling and was ashamed.

Then, to her surprise, she decided she'd quit begging and punch Daniel in the nose. Curling up one discontented corner of her mouth, she paused. The need to sock her husband wasn't like her. She had only wanted to punch Daniel once in their married life.

Honesty forced Grace to admit that wasn't purely true. In the very beginning she'd wanted to punch him pretty regularly. But lately only once. Exactly three years and nine months ago.

A body hurled past the window. The glass in the window rattled, but it didn't break for a change.

She lowered her hand to her stomach, did some quick figuring, and raised her eyes to her husband. And by golly she almost did punch him then.

She narrowed her eyes at him.

"What?" He straightened away from her, alarmed.

"This is your fault."

He arched his eyebrows. "Most things usually are."

"It had better be a girl this time."

Daniel froze, staring at her as if she'd grown a full set of longhorns. Then he screamed and ran out of the house.

Which was only what she expected.

He left the door open so she could watch him as he vanished into the trees. How long would it take him to calm down this time? She also apologized to her little unborn daughter for the torture that was in store for her from her brothers.

The table, teetering on three legs, crashed over on its side. Grace sank back into her rocker, and her eyes fell shut. No way would this baby be anything but another unruly little boy. There was something wrong with Daniel that he could only make boy children.

A stick flew in through the window, shattering the glass. The stick landed near her feet and shards of glass rained down on her. She didn't bother to get up. She could brush the glass off later.

She unfolded Hannah's letter and read it again, more slowly this time. There was no denying that her sister was in reach for the first time in years.

She had to get out of here a few times this winter. Going to see Hannah was the perfect solution.

She looked down at her stomach and conjured up the only voice she had that the boys obeyed. With a jab of her finger straight at her belly, she said, "And there'd better only be one of you in there!"

SEVEN

They were still a merry band when they got to town.

Grant thought they'd made it just in time. Benny ran ahead and as good as erupted into church. Grant saw the minute he followed his last child in that services had already started. Grant, with Libby hoisted in his arms so she could keep up, immediately began shushing the kids to settle them down and let Parson Babbitt go on with his prayers. But Grant had his hands full curbing their high spirits, especially with the two youngest boys.

The parson gave him a kind smile and moved along with his preaching.

Grant had learned to expect a strong shoulder and a kind heart from Parson Babbitt. And the rest of the congregation spared Grant quick glances and smiles. Not all of the citizens of Sour Springs were kind, but the people who worshipped in this little white church on Sunday were good to the orphaned children in their midst.

Grinning down the two rows his family filled, he settled in with his squirming, whispering family and had almost relaxed when he caught the snippy woman from the train depot looking over her shoulder at him. Glaring her disapproval, she might as well have shouted at him from across the room.

Grant realized that his sons all still had their hats on. He reached over and pulled them off Benny's and Charlie's heads. Joshua caught on and tugged his off. As Grant dropped Benny's snow-soaked wool hat onto his lap, Grant realized he still wore his own battered Stetson. Feeling his cheeks heat under Miss Cartwright's glare, he tugged it off, looking straight forward. Miss Fussbudget oughta keep her eyes to the front, too.

About that time, the parson announced that Hannah was the new schoolteacher in Sour Springs and that school would start Monday.

Grant's heart sank. He'd dealt with teachers many times who thought orphans somehow didn't deserve to be given the education that other children received. Try as he might to control his rising temper and listen to the sermon, the devil gnawed at his good nature, and Grant kept looking back at the stiff-necked Miss Cartwright, rehearsing the set-down he'd like to give her. He knew already that his children wouldn't last a week in her school.

Settling into a slouched lump of irritation, he knew they wouldn't last two days. No matter what happened that first day, even if Miss Prim-and-Proper Hannah didn't throw his kids out, some parent would get in a snit about some story a child brought home from school and there'd be a group before Grant got there the next day. Of course, the Brewsters had moved, so it wouldn't get as nasty as most years, but he'd still end up schooling his young'uns at home.

When it came time for music, Josh went to the front by the parson and played his mouth harp for the whole church. It was the only musical instrument in Sour Springs. It lifted Grant's spirits briefly, but once the music stopped his mind went back to being snappish.

By the end of the service, the kids were fairly writhing in their seats as they looked fearfully out of one of the windows, afraid their precious snow was melting while they sat. When the parson said his last "amen" the children fell over themselves dashing outside to the buckboard.

Grant managed to thank Parson Babbitt for the service and apologize for the noise. "It's the snow. They're crazy to get their sleds going."

The parson laughed and clapped him on the arm. "I was young

once, Grant. I well remember the sound of a sledding hill calling to me during church. Don't keep them waiting."

Harold hollered, "I put a bunch of pumpkins in your wagon, Grant. We had more 'n we knew what to do with."

"Thanks, Harold, Mabel." Grant nodded at the couple.

"We're getting more eggs than we can eat, Grant."

Grant turned to nod at Priscilla Denby and her husband. He knew they were sharing their meager supplies, but to save his pride they acted as if they had plenty. "God bless you, Priscilla. We'll eat 'em up fast enough." Grant had chickens of his own, but they could always use a few more eggs.

Grant saw several people setting boxes in the back of his wagon. He never got to church without having people send things home with him. He never asked for help, and he'd have managed without all the gifts, but the clothes and extra vegetables really helped.

"I put a bolt of fabric in your wagon, Pa." Megan, one of his girls, married and soon to have her third child, waved. Before Grant could say hello, Megan was dragged by her five-year-old son, Gordy, toward her husband, Ian, and their wagon. Grant heard the boy yammering about sledding. Ian was one of Grant's, too. That made Gordy Grant's grandson.

"Let me go talk to Grandpa, Gordy."

Twenty-seven and already a grandpa to a five-year-old. Grant had to smile.

Gordy kept tugging, yelling about the snow melting.

Soon to be three children in Ian and Megan's family, the two they had had bright red hair like both their folks. Grant looked at his grown children, the O'Reillys, and saw their young'uns looking exactly like them.

Something caught in Grant's throat a bit to know he'd never have a child who might have eyes the same strange color of light brown, speckled with yellow and green, as his. The odd color of his eyes always made him wonder if, somewhere out there, there might be an older woman with eyes like his, or some other orphan child, deserted just like he'd been. Or could there be a man who never knew he had a child, who lay awake some lonely nights and wished for a son with greenish-yellow eyes?

Benny ran past, storming into the crowd of redheaded O'Reillys, and Grant shook off the silly feeling. *There's nothing about my eyes I'd wish on a child.*

Ian came up with Catherine, his toddler daughter perched on his hip. He clapped Grant on the shoulder. "Two more, huh, Pa? Heard about it."

Grant nodded. Ian, only two years younger than Grant, had lived only a short time in Grant's home. But he seemed to like the sound of the word Pa, even though Grant had told him to stop calling him that several times.

Pointing, Grant said, "The boy is Charlie. He's already helping with the younger kids. And Libby is the little girl." Grant watched as Joshua boosted Libby onto the back of the wagon. "She hasn't talked since we brought her home. She's gonna need special care."

"You're up to it, Pa." Megan came up, winning her tug-of-war with Gordy. She tied her no-nonsense wool bonnet on her head. "Let me know if you need anything."

Megan, his daughter, now gave him advice. It was pretty good advice, too. "Thanks. Appreciate it."

Ian rested a hand on Megan's waist, and she smiled a private smile at him.

That look made Grant's stomach a little twitchy, but he wasn't sure why.

"How'd you get them off the sledding hill this morning?" Megan asked.

"It wasn't easy, especially since I didn't want to quit either. And now we've got to run. They're scared to death that the snow'll melt out from under 'em."

"It probably will." Ian settled his Stetson on his head.

Gordy started jumping up and down, yanking on Megan's hand. "Let's go!"

Ian interceded. "You're wearing your ma out. Dangle yourself from my hand for a while."

Gordy giggled and dived at his father's hand.

Megan rested one hand on her midsection and gave Ian a grateful smile.

"Pa, we've got to go!" Benny barreled into Grant's leg, knocking him sideways.

Grant rested one gloved hand on Benny's shoulder and grinned down at his son.

"Gordy was sledding before first light himself." Megan laughed. "And he's itching to go back. We'd better get a move on."

Grant nodded good-bye as Benny grabbed his hand and dragged him toward the wagon. He plunked his hat onto his head and jogged along with his son. Benny let him loose, obviously convinced his pa was going to do the right thing.

Someone caught Grant's sleeve. He recognized that insistent tug. His heart sank into his scruffy boots. He rolled his eyes but got them under control before he turned around to face Hannah.

"Mr. . . . Grant, I'm coming to visit you this afternoon." She released his coat as if he might infect her with some disease born in filth. "I want to meet all the children I'm going to have in school."

"We've got a busy afternoon, Hannah." He used her first name just for the pleasure of annoying her. "We've got chores, and the children want to spend any spare time sledding. We won't have time for company."

"Mr. . . . Grant, I'm not asking permission," she snapped. "I'm telling you I'm coming out. I want to see exactly the conditions these children are living in on your ranch. Why, you have them dressed in the next thing to rags. Their hair hasn't seen a comb in days and—"

"We didn't take time to change for church is all. They were sledding, and I let them go until we didn't have a second for breakfast or cleaning up." Grant was annoyed with himself for explaining. He didn't have to justify his actions.

"You haven't fed them yet?" Hannah's eyes flashed, and Grant wondered if she'd snatch the whip off his buckboard and thrash him with it. He was sure he could take her, but she had a lot of rage so he didn't want to put it to the test.

"I feed my children, Hannah. And they have decent clothes."

Benny came dashing back to Grant's side, the brim of his woolen hat ripped halfway off the crown. His coat, a hand-me-down through a dozen boys, hanging in rags off his back.

"Can't we go, Pa?" Benny danced around frantic. "I'm cold and hungry."

Heat climbed up Grant's neck. He looked down at his own coat, which was no better. He noticed the tip of his bare toe showing out of his right boot, a hole in the leather opening up to a hole in his sock. Of course they hadn't worn their Sunday best to go sledding, and Benny's coat might be ugly, but it was warmer than his good one, the one handed down through only about four sons.

Grant had to force himself to stand still and listen when his wildly impatient children dashed back and forth begging for him to come. He thought of all the cutting comments he'd rehearsed when he should have been worshipping, and the fact that he'd spent his church time wallowing in the sin of anger was all her fault.

He drew himself up to his full six feet. She wasn't a tiny bit of a woman, at least five-six, but he still towered over her, mainly because his anger made him feel a lot bigger. "Miss Cartwright, I have had enough of your—"

"Pa." Marilyn stood beside the two of them.

She diverted Grant's attention from the scalding comments he wanted to make. Grant had spent the last ten years putting children ahead of himself. It was second nature to set aside what he was doing and listen when Marilyn talked.

"What is it?"

"I'd like for Miss Cartwright to visit. Maybe if she waited a couple of hours, let the children run off some of their steam on the sledding hill, she could drop in for a while this afternoon. The snow will be gone by then anyway."

Grant's teeth clicked together in frustration. He saw the children almost bouncing with impatience and felt the vibration of Hannah's acute disapproval. It was too much pressure coming from all directions. He caved.

He turned with exaggerated politeness. "It would be a pleasure to have you drop by and visit. Come around three."

Marilyn frowned a little at his tone then, with a half-amused shake of her head, went on to the wagon.

"You can stay for an hour. Interview the slaves. . .uh. . .I mean the children. Inspect the prison. . .that is. . .our home. Maybe we'll give you a bit of gruel and some stale bread to eat before you set off for home."

Hannah jammed her fists on her slender waist. "Mr. . . .Grant!"

Grant turned away and jumped up on the wagon seat without letting her finish. He turned back to her. "Are you deciding whether we're worthy of the fine school here in Sour Springs, Hannah? If you are, don't bother. I've already decided that your school isn't worthy of my children."

He released the hand break and slapped the reins against the horses' backs. They snorted, tossed their heads, and jingled the traces, then pulled the creaking wagon away from the church. Grant left her standing in a swirl of snow. He knew he shouldn't have been so rude. Why was it all right for her to be so nasty to him, but somehow he wasn't supposed to be mean back?

"She's just worried about us, Pa." Sadie spoke as if she'd read Grant's mind. "Maybe she's seen orphans mistreated before. If she's really trying to rescue us, then she's not such a bad person. Having her out to visit will make everything better."

"You're right." Grant shook his head slowly, wondering at himself. "But that woman does have a talent for bringing out the worst in me."

Sadie patted his shoulder. "Your worst is still real good, Pa." Sadie sank back to sit on the floor of the wagon box to wrangle with her brothers and sisters about who got first turn on the toboggan.

Grant let go of some of his bad temper. Fine, he'd let Hannah come out and inspect.

Then he thought of the home she'd be inspecting. If she came out to inspect, she'd see his tiny house and his hodgepodge of clothing and furniture. She'd see the scanty food he had on hand and find how many chores he asked his children to do.

His hands tightened on the reins to turn his team around to forbid her to come. Then, with a sinking heart, Grant let the horses go on. He could forbid till he was blue in the face, the stubborn woman would still visit. And whether her problem was disapproving of orphans or disapproving of him, she'd still do one or the other. So what difference did it make?

He sped the horses along and planned on another term of schooling his children himself.

"There he goes." Prudence watched until Grant disappeared, then dropped the curtain and turned to Horace.

Horace sat at the kitchen table scooping stew into his mouth. Prudence looked at him with envy. He got to stay out of sight. He dressed in comfortable clothes and didn't have to take a monthly bath. He had the easy half of this cheat.

"You should'a gone to church." He spoke through a mouthful of food. "Good chance to meet him."

Prudence rolled her eyes and sighed. "*I know!* You don't need to tell me what I already know. I'll go. I figured the storm'd be a good enough excuse to miss this mornin'. I can't stand sitting there all morning listening to that preacher go on and on."

Horace nodded as he shoved a biscuit into his mouth. "I've got the worst of it though." He swallowed hard. "Digging in that stink hole."

"It pays better'n sewing." Prudence paced, her arms crossed, as she tried to figure out how to corner a man who barely showed his face in town and, when he did, was surrounded by that gaggle of children.

"Yeah, but I'm gettin' real sick of it. Can't you get your hooks in that man? You're losin' it, Prudy. Losin' your looks. We've gotta make this score a'fore you're an ugly old crone."

"Shut up!" Prudence picked up a plate off the sideboard and was tempted to throw it at him. Anything to stop his mouth from telling her what she already knew.

"I've had a couple of people in LaMont ask me where I'm finding the oil. Mostly people don't know what it is, or I s'pose they know and just don't recognize its value. And I just put it on the train and ship it out fast so no one pays much mind. But a few have noticed. Last time I had to ride the wrong direction out of town then circle around before I lost a man tailing me. Digging that black gold out of the ground is hard work, and I hate it. But much as I hate it, I don't want to lose it. This is our big score. We need to own it then sell it. We can go to California, buy a hacienda, and settle down for good. No more slavin' our lives away. But it won't happen if you don't get your hooks into that man. You're gonna lose everything for us."

Prudence nodded. "I'm working on it. I may have found a way in, too. The man needs clothes—anyone can see that just by looking at the rags he and his children wear. I'm watching to catch him alone and that's the tricky part. I've already offered to do sewing for him, but so far he keeps refusing. I suppose he's got no money. But I'll offer to work cheap. I'll get him. My business is getting a little better. A few men want me to sew them a shirt from time to time. No more women than there are in town to sew, I'm making a slim go of it. But Grant's never come in with an order."

"Make it quick. You're gonna have to come up with somethin' better than sewin' pretty soon. If you can't get next to the man, how're you gonna get him to marry with you?"

"Yeah, and how am I gonna be a widow who inherits his land if I can't get him to marry me?"

"You've never had trouble before, Prudy. Use your head, use your body, use what's left of that pretty face, and figure out a way to compromise that cowpoke. He don't look like he'll be any trouble to fool if you just once get your chance at him."

"I am using my head. Why don't you use yours? You shouldn't be in here today. Someone's gonna see that I've got a man staying with me. We'll either have to lie about you being here or explain who you are, and then there'll be questions we don't want to answer."

Horace stood from the table, swiping his sleeve across his mouth. "Too bad."

"Well, when you're found out, you'll ruin everything."

"Watch your mouth. I'm holding up my end of the bargain." He strode across the room and shoved her back. "You hold up yours."

"You dig in the dirt and keep your head down. I take all the risks. When he turns up dead, they'll look to me, not you, you stupid oaf." Prudent felt the thrill of fear that came when she goaded him, knowing how he'd react. "And now you're ruining it by being in here. You're a fool, Horace. A lowdown, half-witted, old coot."

Horace backhanded her.

She slammed into the wall. Stars exploded before her eyes. Her tongue touched the blood pouring from her split lip.

Grabbing the collar of her dress, he drew back his fist.

"Not my face, you stinking pig!"

Ruthlessly, he squeezed until he cut off her air.

She clawed at his strangling hand. Her nails drew blood on his rough knuckles.

Wrenching her to her tiptoes, he went for her stomach.

Eight

"Humpf! Take those children right out from under my nose, will you?" Hannah set out in the same direction she'd taken yesterday. Only this time she wasn't blinded by a blizzard. Instead she was blinded by her temper.

All through the ride she talked to herself, working up her indignation. It helped to keep her mind off the unfriendly horse.

She'd barely taken the time to write her usual letter to Grace. Hannah made a point of mailing off a letter to Mosqueros every time it looked as if she'd be in one place for a while. But she'd always moved on before a letter could come, assuming Grace even got it. Assuming Grace was alive and could write back.

In her heart, Hannah knew Grace would never have had time to receive Hannah's letter and write an answer. That gave Hannah hope for the sister who seemed to have vanished off the face of the earth almost four years ago. Had Parrish caught her? Was Grace, even now, back in Parrish's clutches, living as a prisoner, forced into hard labor?

She had a few pennies left. Hannah wanted to send the letter quickly so Grace could have the news if the letter ever reached her.

The horse jumped sideways at its own shadow and Hannah almost fell off. She went back to paying attention to the horse.

And thinking of one ornery beast led her thoughts directly to another. Grant.

"Refuse to send them to my school?" Hannah found the thicket. The horse wanted to nibble.

"Say my school isn't worthy?" She found the wagon wheel. The horse stopped to scratch his backside against it.

Prodding the old nag she'd rented, at last a tiny cabin appeared a mile or so in front of her, tucked in front of a ragged line of mountains. The ramshackle building was about a fourth the size of the barn that stood beside it.

Screaming erupted ahead.

Frantic, Hannah kicked her horse to get it moving. It reacted poorly to that and crow-hopped. It left Hannah behind on the second hop. She landed hard and broke through the rapidly melting snow to an impressive stand of buffalo burrs. Hannah heard her dress rip. The sound almost made her heart skip a beat. It was the only dress she had.

The horse, showing more energy than it had demonstrated up until now, took off running back the way it had come.

Hannah wanted to rub her sore backside and scold her horse and generally cry her eyes out, but the screaming kept her from doing any of that. She leapt to her feet and ran.

Grant dropped the reins on the horse he'd been leading in from the corral and ran.

He got inside the barn in time to see Benny reel backward and land on the seat of his pants.

Rushing past the other children, Grant grabbed Charlie's upraised arm and wrenched the tree branch out of his hand.

"Give it back!" Charlie lunged at the branch.

Grant held it overhead, out of reach. Charlie clutched Grant's arm and used it for leverage to jump at his weapon. Grant grabbed hold of the boy's arms, and Charlie proceeded to kick him.

"Joshua, put my horse up." Grant grunted with the impact of Charlie's flailing hands and feet and glanced over his shoulder at his oldest son.

Marilyn rushed into the barn, carrying Libby. Sadie was right behind them.

"Yes, Pa." Joshua was as tall as a man. Right now his intelligent brown eyes were grave. He went outside to round up the pinto gelding Grant had let loose on account of the screaming.

Marilyn, sixteen and as pretty as she was sweet—and relatively new to the family—said, "Let's go in the house, Benny. We need to wash that cut."

"Not just yet, Marilyn." A sharp kick on the ankle almost made Grant let Charlie go, but he hung on doggedly and the boy finally quit fighting. "We have to settle this."

Grant looked down at Charlie's belligerent face. "There's no call to be so upset. There's room for everyone at the Rocking C."

"I've been on my own before." Charlie resumed his struggle against Grant's hold. "I'm not staying squashed into that stupid house."

"Settle down, son." Grant's heart ached as he caught Charlie's shirt collar to further subdue him. He hated putting his hands on his children with anything other than complete kindness.

"I'm not your son!" Charlie jerked against Grant's hold. "Don't call me your son!"

Benny, too courageous for his own good, climbed to his feet and faced Charlie. "I'll help you hold him, Pa."

Charlie threw himself at Benny and would have hit him if Grant hadn't restrained him.

Grant shook his head. "I've got him, Benny. Thanks."

Libby edged up beside Marilyn. Grant could see Libby was already adopting the oldest girl as a substitute mother, but she had an attachment to Charlie from the train, and worry had cut a crease in Libby's smooth brow.

"Stop it, Charlie." Joshua returned, leading the pinto into a stall alongside the line of well-fed horses. "We've got room for everyone."

"Yeah," Sadie snipped. "Everyone was good to you when you came home with Pa last night. You gotta be good to us back."

Charlie didn't look at his brothers and sisters. He kept glaring at Benny.

Grant spoke quietly in Charlie's ear. "I don't blame you for being angry. It wouldn't be normal if you weren't."

Charlie struggled. Benny wiped at a trickle of blood dripping into his eyes.

"I can see how badly you want a family, Charlie. I know I'm too busy to pay you the kind of attention you'd hoped for from a pa. And you're going to have to share everything. It's not the family you dreamed of."

Some of the fire cooled in Charlie's eyes.

"I can sleep in the barn for a while, Pa," Joshua offered. "Charlie can have his own room. I know how he feels. If it gets too cold, I can get a bedroll and sleep by the kitchen stove like you."

Grant shook his head. "No child gets brought into this home and then gets shoved out into a cold barn."

"But right at first, to Charlie, it's important to have his own space." Joshua came and stood at Grant's side. Grant realized he could look straight into his son's eyes. "I don't need much."

"He don't want you in the barn." Charlie renewed his wrestling against Grant's firm hold. "He wants you inside with him. I'm the one he'll heave out into the cold."

Grant saw the burn of tears in Charlie's eyes. But Grant knew Charlie wouldn't cry. There'd been enough pain in his new son's life that nothing could shake tears loose anymore. Add to that the real fear that a show of weakness would set the other children on him like a wounded animal chased by a wolf pack and there's no way the boy would cry.

"How long have you been here?" Charlie snarled at Benny.

"I've been here almost three years."

Charlie quit struggling. Grant saw his surprise. "You must have been just a baby. They put babies on the orphan trains?"

Benny shrugged. "Pa says I was so young it didn't make no sense. That's why no one chose me. But Pa did."

Benny nodded at Marilyn. "Marilyn's just been here a few months."

Charlie looked at Pa. "The orphan trains come through that often?"

"No, Marilyn was living in an alley in LaMont. I found her there when we drove some cattle in to sell."

"The orphan train doesn't come through this route more than once every year or two," Sadie added.

"But whether we came on a train or some other way, we've all been through this." Joshua wiped the sweat from his shining black brow. He'd been cleaning stalls. "Pa brings new kids home all the time. Sadie 'n' me were with the first group of kids he adopted. We've been here ten years and we've seen lots of new brothers and sisters. He doesn't throw the old ones out or love the new ones more. He has enough love to go around."

"God has given Pa a heart that has more room in it than this whole wide Western land," Sadie said.

Grant's heart ached at hearing Sadie's kind words.

Charlie glanced at Grant, then at his other brothers and sisters, then back at Benny. He scowled.

"We're all orphans," Grant said. "Me included. I know exactly what your life has been like because I've lived the same one." Since the boy hadn't taken a swing at anyone for a full thirty seconds, Grant took a chance and released Charlie, then came around and hunkered down to his eye level.

"All of us have," Marilyn assured.

"We know how it is," Sadie nodded.

"That's why I can't let Joshua live in the barn." Grant silently prayed that Charlie would understand. "I have to treat Joshua right, and I'm going to treat you right, too. Can't you see that a parent who loves one child more than another hurts the child he loves as much as the one he doesn't love? If I treated you better than Joshua, I'd be hurting you both. I'll never desert you, no matter how angry you get. I know what it's like to hate the whole world just because it hurts too much to hope for something good."

"It's all right, Pa." Joshua said. "I can sleep in the barn. No matter where I am, I know you love me and I know God is always with me."

Grant focused on Charlie. "When you're alone in the world, God is a really good idea. It's the best lesson you'll ever learn. God will never fail you. He'll go with you wherever you end up." He smiled at the confused, angry little boy.

A deep longing appeared on Charlie's face then was wiped away by rage. "Why would God love a kid when his own parents don't?" Charlie gave Benny a violent shove, knocked him down, then whirled and ran out of the barn.

The whole family watched Charlie go.

"You think he'll run away?" Joshua crossed his arms.

"Maybe." Grant sighed. "But he can't get far. I'll talk to him. He'll get over being mad."

"I think I'd better go after him, Pa," Benny said. "I'm the one he has a problem with."

"No, he might hurt you again. I don't know all he's been through." Grant frowned and rubbed at the deep furrows that cut across his forehead. "But I can imagine."

"That's okay. I can take it. I'll watch out for branches, and if he wants to take a swing at me, well, I don't mind if he works off a little temper on me."

Grant shook his head, "Benny, thank you, but—"

"You let these children work their tempers off with fistfights?" Hannah rushed into the barn and hurried over to Benny. She immediately pulled a handkerchief out of her sleeve and began fussing over Benny's bleeding temple.

"What kind of a madhouse do you run here, I'd like to know?"

NINE

If this was a madhouse, Grant was the man in charge when he should have been an inmate.

Hannah had a good mind to shove him into a straitjacket right here on the spot.

She dropped to her knees and dabbed at the blood-soaked cut on Benny's head. "This looks ghastly! We need to get him to town to a doctor." Hannah felt her sleeve drop off her shoulder in the back. It was still stitched on the front, hanging by a few threads. She ignored it, too worried about Benny's cut to care about her dress.

"I'm okay, really, Miss Cartwright." Benny patted her hand. "I think it's already quit bleeding."

"You're very brave." Hannah comforted him. "But you're just a child. You can't see how serious this is."

At that moment, Grant caught Hannah's hands and pulled them away from Benny's head, then lifted her to her feet until their noses almost touched. "Quit fussing over him. He's all right."

"He is *not* all right." Hannah wrenched her hands against his steely, work-roughened grip. "He's hurt and bleeding. You can't just stand by and do nothing while these children harm each other."

Grant didn't even seem to notice her pathetic efforts to pull away.

"It's a head wound, ma'am," a black boy nearly as tall as Grant said politely. "Everyone knows they bleed like crazy."

As she jerked against Grant's hold, the last stitch on her sleeve gave up the ghost and the fabric fell the rest of the way down to her wrist. Grant's eyes zeroed in on her bare arm, and humiliated, she looked over at the boy who had spoken to her then looked at all the children who stood behind Grant as if they were lined up against her.

She was making a fool of herself fighting Grant's superior strength. She quit struggling and drew herself up to her full height. She came to Grant's chin.

Grant said with mild menace, "Do I have your attention?"

"You do." She spoke through gritted teeth.

Grant, without looking away from Hannah, asked, "Sadie, what work do you do around here?"

Hannah identified Sadie by the way she stood straighter and took a step closer to Grant. Her dark eyes glowed out of the ebony skin on her face. "I cook the meals with Marilyn and now Libby."

Hannah had been so upset about Benny's bleeding that she hadn't even given her little sister a look yet. She noticed Libby clinging to Marilyn, but when Sadie said Libby helped with the cooking, Libby beamed.

Sadie took the bloody handkerchief out of Hannah's confined hand and pressed it against Benny's head while she went on. "I wash a couple of batches of clothes a day and I keep the cabin straightened. I sew for the family and I ride out with the herd in the afternoon if I have time."

"Do you ever get any time to rest or have fun?" Grant asked, still staring into Hannah's eyes, holding her secure.

A flare of heat climbed up Hannah's cheeks.

Benny took over tending his wound.

Sadie stepped back beside Grant, tugged at her tightly curled black hair that had escaped from a bun, and tucked it behind her ear. "Well, sure, Pa. I go along when there's a church social. And I spend time every evening reading."

"Marilyn, how about you? Miss Cartwright is the new schoolteacher. She thinks I work you children too hard. What do you do around here?"

"The same as Sadie." Marilyn was as fair as Sadie was dark. Her fine hair was pulled into a flyaway braid that hung down nearly to her waist. Every hair that had escaped curled. Her eyes were blue under slim arched brows. Her skin was deeply tanned, and she was almost a foot taller than Sadie. "I'm also working on a patchwork quilt and I help with the younger children, see to their baths and help them with their studies and such."

"Do you have any fun, ever?"

"Since Wilbur's been sparkin' me, I have him over of an evening, and sometimes we go for a buggy ride or the whole family goes to a church social. And I spend time reading, too."

"Miss Cartwright seems to think you're a slave," Grant said in a voice so acid it nearly burned Hannah's skin.

Hannah jerked on her wrists, but Grant didn't loosen his hold.

"A slave?" Marilyn gasped.

The older black boy stepped forward. "Only a person who's never been a slave and knows nothing about slavery would make such a comment."

"That's Joshua." Grant pulled Hannah a little closer until her arms bent at the elbow and pressed against Grant's chest. "He spent the first few years of his life on a plantation. His father was sold when he was too young to remember him. His mother died after a beating from her master when Joshua was five. He escaped with some other slaves running away and ended up living on the streets in New York. Eventually he came here. How about it, Sadie? Do you think this silly woman should be throwing the word *slave* around?"

Sadie, short and black with very old eyes, crossed her arms. "My parents were emancipated before I was orphaned. I was four when they died. Joshua and I and four others lived on the street for a year. Then we found out we could hide on a cargo ship and get out of that cold, awful city. We ended up in Houston."

Grant shuddered visibly. "Sadie and Joshua, living on the street, behind Confederate lines during the war."

"How long did you live on the street?" Hannah's earliest memories were of a Chicago orphanage. Then she'd been under Parrish's thumb. But the last few years, Hannah had been little more than living on the street.

"About a year in New York before we got the idea of stowing away. We'd only been in Houston a little while when Pa found us there and—"

"Yes," Grant interrupted, "one of the boys they were running with tried to pick my pocket."

"Will," Joshua said with a fond smile.

"He was a mighty good thief," Sadie added.

Grant shook his head. "No, he wasn't, or he wouldn't'a got caught."

"He just didn't know who he was dealing with." Joshua shoved his hands in his pockets. "He didn't know he was taking on someone who'd been a hand at thievin' himself for a time."

Hannah knew how it was to be hungry or cold and see something you needed. Things had found their way into her hands, too. She'd never picked anyone's pocket, but a pie left on a windowsill or a dress hanging on a clothesline had come home with her now and then.

She'd known it was wrong and she'd gone right ahead. What's more, to survive, she'd do it again, maybe not for herself. She liked to believe she could put herself in God's hands and even face death from cold or hunger before she'd break another commandment. But if she had children in her care, she wouldn't stand by and let them starve. She couldn't. She asked for forgiveness to God and hoped the day never came again that she was forced to make such a choice. She waited for Grant to make excuses and pretty it up.

He didn't.

Joshua continued, "It's how I survived. It was wrong, and I knew it, but I did it anyway." He nodded at Sadie. "She's fifteen. Sadie is one of the few of us who knows her last name."

"Sadie Mason." The black girl tilted her chin up with pride. "My pa named himself after what he did for a living in New York. Then he and Ma died in a diphtheria outbreak. They were both born into slavery, and they were separated from five children, all sons. Their owner sold my brothers off when he needed a little spending money. I wasn't born until later, after Pa and Ma had escaped north. They told me what it was like, and even though I was mighty young when they died, I remember the scars of lash marks on both of their backs. You're a mean lady to come in here and tell Pa he's treating us bad. You don't know what bad is if you can say such things."

Hannah knew exactly what bad was. She'd lived it herself when she'd been in Parrish's hands. She had lash marks of her own, and she knew a person didn't have to be black to be a slave.

Every breath she took was for the purpose of helping and protecting children. Her heart ached to see these young spirits broken to the point that they'd defend this man. She remembered the times she'd said what Parrish expected her to say and put her whole heart into the lie, because she knew punishment awaited her if she didn't defend her pa.

She looked at the little boy who was standing beside Libby. The bleeding *had* stopped. Freckles sprinkled across his nose, and lank hair drooped across his eyes. His ears stuck straight out from his head, and his brown eyes didn't shoot pellets of rage at her. Stepping nearer to her, he watched her like he was afraid she'd vanish.

"I'm Benny, an' I'm six. Pa isn't a bad man. And I don't think you're a bad lady neither. You came out here because you were worried about us. I think that's nice. We're fine, but you can worry about us if'n you want to." He edged closer.

"You're right, Benny." Marilyn stepped up beside Grant, her blue eyes level with Hannah's. Hannah wondered if Marilyn wasn't almost her age. "She's not bad. She just doesn't know us very well yet. She doesn't understand how things work on the Rocking C."

Marilyn looked sideways at Grant and added with a teasing lilt to his voice, "You seem to have latched on to Miss Cartwright for good, Pa."

Grant looked away from Hannah and arched an eyebrow at Marilyn. Hannah saw the sassy way Marilyn grinned at him and knew for a fact that she'd never grinned at Parrish in such a way. Grant returned the smile, then let loose of Hannah's wrists and stepped away.

Hannah rubbed her wrists distractedly and noticed her sleeve dangling. She pulled the fabric up to her shoulder, but it drooped back down. Ashamed of her arm being bare, she pulled it back up and clamped her arm to her side to hold it as best she could.

Looking from one child to the next, Hannah balanced their obvious contentment here against what she knew their life must be like. She noticed Grant rubbing both his hands on his pant legs, as if touching her had gotten his hands dirty.

She finally ignored the rest of them and said to Benny, "I'm not a bad person. You're right about that, Benny. I didn't like Charlie and Libby coming here when Mr....Grant said there was no mother and not enough room. I still don't think he should have all of you out here."

Grant snorted, clamped his arms across his chest, and shook his head. He opened his mouth, but before he could speak, Joshua said, "So what would have been better, ma'am? All the folks that wanted kids had already chosen. Sour Springs is the end of the line. The only thing ahead for Charlie and Libby was a long train ride back to the orphanage. You really think they're worse off here?"

Hannah glanced doubtfully at Benny's bleeding head.

Suddenly Grant's eyes gleamed. "What is it you'd like to inspect, Hannah?"

That's when Hannah remembered she was usually afraid of men. Up until now, even with his grabbing her and looking at her with that narrow-eyed predator look, she'd forgotten to be scared.

"Why don't you come on into the house and help us get an evening meal on the table?" Grant said it so sweetly the hairs stood up on the back of her neck.

Hannah knew she was being tested. . .or maybe used. After all, there was no woman around to do chores. It was just the worst kind of dirty shame that she had never spent much time in a kitchen.

She wasn't going to admit that. "I'd be glad to stay and help. In fact, I insist upon it."

Grant jerked his head toward the barn door. "This way."

He scooped Libby up in his arms and walked past Hannah without another look. Libby looped her arms around Grant's neck and stared over his shoulder, smiling at Hannah.

Falling into line with the other children, Hannah scowled at the way they trailed after Grant. She decided to catch up and prove herself his equal. Before she could, Benny's hand slipped into hers. She looked down at the little boy.

He was watching her with wide, adoring eyes. "You smell good, ma'am."

Hannah was sorely afraid she smelled like a horse, but Benny didn't want to hear that. "That's very sweet. Thank you."

Benny crowded closer and walked slowly as if he wanted the time with her to last. Hannah's heart melted as she felt his hand cling tightly to hers. As Hannah neared the awful, undersized house, she felt even more that she had to protect these darling children.

With Parrish it had been an apartment, the children confined to their one room nearly all the time while Parrish lived in the other four rooms. This wasn't just about Libby anymore. With Benny pressed up against her, she knew she'd just fallen hopelessly in love with another one of Grant's children.

Her spine stiffened as she watched that awful man walk toward that awful house.

No matter how hard you try, Grant, until I'm sure everything is as it should be, you're not going to get me out of here.

TEN

I've got to get her out of here.

Grant strode toward the cabin, stunned by the way the kids were looking at Hannah. He didn't have to be a genius—he didn't even have to be particularly bright—to get what Benny was thinking.

Mother!

It's a good thing he didn't have to be bright because he was the dumbest man who ever lived. He'd had this little moment of insanity and thought it would teach Hannah a lesson if he made her come in and help make dinner. She would see how great the girls were as cooks. She would see the other children pitching in with a cheerful attitude, and as a bonus, he'd get a little free labor.

Now he was letting the confounded woman into his house, and she was going to see how crowded it was and how sparse and rickety the furniture. She'd see the bedrooms crammed with beds and that there really wasn't enough room for Charlie and Libby.

With a sigh, Grant admitted it didn't matter that he'd invited her. He'd have never kept her out anyway.

After one look at Benny practically wrapped around her, he didn't look back again. He should have looked sideways, because if he had he might have headed off the next question.

"Is that the only skirt you have for riding?" Marilyn asked. "I have a split skirt, and it's way handier." Marilyn tugged on her riding skirt.

"Where did you get that?" Hannah's voice sounded envious. "I've never seen one before."

"I made it." Marilyn smiled. "It's much more modest on horseback."

"You know how to sew?"

"You don't do any sewing, Miss Cartwright?" Marilyn dropped back to walk closer to Hannah.

Grant was sure that the older girls had been annoyed with Hannah just a few moments ago. Now he was feeling deserted. At least Sadie didn't—

"We could show you how, and then we could give you a pattern for a riding skirt." Sadie turned and walked backward so she could look at Hannah, since Hannah was out of sides to walk beside.

Marilyn adjusted Hannah's torn sleeve slightly. "We'll help you get this sleeve put back on. And there's a tear partway across the back. We can mend that, too."

"Oh, thank you. I was worried about getting my dress patched back together in time for school in the morning."

Grant shook his head in disgust. It looked like it was Joshua and him against the women.

"What happened to your horse, Miss Cartwright?" Joshua gave Hannah a concerned look. "I don't see it tied up anywhere."

"It threw me."

"That's how you tore your dress?" Marilyn asked.

Hannah was silent so Grant had to turn around to see her nodding and fiddling with her sleeve.

"You fell off your horse?" Grant snorted a manly snort and exchanged a look with Joshua.

Joshua's eyes were fixed on Hannah. "Are you all right?"

"I was upset when I heard the screaming coming from the barn. I kicked the horse to hurry him up, and he tossed me off his back. I'm afraid he's long gone by now."

"Don't worry about it." Joshua dropped back to walk closer to

Hannah, too. "If you rented him from in town, he'll go back. I'll hitch up the team and give you a ride home after supper."

"Why, thank you, Joshua."

That left Charlie. Grant had no hope. Charlie had taken off somewhere, and if he was here, he'd probably throw in with Hannah just to prove how much he hated his new family.

Grant thought of all the places there were around here to hide. Usually the young'uns picked a favorite, and Grant got onto it and could find them in a pinch. But Charlie hadn't been here long enough for Grant to know where he'd hole up.

"I'd better go find out where Charlie took off to."

"Leave him be, Pa." Joshua looked around. There was no sign of the boy anywhere.

Grant shook his head. "I'd better go."

"I've got a feeling about Charlie, Pa. I think he might be better after he's had some time to cool down." Joshua held Grant's gaze, clearly expecting Grant to listen.

Grant all of a sudden realized that while he wasn't looking Joshua had turned from a boy to a man. Then he counted and realized Joshua would be seventeen in a couple of months—based on the age and birthday Grant had urged Joshua to pick when he'd come here so they could have a special meal for his birthday. For all Grant knew, Joshua could be twenty by now.

Grant had been on his own by that time. In fact he'd adopted six kids the year he turned seventeen. One of them was Joshua, and the boy was a son to Grant in every way imaginable without being flesh and blood.

Grant's older girls talked sewing with Hannah. Benny and Libby had found a new ma. And Joshua had just grown up right in front of his eyes. For the father of six, Grant didn't have much to do. He slumped his shoulders and wondered if he hadn't oughta adopt more kids as soon as possible.

They got to the house, and he remembered why he shouldn't have taken the two he'd just gotten. He shifted Libby to one side while he held the door open, thinking he could at least serve some purpose manning the door. He let the whole family troop past, minus one troubled young boy, plus one interfering female.

He noticed Hannah having trouble getting in the door with her little vine, Benny, clinging to her. She veered a bit too close to Grant while she went in sideways, and Grant got something else in his head to worry about.

Benny was right. Hannah did smell good.

He had a notion to tell her. For some reason it reminded him of that strange, secretive look that had passed between Ian and Megan at church this morning. With only the vaguest idea of what it meant and why he'd think of it now, Grant fought down a surge of restlessness that he'd rarely felt before, being exhausted half to death most of the time.

But somehow that restlessness erased his impatience with Hannah, and he didn't mind her staying around quite so much. His mind swirled with a lot of confusing thoughts he couldn't pin down. And he considered how nice Hannah would look in a split skirt as he followed close after her.

Then Hannah gasped.

He stepped well away and focused his eyes elsewhere. Before she could start in on him, he said defensively, "It's the house my folks left me when they died. I've been meaning to build on, but money's scarcer 'n hens' teeth and time is scarcer yet. I've got three bedrooms. The girls, Marilyn, Sadie, and now Libby, sleep together."

"Parents? I thought you were an orphan." Hannah hoisted Benny up in her arms as if she'd done it a thousand times.

"My folks adopted me off an orphan train when I was fourteen. I lived with 'em for a couple of years before they were killed when their team ran away with their wagon. They left me this house, and it was so quiet I couldn't stand it. I went to enlist in the Confederacy, went as far as Houston and found six kids living in an alley. I just turned around and brought 'em back home."

"You adopted six children when you were sixteen?"

"I was seventeen by then. And later, after the war, I got more young'uns that were leftovers on an orphan train."

Hannah settled Benny more firmly on her hip as if she planned on taking him with her. "That's ridiculous. Who allowed that?"

"Martha was riding with the children even then."

"What was the matter? Did you need help on the ranch?"

Grant stepped close to Hannah. He knew he should back off, but he didn't quite have the self-control. "I had a home. Those children needed it."

"A seventeen-year-old boy isn't a parent. What were you doing? Adopting *playmates*?"

"I'm not saying I was a good parent, but I could put a roof over their heads."

"Children need more than a roof. Mrs. Norris should have been reported for allowing such nonsense."

"Martha will be given jewels in her crown in heaven for bending the rules and letting me take those kids."

"I may report her yet." Hannah tore her eyes away from Grant and stroked one hand over Benny's hair, still soaked from after-church sledding and tinged with blood. "Isn't she answerable to anyone?"

"You leave her alone." Grant's eyes narrowed. "She's the finest woman I've ever known. If you cause her one second's trouble, so help me, Hannah, I'll—"

"Don't you threaten me." Hannah stepped right up into his face. "If my complaint causes her trouble, then what does that say about her actions? If she's got nothing to hide, then—"

"What was the point of me living in a house by myself while they had nothing?" Grant leaned down toward the stubborn woman. "I didn't plan it, but I couldn't let them go all the way back to New York."

Hannah's chest heaved and her eyes flashed fire. She clung to Benny as if she'd be willing to fight and die to protect him.

This little spitfire was as alive and spirited as anyone he'd ever known. Grant couldn't look away.

"If you were adopted, why didn't you take your parents' name? Then all these children would have names."

"My parents' name was Cooper. I can use that if I need to. But I want to remember what it's like to not have a name."

"Why? Why would you cling to that memory? By not claiming a legitimate last name, you're reminded every second of every day of your hardships. That has to be. . .exhausting." Hannah shuddered as if she herself had burdens that rode on her shoulders and never let her rest.

Grant wondered what those burdens were, and if she'd had any luck forgetting. He didn't think so. He thought his way was more honest. "It's who I am. It's *what* I am. Why try and forget something that is unforgettable?"

Her eyes narrowed as she studied him. She glanced at Libby in Grant's arms, and the two females exchanged a long, secretive look.

Grant tightened his hold on his newest daughter. He'd have to keep a sharp eye out or this lady might go to stealing his children. "The second I forget what it's like to be alone, maybe I'll forget there are children in this world who need me. I'll never do that." Grant held Hannah's gaze.

He saw her waver between compassion for the children and maybe some compassion for him. Her eyes hardened and she hugged Benny closer.

His shoulders slumped. He'd picked a life that was one long fight— wonderful but troubled children, unkind townspeople, and contemptuous teachers. He looked at the bedroll he'd shoved under the kitchen table. He didn't even have a room to sleep in anymore.

Disgusted, he shook his head. "I'm through wasting my breath on you. Why'd I think for even a minute you might understand?"

He turned away and set Libby in a chair by the stove. "Just finish your inspection and go, teacher lady. I told you where the girls sleep. Joshua has the back bedroom, and Charlie and Benny sleep in the loft. That's not too crowded."

"You forgot to mention yourself, Pa." Sadie pointed out helpfully. "You're going to sleep where it's warm by the fire. So the off side of the kitchen is your bedroom. That makes four bedrooms."

Thanks a lot. Grant knew Hannah wouldn't let that pass. He shook his head and braced himself.

"A four-bedroom home," Hannah said with a surprising amount of sarcasm for a woman holding a child so gently in her arms. "Why, it's the next thing to a mansion."

Of course Grant's house wasn't a mansion. The kitchen was just barely big enough to contain one long thin table, two benches on each long side, a stool on each short side, a potbelly stove, a dry sink, and a fireplace. When he'd started, he had the cabin, the land, and a few dozen head of cattle left to him by his parents, but not a penny in cash. He'd scrimped and saved, living off the land for years. These days, with his herd growing and a couple of cattle drives under his belt, he had some cash money, but counting pennies got to be a habit and it was a good lesson to teach his kids. So what if they'd never gotten much that was fancy? What furniture wasn't left from his parents' time, Grant had made by hand, like the extra long table.

I know how to make things sturdy, but no one would accuse me of makin' 'em pretty.

The girls' bedroom was on the east side of the house. It had its own door and stretched half as wide as the little kitchen and as long as the bunk bed it contained—the room's only piece of furniture.

Joshua's room was a lean-to on the back of the house that had been meant as a place to hang coats and kick off muddy boots. The loft overhead dropped down a scant few feet from the peaked roof. Benny and Charlie had to shimmy in on their bellies, and it was barely long enough to stretch out in. It had been Grant's bedroom while Benny slept with Joshua, until last night.

Grant saw Hannah inspecting through the wide open door to the girls' room. The orphanage Grant had grown up in had bunks, and he'd done his best to build his own version with no advice or pattern.

And every spare inch of the house—of which there were few—was jammed to the rafters with children and fabric and clothes set to be handed down. Grant couldn't help being embarrassed about the shabby little house. Hannah's disapproval rolled toward him in waves.

Dragging his Stetson off, he hung it on one of the dozen racks of deer antlers lining one wall, coats and hats hanging from them all. "Look, I know it's not much," he began before she could start in on him. "I've been meaning to build on. But the kids need things like books and shoes and we've got a lot of mouths to feed. I'm not spending my money on lumber, and the only available wood to cut is on a slope too dangerous to tangle with. We need to eat and sleep and we've got it. We spend most every minute of the day outside anyway, tending the herd and doing chores."

Grant snapped his mouth shut. He hadn't intended to start listing off the work the kids had to do, but there was nothing wrong with a young'un having chores!

Hannah looked rather helplessly around the little house until Marilyn distracted her by saying, "Let's get started on supper."

Hannah bit her lip and looked uncomfortable. "I. . .I'm not a very good cook."

"We can handle it," Sadie said. "You're company. You just sit and watch."

"No." Hannah removed her bedraggled bonnet and found a spare antler.

Grant really looked at that limp, tattered bonnet for the first time. Of course he'd noticed how Hannah looked. He hadn't done much *except* notice her anytime she'd been within a hundred feet of him. But for the first time he looked beyond the flashing blue in her glaring eyes and the pretty pink of her insult-spouting lips.

The ride out to the Rocking C had been hard on her. Her horse had thrown her. He'd barely registered that when she'd said it, even though Joshua had thought to express concern. There was dirt streaked on her fair skin, and the neat bun she'd had at church was gone. Buffalo burrs clung to the back of her ripped-up dress, the same dress she'd had on yesterday at the train station and at church, although it was travel-stained. It was faded as if it'd been washed hundreds of times and the seams looked nearly worn through. The cuffs and collar were frayed. Grant knew enough about not having that he was abruptly, absolutely sure that this was the only dress Hannah owned.

Marilyn rested a hand on Hannah's arm. "Sit down, Miss Cartwright. While Sadie starts supper, I'll baste this sleeve back on and put a patch on the back of your dress. It'll only take a minute."

"Thank you so much, Marilyn." Her eyes said thank you a hundred times more than her words.

How had she learned the children's names already? Half the people in Sour Springs didn't even bother to learn them. Of course they were as different from each other as night and day, but it took a bit of time and effort to learn someone's name. The good folks of Sour Springs seemed to have no interest in exerting either.

As Marilyn fussed over her, Grant noticed the dark circles under Hannah's eyes. The long train ride she'd finished only yesterday—the same one that had worn Libby and Charlie to a nub—had beaten her down, too. But even exhausted, she hurried out here to check on some orphaned children.

Grant thought again of that look between Ian and Megan. He knew nothing about what passed between men and women, and he had the unnerving notion that maybe Hannah could explain it to him.

Marilyn turned Hannah to face the lantern, and while Marilyn threaded a needle, Grant caught himself studying a chunk of Hannah's bare back that showed through a gaping hole in her dress. His eyes narrowed as he realized what he was seeing—scars.

With a quick, unplanned step, he was behind Hannah, pulling the fabric aside. "What happened here? Did you do this falling off your horse?"

She froze while Grant's hand traced the jagged furrow that disappeared behind the fabric. Then with jerky, uncoordinated movements, Hannah pulled away from him. He hung on until he heard a tear in the threadbare fabric. Not wanting to ruin what must be her only dress, he let go. Furious at that mark, a mark he bore himself, he wanted to see how deep it was and how long and if there were others. And how old it was. No fall off a horse this afternoon put this mark on her.

She turned so her back was away from him—out of reach, out of sight. "It's nothing Mr. . . .Grant. I insist you keep your hands off me." Her tone could have turned water into ice and her eyes were colder still.

But her trembling lip wasn't cold. She was obviously afraid of his question.

"Hannah, tell me what—"

Pleading with her eyes, she said, "Leave it alone."

"Please." Grant took a faltering step toward her in the tiny cabin. No one was far apart, but even so Grant was far too close to Hannah.

Marilyn came up behind Hannah and, after a quick glance at the scar, looked up and shook her head, warning Grant off.

He clenched his fists and saw Hannah look at that sign of anger as if afraid he'd use those fists on her. And that stopped him when no words would have.

He thought of her spunk yesterday and today. But those marks had been put there by someone laying a whip or a rod to her back. Far too many of the children he adopted bore them. So how had she gotten them?

He'd have the answer. . .but not now.

Sadie sneaked a peak at Hannah's back from where she peeled potatoes at the table. She looked quickly away, running a damp, trembling hand up her own arm, which had been scarred by boiling water. A man who caught her stealing food out of the garbage in his alley had thrown it at her.

Joshua came to Sadie's side, gave her a quick hug, took the potatoes and sharp knife away, and started peeling.

"I'll go get us a chicken." Sadie rushed out of the cabin.

Grant looked after her. She needed a few minutes when she got to thinking about her days on the street, more so than the other children. There was a lot she'd never told and probably never would. He let her go.

Marilyn took quick careful stitches on Hannah's dress as the room fell silent. Each of his children lost in his or her memories. Grant had plenty of his own.

Fighting the need to punch somebody, Grant noticed Libby stand from her chair by the stove and limp into her bedroom.

He remembered a job that needed a father's hand. Glad for an excuse to leave the room and break the spell that had settled on Hannah, his children, and himself, he followed Libby into her room. "Let's have a look at your shoe, Lib."

Libby sank onto the bottom bunk and looked at him with wide, scared eyes. Trembling all over, she stretched her little foot out toward him.

It was wrong to hate, Grant knew it all the way to his soul. He was a believer in God and had read the Bible clear through several times. He knew, above all else, God called His believers to love and forgive. But right that minute, Grant hated every person who'd ever made any child fearful. Hannah sat in there not willing to talk about the marks on her back. Sadie shook with the memories that burned more deeply than boiling water. Grant thought of a woman working in his orphanage who had taken the job, he was sure, to have access to defenseless children and feed her hunger for inflicting pain.

And here sat this little girl feeling like her broken ankle made her unworthy of love. Grant knew her silence was rooted in her fear. How many times had she been hurt for speaking the wrong words? What made her hide inside herself this way? What had she seen that was unspeakable?

Grant sank down onto his knees in front of his new daughter and took her tiny shoe in his hand. "I want you to know, Libby, that having a foot that's hurt doesn't make you any less of a wonderful little girl."

Libby dropped her gaze to the floor.

Grant barely fit in the space between the bed and the wall as he slipped off her shoe and inspected. "Does it hurt, honey?"

Shaking her head, her lower lips trembled.

Setting the shoe aside on the lumpy mattress, Grant studied the thickened ridge around her ankle and the thin scars that spoke of medical treatment that helped ease Grant's temper and shake him loose of his memories. At least someone had cared enough to try and help her.

He let loose of her foot and said briskly, so his voice wouldn't shake, "Now, get up off 'a that bed and stand straight in front of me. I think I know a way to help your leg."

Libby stood straight, looking at the wall over his head as if she expected him to hurt her. Grant suspected she'd been hurt plenty in her life. As he reached for her leg, Libby looked away from the wall and out the door to the kitchen. The way Libby's eyes lit up, he knew only one person could be there.

Hannah was inspecting him again.

He wanted to turn on Hannah and order her out, but the mule-stubborn woman didn't obey orders worth a hoot. Instead he ignored her and studied the way Libby stood and experimented with lifting her foot a bit. "Lib, I think your leg must have healed shorter than it was before. I can make the sole on your shoe thicker and maybe you won't limp anymore."

Libby looked skeptical, but Grant knew she was out of practice at hoping.

Grant took Libby's worn-out little lace-up boot and went with it to the kitchen. Gathering his razor sharp hunting knife, he pulled a piece of thick leather from one of the untidy mounds of clothing and fabric. Next he hunted up several tack nails. Settling himself at the kitchen table, since that was where the only chairs in the house were, he went to work.

Joshua set the potatoes on to boil. "I'll have a look around for Charlie. He might have cooled off by now."

"Thanks, son." Grant turned his attention back to the shoe.

Once her dress was repaired to the best of Marilyn's ability, Hannah donned an apron and hesitantly offered to help cook supper.

While Grant repaired Libby's boot, he got to watch the show.

ELEVEN

"I thank you for all your help making my home run better, Hannah." Grant lifted the reins and started the wagon moving.

Hannah sighed and wished like crazy that Joshua had been allowed to drive her home. But the supper had been late—thanks to her. Night had fallen early as it did this time of year, and Grant had declared the trail treacherous. Hannah thought of the long, flat trail to town and wondered where the treachery was—being tormented to death by Grant maybe?

"Ignoring the last two hours was too much to hope for, I see."

"Yep." Grant's gloved hand settled his Stetson more firmly on his head as the wind threatened to whip it off. His dark hair, a ridiculous length for a man, had escaped its pony tail again and now whipped around his ears and collar. "You definitely made it clear to me why I mustn't take a child without first having a wife."

Hannah thought he might be rolling his eyeballs at her. She thanked God for the darkness.

The wind blew her poor battered dress across Grant. Delicately—for a lummox—he pushed her skirt off his leg. He briefly fingered the charred spot around her knee.

Hannah just barely resisted the urge to slap him. "As long as you insist on talking, why don't we discuss sending the children to school?"

As her eyes adjusted to the night, she could now see Grant give her a sideways look. "They'll be there until I decide they shouldn't be."

And what was that supposed to mean exactly? "Why on earth wouldn't you want your children in school?"

"It's not the schooling. I'd love to have some help with that. I know there are some gaps in my own education, since I never went to school myself."

Hannah gasped and turned on him. "You don't know how to read? Is that it? Mr. . . .Grant, I can help you with that. I'd be more than glad to—" Hannah snapped her mouth shut when she remembered Grant reading a chapter of the Bible before they'd started eating.

"As I was saying," Grant said with exaggerated patience, "my children have had some bad experiences with both students and teachers. It's mainly the other children, but some of the teachers have been cruel, and there are people in town who don't want my children mixing with theirs. After all, orphanhood might be contagious."

"I'll see that none of that goes on." Hannah almost liked the man for a second. If only she could be sure he treated them as well when no one was watching. She knew how good a front Parrish had put on.

Grant gave her a long look. "You say you'll do it. I suppose I believe you. We almost always give a new teacher a chance, although one comes and goes so fast sometimes, we don't even get in before she's gone. The Brewsters, the family that treated the kids the worst, left town."

Although he spoke quietly, Grant's tone changed until it was as grim as death. "But the first time one of the kids comes home asking what some ugly word means, and I have to explain it means his daddy wasn't married to his mama, well, I'll just keep 'em home."

Hannah could feel the fury in Grant. It exactly matched hers. She'd been called that word. The main person to call her that had been Parrish, the man who insisted she call him pa.

"There will be no crude talk like that in my school, Mr. . . .Grant."

"Maybe you'll try, Hannah." Grant took his eyes off the trail and met her gaze. "Maybe you will. But you can't watch all of them every minute."

Hannah knew that was true, and she wouldn't make a promise to Grant she couldn't keep. Grant fell silent and seemed to concentrate on his driving. They got to the end of the first stretch of trail and, instead of Grant turning and going the way she'd come, he followed a trail that was nothing more than a pair of wagon tracks. In the moonlight, the trail seemed to head directly for an impassable mountain.

"This isn't the way back to Sour Springs." She looked at the trail they were slowly leaving.

"Thank goodness you're here, Hannah," Grant said with mock relief. "I've only lived here for twelve years. I might not be able to find my way back to town without your able assistance. After all, you've been a resident of Sour Springs for. . .how many hours now?"

Hannah fairly vibrated with annoyance. She was really tired of Grant's overly polite chiding. "I *demand* to know where you're taking me, Mr. . . .Grant."

"That's not my name, you know." Grant hi-upped to the horses and slapped the reins gently across their backs. The traces jingled; the horses picked up speed. He didn't turn back.

Hannah looked at him. "Grant isn't your name?"

The corner of his mouth turned up in a smile as rude as it was unamused. "No, Mr. . . .Grant isn't my name." He greatly exaggerated the pause between Mister and Grant.

"Excuse me for having manners, Mr. . . .Grant." Hannah could feel that one coming, but she couldn't stop herself. "If you don't want me stumbling over your name, then you should pick a proper one." Hannah settled in her seat prepared, now that she'd spoken her mind, to ignore him all the way to town.

"You're very brave for a woman who is probably being taken out into the wilderness to be abandoned." Grant rested the reins on his ragged pants, the knees patched and the patches worn through. The calm, cooperative horses seemed to know the way without much guidance from him. Maybe he dumped people off in the wilderness regularly, especially unwanted children.

Hannah grabbed the seat and whirled to face him. "I knew this wasn't the way to town!"

"Well, that's a nice surprise." Grant shoved hair out of his eyes. "There *is* something you finally know. What a relief."

"I'm sorry about the potatoes." Hannah should have been more afraid, but for some reason the only feeling Grant seemed to stir in her was anger. She clenched her fists in her lap. "How many times do I have to say that?"

"How about once for every one of my kids who didn't get a full belly because of you."

"Marilyn made more!" Hannah knew she was out of line, but he kept goading her and she'd apologized nearly once per child already.

"That's good then. We grew enough potatoes to feed the whole family several times over. It's probably best to burn some of them up. If it weren't for the stink—"

"I'm sorry! I'm sorry! I'm sorry! That's three. How many children did you have again? Too many for a mere schoolteacher to count at a glance. Was it six? I'm sorry, I'm sorry, I'm sorry."

"At least you chased down the ones you spilled all over the floor. Having you crawl around under the table was kind of like having a pet. The kids have been wanting a dog."

Hannah didn't hit him, and he was too dense to know what a lucky man he was. "Not everyone was born being at home in a kitchen, Mr. . . . Grant." Okay, she was going to stop doing that. It went against the grain, but she was going to have to start calling him Grant without the mister.

"Yes, Missssss. . . Cartwright, I could see that cleaning a chicken was a mystery to you. I believe you ended up wearing the few feathers you managed to separate from the poor bird."

"I have skills. . . Grant. They just don't extend to gutting chickens." She could thread a weaving loom so fast no eyes could follow her fingers.

She hoped to never have to thread one again.

"No need to point that out, Hannah. I got that plain as day."

Hannah sniffed at him. "Cleaning a chicken is disgusting. I refuse to be ashamed of not having such dreadful knowledge."

"You do admit the hypocrisy of *eating* a chicken when you can't bear the thought of getting it cooked."

"I admit no such thing. I'm not stupid. I'm just untrained. I could learn to clean a chicken and boil potatoes without scorching them and—"

"And to stop slicing the bread just one tiny, little second before you get to your hand."

Hannah looked down at her throbbing thumb. Why had Grant insisted on bandaging it himself? Surely his daughters usually handled the nursing. She had the clumsy knotted rag on her hand to prove Grant didn't know what he was doing. And she was left with the warmth of his hands on her—a warmth that lasted long after he'd quit touching. Of course Grant had been obnoxious the whole time he'd done his crude doctoring, but Benny had pressed against her side and murmured comforting words.

And all of that might have been forgotten, since the girls took over and did the meal with her safely settled out of the way, if she hadn't tried to redeem herself by pulling the pot of coffee out of the coals and—

"How exactly did you manage to set your skirt on fire?"

Hannah was done with being badgered. "You were right there and you know good and well how it happened!"

The team slowed as it began pulling them slightly upward. The trail didn't go right up the side of the hill; it slanted across the face of it. They were sloped sideways with Hannah on the uphill side, and they skidded occasionally on spots left slippery with melting snow. Hannah couldn't stop herself from leaning hard against Grant, despite her struggle to keep her distance. Grant's shoulder was like solid iron beside her. Warm, solid iron.

Grant seemed supportive of her efforts to stay away from him because he gave her the occasional strange look that she imagined must mean, "Get over."

But now she understood what Grant had meant about the treacherous trail. The good side of that was Grant was too occupied driving the team to torment her.

With a sigh, Hannah wondered how she'd come to a point in her life that she had to choose between hugging up against a man who delighted in insulting her or rolling off a cliff. One prospect was as unpleasant as the other. In the end she just clung to the seat.

Just when she thought her spine had taken such a beating that she'd be permanently tilted to the left, they came out on top of the bluff, and Hannah could see the brightly lit windows of the little town of Sour Springs right at the bottom of the hill in front of them.

"I rode that horse nearly ten miles!"

"Zeb at the livery gave you directions?" Grant's brow furrowed, and though his expression held its usual grouchiness, for the first time it wasn't aimed at her.

"No, Zeb didn't tell me. It was Harold at the general store. He said there was another way, but it was confusing."

He pressed down on the wagon brake and sent the team over the crest. Now they were tilted sideways in Hannah's direction.

"Ah, Harold." Sawing the reins with one strong hand encased in a worn-out glove, he leaned hard on the brake and kept his eyes strictly on the trail ahead. "He's easily confused."

After a brief pause, Grant added, "But it was Zeb who rented you Rufus?"

Something in his tone made Hannah glance at him. "Was that the horse's name? We were never introduced."

Grant turned away from the crazy trail and grinned at her. It was definitely the first time he'd done that—of course he'd laughed at her quite a bit, but that wasn't the same thing at all.

"A swaybacked, gray horse with a white blaze, one white front leg, and a bad attitude?"

"There are, no doubt, several horses in the livery that fit that description." Hannah had the sudden urge to protect Zeb, and she didn't know why.

"Nope. I think Zeb saw an easy two bits and landed old Rufus slap on top of you." Grant added in a grim tone that didn't bode well for Zeb, "He hadn't'a oughta done that."

The trail canted. Grant leaned against her, and she didn't think he was making the least effort to prevent the contact. She braced her arm against the seat and held them both on the wagon.

After far too long of brushing hard up against him, they reached the bottom of the bluff and within minutes were at the edge of Sour Springs.

"You can probably get the worst of that scorching out just by washing the skirt." Grant paused while he straightened the team out and headed for the diner as if he already knew where she lived. Most likely he did. It was a small town. "You do know how to wash clothes, don't you?"

Hannah would have given her first month's salary, all twenty dollars of it, to have a washboard and a few minutes of freedom with Grant's head at that moment. She glared at him, and he laughed in her face as he pulled the team to a halt.

He swung down and came around to help her. Hannah hurried to arrange her skirts and climb down before he got there. She didn't so much climb down off the buckboard as she fell. Grant caught her.

He steadied her feet under her and said with a smug grin, "Thanks for the help with dinner, ma'am." He deepened his Texas drawl and did his best, Hannah knew, to sound as dumb as a post. "Shore am glad we had a woman around for a change."

Hannah didn't have the energy to hit him. She stiffened her spine and became aware that Grant was still holding her up. He was so strong she could imagine leaning on him forever.

Just because she'd made a fool of herself didn't mean she wasn't right about Grant and his children. "You have to do something about the conditions those children live in."

Grant dropped his hands from her waist, far too slowly to Hannah's way of thinking. He kept up the dumb act. "So you're gonna let me keep 'em now? You just want me to keep 'em better. I reckon that's progress."

His comment surprised her because he was right. Somewhere in the middle of the girls mending her dress and making dinner in such a competent manner she *had* changed her mind. She had no intention of admitting that.

She also noticed Grant rubbing his hands on his pants leg again. Touching her must be repulsive. No doubt he'd wash his hands for an hour as soon as he got home. . .that was assuming the untidy man washed at all.

"Surely it doesn't cost that much to add on a couple of bedrooms." Hannah walked toward her boardinghouse wishing he would leave so she could go upstairs and be alone with her humiliation.

"It doesn't cost much, just more than I have," Grant said. "As I already told you, I could cut down the timber to build on, and it wouldn't cost me nothing but time and a few aching muscles, but the stand of trees fit for building is on a slope so steep I'd have to risk my neck to get at 'em. My children have a roof to keep the rain off their heads and plenty to eat. Well, 'cept for today. Today was kinda slim pickins, what with you burning most of it to a cinder. I never knew how tricky all this woman stuff could be. Guess that's cuz it all came so easy to me and it being so easy to teach to all my many mistreated children."

Hannah whirled on him at his last dig. "I know I don't have womanly skills! I accept that about myself."

Suddenly Grant's teasing smile faded, and he spoke so softly that it was almost a whisper. "When are you going to tell me how you got those scars, Hannah?"

A dog barked, breaking the silence that lay like death between them. Grant's team shifted as they stood, and the hardware of the traces clinked together.

"That's none of your business, Grant. I'm never going to talk about it and you shouldn't have seen my. . .uh. . .shoulder uncovered."

Grant's eyes narrowed and Hannah prayed he'd let it go. He studied her, waiting, thinking, wondering. She saw his frustration. He wanted answers, but she wondered if maybe he also *didn't* want to know. If he'd been an orphan, he knew children had stories they didn't want to relive, either by speaking of their own experiences or listening to someone else's. She thought of all she'd suffered at Parrish's hands, and the words wanted to flood out. Her throat clogged shut with anger and pain and heartbreak. She understood all too well how Libby could choose to not talk. Sometimes the words were too awful to be spoken aloud.

"I know it's none of my business." Grant tugged off one glove and ran a finger over the seam Marilyn had sewn in Hannah's dress. "It's just that—"

"Go home, Grant." She could do it. She could be tough and resist the temptation he offered to lean on his broad shoulder. She needed him to go away. This day and the kindness of his children was all she could handle. "Make sure you have your children in school tomorrow. If you keep them home, I'm going to—" Her voice broke.

Surprise flashed in his eyes, and she turned and marched toward the back door of the diner. He wasn't allowed up, thank heavens. Tears burned behind her eyes and she hurried all the more. Hard fingers closed on her arm before she got inside.

She turned back only because he made her. She stared at the second button of his shirt, fighting back the unexpected tears and waiting in rigid silence for his sickening pity.

Grant tapped her chin until she lifted it and met his eyes. He said softly, "Let's just hope you can teach school better'n you can cook."

Hannah's mouth gaped open on a gasp, and she made a fist that she would most likely have used on his smirking face if he hadn't headed back for the buckboard, laughing like a maniac every step of the way.

He drove off with a jaunty wave.

She watched him go and noticed he went to Zeb's livery instead of heading back up the steep trail. It took her a moment, but she realized she was standing in the alley behind the diner staring after the man. She whirled around and rushed inside. It was only as she climbed the stairs to her tiny, lonely room that she realized Grant had headed off a bout of tears by deliberately insulting her. It was by far the nicest thing he'd done so far.

And anyway, she desperately hoped she *could* teach school better than she cooked because she'd never done it before, either.

"Is the gap melting down at all?" Grace thought her throat might shut up completely.

"Nope, sky-high and no getting out of it. It's been too cold for a thaw."

Grace stepped away from Daniel as if he were aiming a gun at her. She didn't rest her hand on the baby in her belly because Daniel tended to run screaming when she made any reference or gesture that reminded him of the young one.

"So, how about the pass?" Grace twisted her hands together as if she were wringing a wet dishcloth. Or Daniel's neck.

"The high pass, Ma?" Mark looked up from the fireplace. He and his brothers were thawing out after they'd ridden out to inspect the cattle. They'd be warm and back outside in a matter of minutes. Grace had a strange urge to beg them to stay inside and talk to her. She felt so alone, trapped, strangled, desperate.

Okay, calm down!

103

She pulled a long breath into her lungs. "Well, what would you boys like for dinner? I've got a mind to make a cake."

The boys cheered and beamed at her. She had their undivided attention.

"We're well stocked with honey and flour and eggs."

She thought of the high pass. In fact, she thought she heard a voice whispering to her through the tall pines that lined the canyon. Calling her to come up, come over, go see Tillie or Sophie.

Go see Hannah.

That letter had been driving her close to mad, knowing Hannah was so near. She'd calculated that it would be a three-day train ride only. Simple.

She shook her head before she raced outside to follow that voice.

"Maybe one or two of you boys would like to stay in with me and help me mix the batter."

A chorus of groans almost deafened her.

"You stay and help her. You're a baby!" Mark shoved Matthew straight toward the fire. Matthew lurched to the side and toppled into Abe, who slugged him. Matt did a sideways dive that would have made a circus acrobat proud then fell over backward into Mark, who screamed as if he'd had an arm severed.

The whispering outside grew louder. Grace smiled. She felt almost insanely calm as she decided it was wrong of her to be the only one in control of herself in this family. Why, it was almost a sin. If she really loved her boys and Daniel, she'd be out of control, too. It was the right thing to do.

Her smile fixed firmly. "I need some fresh air."

Grace snagged her coat and boots as she dashed outside. No one noticed her leave, being involved in a riot as they were. A foot, or maybe a body, slammed into the door just as she swung it shut.

She slipped on the boots then pulled on her coat as she started walking toward the high-up hill. She didn't bother catching up a horse.

It was only a mile or so.

Then she got to the part that was mostly straight up, with icy ledges and treacherous toe holds buried in snow. She should probably wait for a thaw, but that thought didn't even slow her down. She reached the first clump of trees and began singing as if the trees were a chorus of angels and she was lead soprano.

Daniel didn't catch her until she was up and over and within a mile of Adam and Tillie's house. He grabbed her arm. "What in the world are you doing, woman?"

Grace's ears had quit playing with her mind—or was her mind playing with her ears—as soon as she'd topped the high pass. She turned and smiled at her husband, not wanting to punch him at all. "I believe I mentioned that I'd like to get out and see Sophie once or twice this winter. Being snowed in is a bit—" Grace quit talking before she told him the truth. That it was possible she was losing her sanity. That it was possible she'd start screaming or maybe beating on him while he slept. She rubbed the back of her neck while she stood there facing her husband.

He pulled his hat off his head. The wind whipped through his overlong blond hair, and Grace tried to remember the last time she'd made him sit for a haircut. She'd thought of it a few times, but her hand had gotten a bit shaky at the thought of standing behind Daniel's back with a sharp object. She brushed her hand over his hair.

"Grace, I've got chores."

"I'm over the treacherous part, Daniel. You should have just gone on back to your chores and not worried about me."

Grace saw Abe, a mile or so behind them, dropping down the cliff with reckless speed. She didn't even cringe when she saw Matt strapped on Abe's back. They'd be fine.

"No, it's a long walk to Adam's. There're dangerous animals out here, Grace. What kind of husband would I be if I didn't protect my family?"

With a loud snap, a branch Abe was using for support broke. Her oldest son fell forward and slid on his belly the rest of the way down the cliff. Matt screamed and laughed and slid for about a hundred feet as if he was on a sled and Abe had fallen specially, just to make the trip fun.

Daniel glanced backward but didn't react. Fine job he was doing protecting any of them.

"Uh, Daniel, the whole bunch of us Reeves seem to have a knack for survival. I think I'll be okay."

"The boys are sturdy enough, but wives are puny, sickly things, and I think I'd better stay close."

Mark topped the canyon wall.

Grace felt her lower lip begin to tremble. "So, are all the boys coming?"

Daniel settled his Stetson more firmly on his head. "Once we figured out you'd cleared the canyon rim, I sent 'em back to do the chores and told 'em to come on along once they were ready."

Abe picked himself up, and Matthew shrieked and kicked his brother's sides and yelled, "Giddup!"

John's head popped up atop the rocks.

"Let's go then." She turned and strode toward Adam's, planning to make a better headstart for herself next time. Maybe if she snuck out in the night—

"You know there are mountain lions in these parts. It shore were a stupid idea for you to set out on your own." Daniel fell into step beside her and rested an arm along her shoulders.

Grace nodded. "Not the first stupid thing I've done." She gave him a significant look, but he smiled and didn't seem to get the hint that *he* might qualify.

"Reckon that's true enough." He pursed his lips and pulled her a bit closer. "And reckon it won't be the last."

Grace picked up the pace, but the boys still caught them before she was even close to Tillie. Somehow she didn't mind. Now that she was going visiting, she liked having her family along.

Gingham Mountain

When Adam's neat cabin came into sight, Adam was outside tending his livestock and he straightened and waved. He was too far away from them for Grace to see his face, but she could imagine his pleasure at having company.

Adam, a black man who was good friends to the Reeves and a right hand man to the McClellens before he started his own ranch, waved again, then walked briskly toward the house, telling Tillie the good news no doubt. By the time Adam vanished inside, the boys had whooped at the sight of their friend and started racing toward the house.

Grace made only the barest notice of Adam stepping outside and shuttering the windows. He'd barely closed one when Mark sent a branch he'd been using as a walking stick straight at Ike's head. It missed Ike and slammed up against the shutter.

Adam finished securing the shutters and turned to face them. "Well, hello there, neighbors. Didn't figure to see you again until spring."

Tillie came outside, and Grace saw that Tillie's stomach got out the door well ahead of her.

"You're expecting a baby?" Grace gasped and ran toward Tillie.

Bright white teeth flashed in Tillie's dark-skinned face as she laid one hand on her belly. "Yes, I am. We haven't been to town in a spell, and of course Adam never thinks to mention it, so the word is just now getting out."

"I'm so glad to s—see you." Her voice broke and she launched herself into Tillie's arms.

Tillie hugged Grace closer. Tillie was enough older than Grace that Grace almost felt mothered. Tillie turned, Grace still in her arms, and walked with her toward the cabin. "I'll make us a nice cup of tea."

Abe opened the cabin door.

"Hey!"

Adam's voice startled Grace. She noticed the boys stopped in their tracks to look at him.

Once he had the boys' attention, he said, "Uh. . .sorry, didn't mean to yell. Uh. . .I was just thinking, I could saddle you boys each a horse, and we could ride out to look at my herd. We could let the women have an hour or so of hen talk."

Grace thought Adam seemed on edge, but she could imagine why. The boys whooped and charged toward the barn.

Tillie dragged Grace inside and shut the door quick. She settled Grace at the table then reached up to a padlocked cupboard and opened it to pull out a heavy pottery coffee cup.

"Why do you keep it locked? No one would steal glassware."

Tillie bustled about filling the kettle with tea. "Uh. . .*Adam* has on occasion been known to break a bit of glass. Clumsy men, you know."

"Oh my, do I ever know."

Tillie came and sat down straight across from Grace. "So, tell me what brings you here."

Grace felt like wings sprung straight out of her heart. These were the exact words she wanted to hear from some woman, any woman. Maybe she wouldn't have to go all the way to Hannah's after all. Not on *this* visit.

TWELVE

Horace sneaked out of Prudence's house before first light. He didn't like getting up early, he didn't like hard labor, and he didn't like Prudence being a stand-up citizen while he went slinking around in the dark alleys like a rat. He was sick of it all. This plan needed to work, and soon.

He slipped out of town on foot. He'd left his horse nearly two miles away. Horace chained it overnight in a stand of scrub pines. The horse didn't like it, but the nag had all day to graze.

After the long trudge in the cold, Horace rode the rest of the way to the oil seep. The closer he got, the worse the stink. He had to fill another couple of barrels today if he wanted to keep up the rent on Prudence's store, but he couldn't stand it so early in the morning.

He got to his work site, tucked into a canyon behind the Rocking C—this whole area was Grant's property. Knowing he should go straight to work, instead he veered his horse toward the rocky game trail that led to the top of the bluff surrounding the reeking, oily waters of the spring. The sun was up enough to look down on the world.

He reached the top and saw, a mile away, the shack full of children ruining his plans. He saw Grant emerge from the hovel and head for the barn. Two of his boys tagged him, a familiar little boy that looked barely school age and a new one, a skinny blond Horace had never seen before.

Where was the bigger boy? Horace sneered at a man taking in one of *that* kind. Grant was trash and his whole family was trash.

The black-skinned boy, more man than child, was always along with Grant. Working as if he'd never been freed from slavery. Of course Grant worked like that, too. Fools, when there was a living to be had on other men's sweat. Horace could only feel contempt for the mess of a family.

Horace climbed down off his horse, chained the beast up good and tight, and walked to a better spot where a steep, rugged trail led down the bluff on the Rocking C side. Horace had never gone down. No sense leaving a track for anyone in that family to find. The whole bunch of them ran wild in these hills, but the smell of this area and the rancid water kept them and their herd away from this black spring.

As he neared the overlook, Horace heard rustling just over the rim. He ducked behind a boulder. Deer most likely, but no sense being caught by surprise.

The black boy topped the trail. Prudence had found out about the family. This one's name was Joshua. The boy crawled up the last sheer stretch using finger and toe holds.

Horace watched and knew the instant Joshua'd seen the horse. The boy scrambled to the top and took a step forward. Horace's hand closed over the butt of his revolver. The boy walked toward the nag. He'd go straight past Horace.

Joshua stepped alongside Horace's hiding place. Horace lunged and smashed the gun over the boy's head. The dull thud was satisfying. The boy staggered backward. A trail of blood gushed down the side of his face, the red vivid against Joshua's dark skin. His dazed eyes fixed on Horace and focused.

The boy had seen his face. Glad for an excuse to dispense more pain, Horace realized he couldn't let a witness go.

Horace lunged to grab Joshua, but his fingers slipped on the slick, blood-soaked shirt. Instead of catching hold, Horace shoved him backward, and the boy reeled over the edge of the cliff.

Horace dashed to the drop-off and watched the body tumble and bounce. It slid nearly a hundred feet then landed in a thicket of mesquite. Horace didn't like the way the boy had landed—flat on his back and with that thicket breaking his fall. The impact wasn't hard.

With a long look at the climb, Horace dismissed going down. He took careful aim with his revolver. It was a long shot, and Horace wasn't the best marksman. He liked living by his wits, not his gun. Besides, he didn't want to shoot. A gunshot would draw attention. And a bullet hole in the trash at the bottom of this cliff would be proof positive this wasn't an accident.

In the growing sunlight, Horace eased off the trigger and watched the still form. Blood coated the boy's face and shirt. Seconds ticked past, then minutes with no movement, not even the rise and fall of the boy's chest. Finally, with a satisfied grunt, Horace decided the job was done better if there was no gunshot, no bullet to explain.

A boy, playing, taking a fall. No reason anyone would question things. If there was any blame it would land on Grant. Any father worth his salt would make sure his young'uns stayed well away from this area.

"What were you doing up here anyway, kid?" Horace asked the motionless young man.

Horace'd best not be in the vicinity if they came hunting the boy. He had most of a load of barrels. He'd planned to finish filling the wagon before he took them in, but now it seemed like a good day for a ride to LaMont.

A movement caught his eye. Horace looked overhead and smiled. A vulture.

Watching the flesh-eating animal circle high above, Horace laughed. "Well, there's proof."

Horace made his way down the steep trail, gloating at getting rid of the first of those worthless ophans. Glad for an excuse to quit working and get away from the stinking springs, he untied his horse, hitching it to the buckboard and headed for LaMont.

He carefully wiped out his faint tracks on the rocky ground as he left. He'd earned a break with this day's work.

"Where's Joshua?" Grant went into the cabin for breakfast. "I sent him to scout for that stubborn roan longhorn. The one who thinks she's a mountain goat. She's probably wandered off to have her calf."

Marilyn shrugged as she stirred the oatmeal. "He must be late, Pa."

Sadie, picking up a stack of bowls, paused. A furrow cut between her brows. "He wasn't going far. He should have been back."

Grant nodded and realized he had an itch between his shoulder blades that made him feel like someone had a rifle trained on his back. "I'll ride out and check. I've got the wagon hitched. Marilyn, can you and Sadie drive yourselves to school?"

"Sure, Pa." Marilyn looked up from her steaming pot. "But don't you want us to help hunt?"

"No, he probably just found that stubborn old cow and he can't get her in. I'll meet him coming home, trying to drive her. I'll let him ride the buckskin into school. He'll probably catch you before you get to town."

"No, I don't think so, Pa." Sadie set the stack of bowls down with a hard crack. "Joshua isn't one to be late. You know him better'n that."

Grant knew a person could get held up working cattle, but Joshua was a boy. . .man. . .who was always ahead of time. It wasn't something Grant had taught; it was just part of the boy's character. A niggle of worry grew to about ten times its size. Grant's calm snapped.

"Set the breakfast aside, Marilyn." Grant raised his voice. "Kids, I need help."

Charlie poked his head out of the loft above. Benny came running in from the back bedroom. Libby limped into the kitchen. Grant couldn't leave her and he couldn't let her hike. He plucked the child up and wrapped her coat around her.

"You'll ride with me." He looked at the other children. "We're gonna hunt down Joshua. If we find him along the trail with no trouble, we can all enjoy pestering him for being late. If there's trouble, I might need extra hands."

Marilyn shoved the pan of oatmeal off the heat and efficiently stripped off her apron. All of the children scrambled into their outer things with Marilyn helping.

Sadie strode toward the door, pulling on her coat. "I'll start saddling the horses."

"Libby and I'll head out now in the buckboard. Benny, you ride along with us." Grant followed Sadie out the door, fear goading him to hurry. Sadie was right. Joshua wouldn't be late.

There was trouble.

Standing in the entrance to the little schoolhouse, Hannah hesitated. This mess in Sour Springs had sidetracked her from her plan to move to Mosqueros and search for Grace.

When Chicago had gotten too cold and miserable for Hannah to bear, she and Libby had begun their odyssey to save her sister. First stowing away on a train headed to Omaha, they'd found themselves on a car carrying orphans. Hannah realized that rather than hide for the whole trip they could move around the car, pretending to the conductor that they were with the orphan train and pretending to the orphans that they were passengers. They'd mixed with the huge unruly crowd of children, even so far as sharing their food. The first stop to meet prospective parents was in Omaha. Then, because the train was going on west and Grace was south of them, they slipped away.

There was no opportunity in Omaha to hitch a train ride south.

The security was too tight, especially because nothing like that orphan train came through again. Hannah and Libby lived in cold alleys and tried to earn enough for two tickets.

Libby had stood on street corners wearing a sign asking for money. Hannah had carried groceries and washed clothes. She'd swept sidewalks and washed windows. None of the jobs lasted. None of her bosses were interested in Hannah's problems, and she learned to keep them to herself. Hannah was none too clean, and she knew there was a desperate gleam in her eyes that she couldn't quite suppress. . .and that didn't inspire many to give her a chance.

Hannah and Libby wore rags and starved themselves trying to scrape together cash enough for tickets. They lived in alleys and sheds rather than spend their precious earnings on themselves. It had taken them a year.

Finally they got to Kansas City. The money was harder to come by, and it took them a long time to raise a few pennies. Despairing of paying their way, with luck and a ridiculous amount of risk and with a determined sheriff on their trail, Hannah and Libby snuck onto a train and made it to St. Louis. It was a step in the wrong direction, but they'd needed to get out of Kansas City.

In St. Louis, after working and struggling until it looked as if they'd never afford the next step of their journey, they ran into another trainload of orphans, this group headed for Texas—a giant step toward Grace. They fell in with them, and it went well until Martha identified Libby as being an orphan. She'd pulled Libby in with the group. Hannah had stood by and let her because Martha was feeding the other children, and for the first time in years, Libby ate well.

No one would adopt Libby, of course, not with her limp and her unnatural silence. She had planned for Libby to slip away from the train in a bigger town, much as she'd done in Omaha on the first leg of their arduous journey to find Grace. From there, they'd plan the final journey to Mosqueros.

Then Grant had done the unthinkable and adopted a little girl who wasn't perfect. They'd made it this far, after all these years, and there was no way to get Libby away from Grant and head on toward west Texas.

And now Hannah had a school to teach. She took one step into the school and almost turned around and ran. She'd been teaching children all of her life, but she didn't have the slightest idea how a school worked since she'd never been in one.

Before she completely lost her nerve, she hustled to the front of the room. She started the stove going first, pleased to see that the school was supplied with plenty of wood. When the fire was crackling cheerfully, she found a stack of books on the teacher's desk.

From her own satchel, she produced careful notes she'd made for her Easter pageant. It was the dearest dream of her heart to watch the children singing and acting out the parts of the Resurrection story. She'd heard a new name for such a pageant, a passion play, and she'd always wanted to be part of telling the story of Jesus' victory over death. These notes and papers, which she'd written so carefully for children, had stayed with her as she'd traveled across the country.

She laid the papers aside and studied the room. There were fourteen desks in two neat rows of seven, with a center aisle between them. Each desk held two children, although three students could be squeezed in a two-person desk if the students were small.

If Mabel's estimate was correct, this room was going to overflow. Hannah spent the next hour looking through each book, knowing she'd have to find out where all of the students were in their studies before she could set their lessons.

She had the school warm and her confidence fully in place an hour before the first child came in the door.

She said a prayer that Grant would let his children attend school. If they didn't show up, she'd go after them. There was no reason good enough to excuse them from being here.

THIRTEEN

"Josh!" Grant yelled over the roaring in his ears. He dragged the team to a halt, locked on the brake, leapt off the high buckboard seat, and ran.

His son.

Joshua had been with the first children Grant had adopted.

Now here he lay, coated in blood. Broken. Dead.

"Josh, can you hear me?" Grant skidded to his knees beside the boy. Pressing his ear against the boy's chest, Grant prayed. Nothing, no heartbeat.

Grant tore Joshua's coat and shirt open. The acrid smell of blood sent Grant's stomach churning.

Benny dropped to the ground on the opposite side of Joshua's inert body. He reached to help Libby down to her knees.

Grant listened to Joshua's chest and finally caught a faint noise. "He's alive." Grant looked up. "Josh is alive! His heart's still beating." Grant looked at the steep bluff looming overhead and knew the boy must have fallen. He'd been trailing that agile, wild cow, or possibly looking for a high spot to study the terrain. Most likely the latter. The boy loved to climb.

Grant jerked off his gloves and tucked them under his belt, threw off his coat, tore at the buttons on his shirt, and then dragged it off. He ripped the shirt in half and pressed the worn fabric gently against Joshua's bleeding head.

The cold bit into Grant through his tattered union suit and he shuddered. But it wasn't from cold. So much blood. Grant's makeshift bandage was soon soaked.

"What'll we do, Pa?"

"Can you run back for the girls? We need— No, wait." Grant looked straight at Benny. For the first time ever, Grant was scared to send one of his children off on his own. Something had happened out here. Something bad. No way did his nimble son fall off a cliff. A bird had a better chance of forgetting how to fly.

"What, Pa? I can help."

Think. Think. Think. Grant's heart pounded. He couldn't catch his breath, driven by fear he needed to control now of all times.

He inspected Joshua's battered body. His head and neck were scraped badly, his clothing cut to ribbons. The gash on Joshua's forehead bled crimson against his son's coffee-dark skin. It looked like Josh'd been struck over the head. Joshua's left arm hung at an odd angle. The boy's heartbeat was weak but steady.

"I know you can help. There's just no point telling the girls to go for bandages. We'll have to get Joshua back to the house." Grant nodded at the rags of his shirt. "Can you hold this bandage?"

Benny reached his small hands in and held the cloth.

"Something else you can both do." Grant staggered to his feet.

Benny and Libby looked up.

"Pray. Joshua needs all our prayers."

Libby clutched her hands together and closed her eyes. Her lips moved silently.

Stomach twisting with dread, Grant eased the broken arm across the boy's chest. Binding it with remnants of his shirt, Grant jostled his son as little as possible.

Once the task was done, he dared to breathe again. "Okay, Benny, Lib, I'm going to lift him into the wagon box. I need you to step back." Grant took over with the bandage.

Benny put his hand on Libby's shoulder and the two of them rose to their feet and stepped away.

Grant bent down. His son was reed thin but muscular from long hours of hard work on the ranch. And he was as tall as a grown man. Grant said a prayer for strength, then slid his arms under Joshua's shoulders and knees and lifted the boy, grunting with the effort. Doing his best not to disturb the arm, it took every ounce of Grant's strength to lift him. Grant eased his son onto the wagon bed.

He turned to the young'uns. "Benny, Libby, hop in. I'm going to start for home. You watch Joshua."

Benny boosted Libby up over the side of the wagon. Grant stepped over and hoisted the little girl the last few inches while Benny practically took flight over the edge of the box.

Grant fastened the tailgate, the hinges creaking as he lifted the flat slab of wood, the metal sounding rusty as he shoved the five-inch-long pins into the iron hooks that held the gate closed. He'd left Joshua close to the back end, to avoid moving him one inch more than necessary.

Grant vaulted to the wagon seat and gave a tiny shake to the long leather reins, holding the horses to a slow start. They headed toward the Rocking C. The horses had caught Grant's terror and tried to speed up. Pulling them to a walk, Grant feared every jounce might shake something inside of Josh and kill him. Grant glanced over his shoulder every few steps.

They met the girls riding toward them. Charlie peeked out from behind Sadie.

"We found him." Grant jerked his head toward the wagon. "He's been hurt."

Both girls gasped. Charlie scowled. They rode up beside the wagon.

"Is he alive?" Marilyn asked sharply.

Sadie cried out, covered her mouth with one hand, and began to weep softly.

"He's alive." Grant kept driving and praying. "Marilyn, ride to town for Doc Morgan. Tell him to bring his plaster. Josh's arm looks broken. And get Will and Ian. I may need some help."

Marilyn whirled the horse in a tight circle, slapped her reins against the animal's hindquarters, and tore off, bent low over the roan's shoulders.

As she dashed off, it struck Grant again that he shouldn't let her go off alone. There was danger out here. But the thought came too late. Marilyn was out of sight and out of earshot.

Sadie rode close, her eyes riveted on Joshua, but Grant had other ideas for her. "Head for the cabin and get some water hot and tear up a sheet. We'll need to sterilize his wounds, and the quicker the better. The doc will need to sew him up and put a cast on his arm."

The look of stubbornness on Sadie's face surprised Grant. She'd been with him as long as Joshua, and she'd always been the first to lend a hand. Before Grant could repeat his order, Sadie looked away from Joshua. Grant caught sight of the tears streaming down the girl's face. She yelled to her horse and went for the cabin at a full gallop, with Charlie holding on for dear life.

The wagon took the rest of them slowly home.

As they finally arrived, Marilyn was just riding up with the doctor.

Grant pulled up as close as he could get to the front door. Grant saw Ian coming fast up the trail. Other horses came behind him.

"Benny, get up here and hold the reins." Grant put on the brake then jumped to the ground.

Benny scrambled over the front of the wagon box to the high seat.

Grant came around to the back just as the doctor swung down off his horse. Grant opened the tailgate.

Ian pulled his horse to a stop.

Will rode up and dismounted. Will was another of those first six children. Joshua was his brother in every way that counted. "What's happened?" Will's gaze was riveted to Josh's still form.

"Thanks for coming." Grant couldn't think clearly enough to answer Will.

"Let me look at him before we move him." The doctor edged in between them.

Grant realized he'd blocked the man away from Josh.

The doctor leaned close.

Ian joined them. Grant's heart eased just knowing his family was gathering to lend a hand. He had a lot of trouble with the folks in Sour Springs, but not everyone was unkind. In fact, most of them were generous, decent people. But a few could make a lot of noise.

Another horse drew near, ridden by Parson Babbitt.

The sudden tightening of Grant's throat caught him by surprise. He hadn't cried since he was five years old, but these men coming to help meant a lot.

The parson came to look over the side of the wagon, and Grant saw his lips moving. As soon as he assessed the situation, Parson Babbitt gave Grant a serious nod of his head then went around the wagon to stand with the children. He picked Libby up, rested a hand on Benny's shoulder, and spoke quietly to the youngsters.

"The shoulder's dislocated, not broken." Doc Morgan stepped closer and leaned over Josh, touching the gash, checking his heartbeat and breathing, running his hands over his legs. A firm push on Josh's ribs forced a moan out of the boy.

Grant's heart raced. It was the first sound out of his son.

"There could be internal things but, barring that, it looks like he's going to be okay once we patch him up." Dr. Morgan looked over his shoulder at Ian, whose arms were thick from working his anvil. "I can use your strength here. I'll show you what to do. We'll put this shoulder back in place before we move him. I'll bind it up good and it'll heal fast. Then I want him inside for the stitches."

"Kids, make sure the kitchen table is clear." Grant looked up.

"I already checked, Pa. It's good." Marilyn stood with her arms crossed, watching the doctor with wide eyes.

Grant noticed Charlie's usually furrowed forehead was smooth. A look of wonder had settled on his face as he watched the family hover around Joshua. Grant suspected the boy had never seen so many people worried about an orphan.

Ian followed the doctor's orders and grasped Josh's hand. Grant saw the sheen of sweat break out on Ian's forehead, not from effort but from worry. Resetting a joint was going to hurt Josh bad. But it had to be done.

The doctor explained what he expected. With a hard pull from Ian, a cry wrung out of Josh and the joint snapped audibly into place.

Grant's knees sagged, and Will was there with an arm to support him. Grant ran both hands into his hair, slick with cold sweat. He knocked his hat off his head. "I was fine handling Josh until someone took over."

Will nodded. "Tell me what happened."

"Not now," the doctor interrupted as he rested Josh's limp arm on his chest and then moved aside. "We need to get him in and I don't want him bumped around. I suspect he's got broken ribs, and there are other things inside that could be busted up. He might have broken his neck while he was at it. Ian, you pick him up. Be real smooth about it."

The doctor jabbed a finger at Will. "When Ian gets him up, come over to the other side and steady him. Grant, help ease his feet off the wagon when Ian lifts him away. Hold them straight all the way stretched out until we get him laid down inside."

With Ian's strength and Will on hand, they moved Josh inside easily. Ian stretched the boy flat on the table. Everyone moved inside. All but the doctor stepped to the far side of the room, which wasn't all that far.

Parson Babbitt just poked his head in the door. "You youngsters come on with me to the barn. They haven't got room to move in here."

Grant saw mutiny on his children's faces, but they did as the parson asked. Libby, Benny, Charlie, and even Marilyn minded the man of God.

Sadie gave Grant a beseeching look. "I want to stay, Pa."

The doctor looked up. "I might need a hand."

Grant nodded and settled in to endless, silent prayer for God to hold Joshua in this side of heaven.

Minutes stretched as the doctor bound Josh's ribs, moving him as little as possible, then put a sling on his arm. When that was done, he cleaned Josh's cuts, taking pains to make sure there wasn't a speck of dirt left in the head wound. Half the morning was gone before he straightened. "All right, Sadie, I could use a nurse here if you're willing."

Sadie stepped up. The doctor began issuing orders. Sadie pulled threads, ointments, and bandages out of the doctor's bag, whatever he asked for.

The doc was just clipping the last thread when Joshua's eyes flickered open.

Sadie inhaled sharply and leaned down. "Josh, you're awake."

Grant was struck with another unlikely burn of tears. He rubbed the heels of his hands across his eyes to ensure no embarrassment. When he finished, he noticed Will doing the same thing.

Doc leaned down over Joshua and lifted one of the boy's eyelids. "Can you hear me, Josh?"

Josh nodded once then gasped. A moan escaped his lips, but even that was cut off quickly as if even using his vocal cords hurt.

"Lay still. You took quite a tumble. I've got you patched up, but you're going to have to give yourself time to recover."

Josh didn't so much as nod his agreement.

"I'm going to give you some laudanum for the pain. Not much, just enough so your pa and brothers can get you moved to your bed. Then you'll have a long sleep. You're going to feel puny for the next few days, but you'll heal."

Sadie handed the doctor a brown bottle and a spoon.

The doctor administered the laudanum, and Josh shuddered from the taste, winced, and then slowly let his eyelids fall shut.

Doc straightened and turned to Grant. "Be as easy as you can with him. Let's get him to bed."

"Can I talk to him for just one second, Doc?" Grant moved up beside Josh.

Doc nodded and stepped back. "Make it quick. That drug will kick in, and he won't be making any sense for a while."

Grant bent over the table. "Don't try to talk, son. Don't nod your head or so much as budge. Just blink your eyes, once for yes and twice for no. Do you understand?"

Josh's eyes blinked once.

"I know you didn't fall of that bluff, Josh. Did someone push you?"

Sadie gasped.

Will stepped closer behind Grant.

Ian asked from behind them, "You think he was pushed?"

Josh opened his eyes.

Grant saw the hesitation. "Do you know?"

Josh blinked his eyes twice very deliberately. Then the dark brown pupils dilated.

"No. Okay." Grant leaned closer. "Did you hear anything? I'm going up there to scout around, but do you remember—" Grant stopped, frustrated by the inability to really talk to the boy. "Do you—"

Very slowly Josh's lids slid closed.

"Josh, wait. I need to know. . ."

"No more, Grant." Doc's hand settled on Grant's shoulder. "He's asleep. Even if you could get him to blink, you couldn't be sure he'd know what he was doing. The drug can make you mighty confused. Pretty common after a knock on the head to forget what happened just before the blow, so he probably wouldn't answer you anyway. After he gets some rest, you can question him again."

Grant straightened and looked in Sadie's eyes.

He was surprised by the flowing tears. . .and the fury. She asked, "You think someone deliberately pushed Josh?"

Will moved closer to Josh. All the protective instincts of a big brother shone in his eyes. Looking between his two children, Grant said, "Josh is like an antelope on those hills, surefooted and careful. He didn't just fall off that mountain."

"I'll go with you to do your scouting." Will jerked his chin. Ready to fight for his brother, just like he'd been fighting for him ten years ago when they'd been living on the street. Will had realized the peril two black children were in on Houston's streets, and he'd been ready to fight and die then for Josh and Sadie. When Grant had taken them to a diner to feed them, Will was the one who wouldn't let his little brother and sister go in. Will was the one who stood his ground and made Grant understand the consequences.

"Me, too." Ian hadn't lived with them long. He was nearly a man grown when Grant took him in. But his wife, Megan, had been part of the family for five years before Ian had swept her off her feet. Ian was one of them.

The three of them exchanged a long look. Then Grant turned back to the doctor. "I don't think we should mention this in town. I'll have a talk with the sheriff, but if whoever was up there lives in Sour Springs, we don't want him to know we're onto him."

"You're jumping to conclusions, Grant." The doctor busied himself rolling down his sleeves. "Anyone can take a fall. Rocks slide unexpectedly, the dirt crumbles on a trail."

"Maybe it happened that way, Doc. But I know my boy. I'm going to go have a look. Would you mind not talking about my suspicions in town?"

"I'll keep my mouth shut. Nothing to tell anyway, as far as I can see." The doctor slipped his arms into his black suit coat then added a heavy sheepskin on top of that. "I'll be back in the afternoon to check on Josh. If you need me before that, send someone running. Everyone in town's going to know he's hurt. I'll just let it out that he took a fall."

When the doctor said everyone, for some reason Grant thought of

124

Hannah. He wondered what that little snip would think about this. He'd promised to have his children in school and he'd failed. Now Josh was hurt, and she'd probably find a way to blame Grant for that. She'd be riding out here, scolding and insulting him before the end of the day. She'd probably try to take Josh and the rest of the children home with her.

A twinge of regret that she was always going to find him wanting as a father twisted his heart. He *was* wanting as a father. He did his best, but it was true he didn't have enough room for them. He knew they all worked hard, maybe too hard. Their clothes were torn and patched as often as not. He knew all of that. But he'd never gone to beating up on himself for it. He was better than nothing, which is what these children had before.

At least he'd never gone to beating up on himself till Hannah. He wished she were here to worry alongside him.

Grant's eyes widened and he straightened his spine. He did *not* wish she were here. He wanted the woman to stay as far away from him and his young'uns as possible.

Grant shook his head to clear it of notions that he didn't have time for. It didn't matter what the woman did or said. He managed as best he could. Grant knew that for the honest truth. And no amount of nagging could change that, whatever his shortcomings as a father.

And Grant prided himself on being an honest man.

He was a shameful, lowdown, lying polecat. None of Grant's family had come. He'd promised they would.

Hannah looked at her mostly empty room. She'd expected thirty or more children here today. There must be others missing, too. "Children, take your seats, please." Hannah stepped to the front of the room.

Five children, most fairly young, looked up with wide eyes.

Hannah honestly didn't know quite what to do about her absentees.

"I thought there would be more students here today. Was I mistaken?"

One little girl with two dark braids hanging down nearly to her lap shook her head. "Lots of kids didn't get here cuz of the trouble."

Hannah gasped. "Trouble? What happened?"

Another young boy, this one buck-toothed with serious eyes, said, "Someone came riding in for the doctor. They both tore out of town so fast no one had a chance to ask her what happened. Ian from the blacksmith shop tore out next in the opposite direction. Then he come back through town with Will, Ian's brother. So we knew it meant trouble. Will would'a brought his family to school. But Will lives a ways out so, without him, his kids couldn't come."

Another child chimed in. "And the doctor's got four in his family, but his wife keeps them to home when there's a ruckus. My ma says Mrs. Doc gets notional and we all just have'ta let her do what she wants."

"And the blacksmith's wife is getting on with a baby," the dark-haired girl added. "So like as not she won't try and get Gordy to school on her own."

The children added new names, all kept home because of the trouble. Several said their fathers had headed out of town after the doctor.

"Why would everyone follow after the doctor? Surely he doesn't need that much help."

"Can't never have too much help, Miss Cartwright," the dark-haired girl said.

The serious boy said, " 'Sides, they're mostly all family. I mean not all, but those that ain't connected still might want'a ride out and see what's what. So it's not likely they'll send their kids if they're busy waiting on news."

Hannah kept the scowl off her face by pure will power. "School should be a priority." First the town had no school. Then it hired her with no care. Now they didn't send their children. She started working up a nice head of indignation.

"Well, they've all made a mistake. This town needs to realize that education is important. Where did the doctor go? Who exactly is it that's more important than school? I intend to tell them that they've got their values all wrong. They need to change their ways and make sure that nothing short of God comes between children and schooling, and that's that!" Hannah's voice rose as she worked her fury up to a full boil. "Where did the doctor go? Who exactly is it that's more important than school?"

"One o' them orphans from out to the Rocking C."

"Class dismissed!" Hannah slapped her hand flat on her desk.

The children erupted from their desks, gleefully screaming in delight.

Hannah barely noticed, her heart thumped until it pounded in her ears. She hurried after them. What had happened? "Libby!" Hannah broke into a run. What if Grant had finally realized fully what it meant that Libby couldn't talk or do heavy work? What if he'd done something to her? Maybe Grant had gone too far with a thrashing.

Hannah dashed toward the livery. She needed to save her little sister and all of those other poor children!

FOURTEEN

Grant, Will, and Ian left the cabin and found half the town standing outside waiting for news. Someone had set up a makeshift table, and ladies had brought food and were serving the children breakfast. Several men came forward to see if Grant needed any help. Grant noticed a new pile of food, clothing, and supplies in the back of his wagon.

Harold Stroben from the mercantile lumbered over. "What happened?"

"The boy had a fall. He's badly battered, but the doc says he's going to be all right. Thanks for checking, Harold."

Grant waited until the first flurry of questions and concern had passed, not wanting to raise suspicions. Impatience beat against his chest, but he waited until everyone seemed satisfied.

"I need to ride out to where he fell." He pulled his gloves on with hard, jerky motions. He only held his temper through years of practice.

As he, Will, and Ian walked to the barn, Will said, "Joshua didn't trip and fall off that north bluff."

Ian snorted. "Not possible. My little brother could scale a greased rainbow."

Grant took a second to note Ian's bright red hair and the freckles so thick on his face it was hard to tell where one stopped and another started. Ian and Josh, brothers? Only at the Rocking C. But this *was* the

Rocking C and they *were* brothers, as close as blood. Grant would have smiled if he had one ounce of humor left in his body. "I'm gonna scout the trail up that hill."

Will untied his chestnut gelding from a mesquite bush. Ian swung up on the back of his paint mare. They met Grant as he emerged from the barn on his roan.

Grant looked over his shoulder to see two more of his sons riding up. Several folks were heading back for town. Sour Springs had a lot of good people, Grant decided. A few bad apples had forced him to stay isolated. With the Brewsters gone—they'd been the source of so much trouble—maybe he needed to give the whole town another chance. Including the school.

Will set out at a gallop for the bluff, Ian hard on his heels. Grant fell in behind and he heard more hoofbeats following. His family. He'd created it out of his desperate loneliness. But created it he had. He'd done a good job.

He never had to be alone again.

"Just wait until I get that man alone!"

Trying to dismount, Hannah swung her leg over the horse's rump. She'd been pleasantly surprised at the amiable nature of the horse she'd gotten from Zeb Morris. A far nicer mount than Sunday's. Zeb had acted nervous when she'd come in. He'd apologized for her trouble with Rufus and given her the use of the horse for no cost. He'd also boosted her on.

No one was handy to help her down. Her boot heel hung up on the back of the saddle and she shrieked as she toppled backward and landed with a dull thud in the dirt. She blinked her eyes and looked up at people rushing to her side.

"Are you all right, miss?" A man carrying a doctor's bag crouched by her side as if ready to examine her.

She gave her head a brisk shake to clear it and sat up. Everything seemed to work. "I think I am."

Several smothered giggles drew her attention to Charlie, Benny, and Libby. Libby laughed behind her hand. And her little sister was also, obviously, not hurt. The panic cooled inside of Hannah, and her cheeks heated up with a flush of embarrassment.

If Libby was safe, then what had happened out here that needed the doctor? There were a lot of children Grant could have been too harsh with. Hannah sat up.

"No, wait, we should check for broken bones before—"

Hannah was on her feet looking down at the crouching doctor. "Before what?"

"Never mind." The doctor stood. "You seem fine."

"Of course I am." Hannah gave one fast jerk of her chin in agreement. "What happened? Who was hurt?"

The doctor looked back at the cabin. "Joshua. He fell off a bluff this morning. He's pretty beaten up."

"You're sure it was a cliff? He wasn't hurt by someone. . .you said beaten."

Several people gasped.

"Grant actually—" The doctor cut off whatever he was going to say. "He fell. Yes, he was found at the bottom of a steep bluff. He was out chasing strays."

Hannah could tell the doctor had started to say something. Would he lie for Grant? She well remembered people ignoring her plight. "Who found him?"

"Grant."

So there was only Grant's word for it that Joshua had fallen. Hannah thought of Grant's teasing last night. She'd decided he wasn't so bad. It hurt her heart now to consider that the man, although certainly not a proper father, might have that cruel side. But Hannah knew she couldn't let her feelings rule. "Where is he?"

"Grant?"

"No, Joshua." Hannah resisted the urge to roll her eyes. Why would she want to see Grant?

"He's asleep."

"I'd like to take a turn sitting with him if I may."

The doctor nodded. "Sadie's with him now, but I shooed everyone else outside. I'll bet she'd appreciate the company."

"Thank you, Doctor." Hannah brushed at her dirty dress, wondering if she'd ever dismount a horse without it leading to disaster.

She headed for the house, taking one long look backward to reassure herself Libby was alive and well. Libby grinned at her, waggling her fingers in such a lighthearted way Hannah had to believe her little sister was reasonably well treated. Libby turned to chase after Benny. Hannah noticed that with her boot fixed Libby hardly limped at all.

Hannah went inside, not to sit with Joshua but to guard him. And she wasn't budging until she'd gotten the truth out of someone in this strange family.

"That's blood!" Will rushed past Grant.

Grant jumped aside as Will charged past him. They'd just now topped the cliff, and immediately his eyes had gone to a red splash on a large rock.

Ian crouched by the man-sized boulder and touched the still damp blood splattered on the stone. As he knelt, he flinched and held up a harmonica from under his knee.

"Josh's." Grant recognized the prized possession. "He was playing it just last night. That proves he made it to the top. It proves he somehow started bleeding up here, not from the fall."

"What it proves is," Will said, his mouth a grim line, "someone hit Joshua and shoved him over the cliff."

A tense silence fell over the threesome as they looked at the evidence of attempted murder.

"If someone pushed Josh over that cliff, he'd expect the fall to kill him." Ian rose and handed the harmonica to Grant.

"And when he learns it didn't kill him," Will said with a scowl, "he may worry about Josh turning him in to the sheriff."

The words burned. So furious he barely trusted himself to speak without raging, Grant said through clenched teeth, "Ian, you're in town all day. Put out the word that Josh lost his memory. Talk to anyone who comes into the blacksmith shop then stop at the diner, the mercantile, Zeb's livery, anywhere you can think of. Tell 'em all Josh doesn't remember a thing. Maybe that'll keep him safe. The doc needs to know so he can back our story. Ask him to spread the word, too." Grant turned the metal and wood instrument that had meant so much to Josh over and over in his hands. "I want everyone in Sour Springs to know about this before the day's out so whoever tried to kill him loses his reason for finishing the job."

"I'll talk to Doc Morgan," Ian offered. "Megan was going to have to see him one of these days because of the baby, so we'll use that as an excuse."

Grant's eyes strayed from the mouth harp to the blood-splattered stone, and his boys turned to look at the grim evidence of treachery.

Grant broke the silence first. "You can do that later. For now, we don't leave here until we trail this varmint to his lair."

Grant and his sons rode to the ranch house, exhausted, demoralized, and furious.

The ground was too rocky for a trail to show anywhere around that bluff. There was nothing to identify Joshua's assailant. They'd climbed all the way down the other side of the hill, past the stinking oily water of Sour Springs, and found nothing.

Will and Ian had stuck with him well into the afternoon. His boys headed on home while Grant rode up to the cabin, saddle sore, filthy, and starved.

He recognized another horse from Zeb's and barely suppressed a groan. Soon he'd be praying for a return to this blissful condition.

Hannah.

He had no doubt the woman came to snipe. He fought the temptation to ride back out. Maybe snare a rabbit, do some fishing, live off the land for a week or two. She'd go away eventually.

Resigned to a few hours of nagging, he stripped the leather off his horse, brushed it down for far, far too long, and then gave it a bait of oats. He headed in feeling like he was taking that long, last walk to a gallows.

Maybe it wasn't her. Someone else could have rented a horse. He swung the door open daring to hope.

Inside, instead of hope, he found Hannah.

Sitting in the one and only rocking chair reading *Oliver Twist*, she held Libby and Benny on her lap. Charlie leaned against the stones of the hearth. Sadie worked next to Marilyn at the stove.

Despite his daydreams—he was a realist, he'd known it was her—Grant was caught by how right the family looked with Hannah in the center. His eyes burned. He blinked away the shocking desire to cry. Hannah would think he'd gone soft. And he was only acting like this because of the upset of Josh.

The thought of Josh snapped him out of the emotional weakness. His injured son was nowhere to be seen.

What if. . . Could he have. . . Grant nearly panicked. "Where's Josh?"

A movement brought Grant's head around to the back entry–turned bedroom. Joshua stepped through the little door that led through his room and out the back of the house. His arm in a sling, his face haggard,

Josh had a tidy bandage on his forehead. The gauze glowed white against his black skin. But he was standing.

Grant's knees almost buckled. "You're looking a sight better, Josh." Grant had his hands full keeping his voice steady. "You're gonna be okay then?"

"Yep." Josh didn't so much as shake his head. "I'm still seeing two of everything. Doc Morgan stopped by this afternoon and said that's normal. My ribs feel like I've been kicked by a mule and my shoulder's on fire. It's nothing that won't mend."

Grant could tell the boy still hurt. . .and badly.

Hannah stood carefully, mindful of easing the children to the floor. "Here, take this chair."

"No thanks, Miss Cartwright. I think I'll go back to bed. I just heard Pa ride up and decided if he could see me standing he'd quit worrying." Joshua smiled then turned back to Grant. "I woke up in there awhile ago and lay listening to her reading to the young ones. I was awhile working up the nerve to try and stand, but I did."

Grant managed a half smile and hooked his fingers through his belt loops. "You know me well, son. It does put my mind at ease to see you up. But I wouldn't have made you get to your feet." Grant felt the harmonica in his pocket and produced it for Josh. "We found this."

Josh lit up then flinched in pain.

Grant was at his son's side in an instant. "I'll put it by your bed."

With a heavy sigh, Josh said, "Thanks. I'm not up for much. I didn't get up just for you. I needed to prove to myself that I could stand on my own feet. I'll go back to bed now though. I ache like I took an all-day beating. Sorry I won't be able to help around much for a few days. But if you'll give me some time, I'll be back at it." Josh quirked a pained smile at Grant, and they both acknowledged his weak effort at a joke. Of course he'd have all the time he needed.

Grant noticed Hannah's eyes narrow at the word "beating." Grant glanced at Hannah, and those narrow blue eyes were aimed right at him. He wanted to exchange a look of concern with her. Instead, she as much as accused him of beating his son.

His jaw tensed, and Grant had to force himself to smile and speak easily to Josh. "You'll have all the time you need."

"I'll bring your supper in as soon as it's off the stove, Josh." Sadie flashed him a smile. Grant could see the worry on her face, but she did her best to cover it.

"Thanks." Joshua turned slowly and made his way back to bed with as little jostling of his battered body as he could manage. Grant set the harmonica close, and as Josh settled on the bed with as little movement as possible, Grant spoke low enough no one could hear him. "Have you remembered what happened out there?"

Josh closed his eyes. "No. I remember setting off to track that cow, but nothing after that."

Grant knew Josh was in danger until he could name his attacker. "Doc says that's normal. It'll most likely all come back to you soon."

Josh's eyes slid closed and he didn't respond.

Grant whispered, "Good night."

As he left the room, Marilyn spoke up. "Miss Cartwright, you asked if you could help. Would you mind setting the plates and forks around?"

Throwing a quick prayer of thanks to his Maker that Marilyn was smart enough to only let Hannah handle things made of tin, Grant went to the washbasin and scrubbed his face and hands. He took his time. He straightened as Sadie disappeared into Josh's sickroom with a plate. Marilyn called the rest of the family to dinner.

Hannah, it appeared, was staying for another meal. Grant was tempted to charge her room and board. The light was failing; that meant he'd need to ride beside her into town. Stifling a groan, Grant headed for the table, hoping Hannah didn't burn anything to the ground before he got her out of here.

FIFTEEN

Hannah had to ask. She wouldn't respect herself if she didn't.

She'd seen the way the children interacted with Grant. It was almost impossible to believe they harbored an ounce of fear of him. But he had barely spoken to her during the meal and now he sat beside her grim and stiff, frowning as if she smelled bad. . .which she no doubt did.

Still, she had to ask.

Struggling to be diplomatic, she said, "So what exactly happened to Josh?" There, that was nice. Of course she'd like to know. She was only a caring neighbor. She was proud of herself. Grant was a decent man. He'd be polite.

"You mean did I thrash him within an inch of his life for not working an eighteen-hour day? Did the boy ask for a crust of bread and I took a belt to him? Just say what you're thinking."

He had the manners of a warthog.

Grant gave the reins a hard shake and the horses picked up their pace. His jaw was so tense Hannah expected his teeth to crack.

"I am not thinking that." She was, but she had no interest in admitting it. "The children seem very content with you. I apologize for being unhappy about all those children without a mother. It sets wrong with me, but I can see they need a home. I don't think you've got any right to hate me for worrying about them." She felt her temper climbing and clamped her mouth shut. She'd break a few teeth of her own before she spoke to the surly man again.

Then she thought of something else, and since she hadn't told Grant about her plan to give him the silent treatment, she felt no compulsion to live with that decision. "And I didn't force my way into a dinner invitation. The children wanted a story. Sadie and Marilyn were upset, and at first they were caring for Josh. Then they had to catch up on chores, and Libby and Benny were acting up, probably because they were so fretful about Josh. You should have been there with them when they were so upset. But no, you were off doing who knows what! I stayed because I thought I could help, you. . .you big. . ." She snapped her teeth together again.

They were coming up on the steep climb over the hill and down to Sour Springs. Grant suddenly pulled back on the reins, and when the horses came to a halt, he turned to her. "I'm sorry. You're right. Having you there did help out."

He couldn't have surprised her any more if he'd sprouted a full white beard and left her a sack of Christmas presents.

"Well. . ." Speechless, because she had a hard time thinking of anything to say to Grant that wasn't rude, she fell silent. She wanted to rub his nose in his rudeness. She looked, glared probably, at Grant and saw how tired he was. She remembered the worry on his face when he came in and didn't see Josh.

It hurt a bit, but she managed to say, "Thank you."

Grant nodded then turned to look between his horses' ears. "It helped *me* having you there, too, Hannah."

Hannah should have corrected him and insisted on "Miss Cartwright." Everyone in town needed to treat her with the dignity due a teacher's station, to set a good example for the children. But he sounded too weary and kind.

"When I saw Josh lying there—" Grant's voice broke. His chin dropped to his chest, and his shoulders rose and fell as if he hadn't taken a breath in hours and was only just now remembering how. He whispered, "I thought he was dead. I thought my son was—" Grant's gloved hand came up and covered his eyes.

Hannah didn't know what to say. She wanted to hold him, comfort him. But it was completely improper. His shoulders trembled.

Her arms went around him. "I'm so glad he's going to be okay."

The touch must have helped because he lifted his head and glanced down at her. They were too close. The silent night, the bank of endless stars, the gentle cold breeze, her warm arms, their eyes. . .

She jerked away. Faced forward. "We'd better get home. I've got school tomorrow." Because something had stirred in her, in a deep place, a place she didn't know she had, she spoke brusquely, "And your children had better be there. No excuses."

Out of the corner of her eye, she saw Grant give his head a shake and scrub his face with his hands. "They'll be there, Hannah."

Hoping to regain the distance she wanted between them, Hannah did her best to annoy him. "It's Miss Cartwright."

There was an extended silence. Hannah refused to look sideways to see what Grant was waiting for. She was afraid she knew.

At last he sighed so deeply the air might have come all the way from his toes. "Fine!" With a slap of leather, he set the team trotting. They started the ascent up the mountain at a pace far faster than the last time.

The snow was melted mostly away so possibly this was a normal speed for the horses, but Hannah suspected it had a lot more to do with getting rid of her. For the next few minutes, Hannah had her hands full keeping her seat.

They came down the other side, and as they leveled off, Grant said in a voice that sounded like he had to drag the words out of his throat, "As to your none-too-sneaky hint that I might have given the boy a beating, I didn't. I was gone because I spent the afternoon hunting for answers. Josh isn't a boy to go falling off a mountain. He's agile and quick. The trail was one that'd make a mountain goat think twice, but Josh scaled it all the time. What happened to him was no accident."

"You mean someone attacked him?"

"Yes, that's exactly what I mean."

"But who?" Hannah's breath came in shallow pants as she remembered so many experiences with violence in her past.

"I don't know, but I intend to find the truth. But I should have stayed with the children. You're right. They needed me."

Grant sighed as the wagon pulled into Sour Springs. "Please don't repeat what I've said. For now, until we can figure out what happened, we want everyone to believe Joshua fell by accident."

As Grant stopped the horses in back of the diner, a swish of skirts drew Hannah's eye. The seamstress who had been in Stroben's Mercantile that first night came out of her shop and headed for them like she was a magnet and Grant was true north. Grant saw the woman—Prudence, Hannah remembered—and jerked as if he'd been bee stung. The woman must mean something to him.

His shoulders slumped, and he swung himself down off the high seat. He made a move to round the back of the wagon, but the tall, slender woman cut him off. A trained cow pony couldn't have done it better.

"Grant, I saw you coming into town. I wondered if you'd like to come over tonight. Last time the weather stopped you."

"Uh...hi there...uh..."

There'd been a last time? They must be seeing each other. That moment on the drive, when their eyes caught, flared to vivid life—if he was seeing Prudence, he shouldn't be looking at Hannah that way. Heat crawled up her neck, and she was thankful for the dark that covered her blush. Of course someone as handsome as Grant would be thinking of finding a wife. But where in heaven's name did the man intend to put her in that tiny house?

Prudence rested her hand on Grant's arm in a way that Hannah found far too familiar for a public street. Of course there was no public, only Hannah, and she quite obviously didn't count.

All Hannah's haranguing about having no mother for his children now echoed like pure foolishness in her ears. But why hadn't he told her? Why had he let her go on and on if he was already thinking to take a wife? And a tall wife, graceful and beautifully dressed, too. Nothing like Hannah in her rags.

Hannah realized she was staring. She also realized she'd expected Grant to help her down off the wagon. He had last night. Well, she'd fall down before she'd stare at the couple a second longer.

She heard the murmur of voices, which she studiously ignored. She reached the ground with just enough clumsiness to feel even more foolish than she already did. Her skirt snagged on a step and she pulled it quickly free. But there was no reason to be embarrassed; the couple never glanced her way.

She took a quick peek and saw Prudence snuggled up against Grant. Hannah hoped he didn't behave like this in front of his children.

Hannah's temper rose. She squashed it. And she wasn't going to just run away. She lifted her voice so Grant could hear her over the sweet nothings he was no doubt whispering to Prudence. "I'll expect your children at school tomorrow, Grant. If they're not there, I'm coming out to get them."

Grant lifted his head and took a step toward her, dragging Prudence along as if she'd forgotten to take her claws out of him. Prudence was enough of a drag to stop him, and he didn't seem inclined to fight her off. "I'm planning on them being there."

Hannah jerked her chin up and down—which he might not have even seen in the darkness, especially with Prudence as a distraction. Then Prudence closed any gap that there was between her and Grant.

Hannah turned and rushed inside—which was completely different than running away.

Feeling pure envy, Grant watched that pest Hannah run away.

Sure, she was running from him, but she had the extra treat of getting far away from Shirt Lady. Grant wanted to run himself. If he could only dislodge the woman's fingernails. He gave a second of thanks to God that he was wearing a coat or she'd leave scars.

Her grip reminded him of last Saturday when he'd had to practically fight her off to get Charlie and Libby. It also reminded him of his bucket of eggs and the impression he'd had of someone lurking around his wagon that night. His chickens were doing well, and he'd planned to do some trading in the general store. He didn't think much about the eggs. But the bucket hadn't turned up along the trail, so they hadn't fallen out of his wagon. Right now he'd rather be talking with an egg thief than dealing with this woman and her fingernails.

He endured Shirt Lady's brainless chatter for as long as he could, worrying about getting home to Josh and thinking about what a nuisance Hannah was and how nice it was that she'd brought her little nuisance self out to watch his children today. Now the young'uns were home alone while Grant stood here trying to be polite to a woman whose name he'd made a deliberate effort to not learn. All he knew was the lady was always and forever talking about making him a new shirt.

Grant glanced down, remembering he'd torn to shreds his best shirt to make bandages for Josh. That now-destroyed shirt was little better than a rag before he'd taken it straight off his back but a lot better than the one he now wore.

The woman finally took a breath, and Grant near to knocked her over taking possession of his arm. He thought she might have left scratch marks, even through his buckskin coat.

"I've left the young'uns alone too long." He vaulted onto the wagon seat. It occurred to him that Shirt Lady hadn't come out to check on things today. Half the folks in town had come. They'd offered food, their strength, their support, their prayers. Shirt Lady hadn't so much as asked after Josh, even now. No possible way she could have missed what happened with all the effort Ian and Will had made to put the word out Josh had amnesia. Any decent person would now ask which boy was hurt and inquired after his health. She just hadn't cared.

He saw that same sour expression on her face that had been there before when he'd talked about his children. She looked up at him on the high seat. "But Grant, what about coming over?"

"I've got to get home." Why would she even want to pass a moment of her time with him if she didn't like children? It just didn't stand to reason. It was on Grant's tongue to say something mannerly about "another time," but he feared if he started talking something rude might come out. The best he could manage was, "Evenin', Miss. . . ." He jerked on the brim of his Stetson and slapped the reins on his horses' backs so hard he owed the poor critters an apology. Well, too bad. They weren't gettin' one. Helping him escape was part of their job.

He saw Shirt Lady jump back. She dodged the wagon. Good, if he'd run over her toes he'd've had to stop and take her to the doctor.

Grant promptly dismissed What's Her Name from his thoughts and quarreled inside his head with Hannah all the ride home.

SIXTEEN

"You may close your books, children. Class dismissed for recess."

The children dashed out the door.

Hannah waited until the last one left, then buried her face in her hands and wept. She did her best to muffle the sound, but she couldn't control the shuddering of her shoulders and the quiet, choking sobs. She gave herself up to it completely, knowing these tears would just have to run their course. She'd be fully recovered by the time her students came back.

A hand rested on her shoulder, and she jerked her head up, mortified. Marilyn looked down at her with a kind smile.

Hannah had a split second to wonder if this particular student was older than she. Then she took another split second to wonder just how old either of them was. Chances were no one really knew.

"Don't cry, Miss Cartwright. You should be happy. You're a wonderful teacher."

Hannah really needed to cry for just a few minutes, but with Marilyn watching, she got a grip on herself. Her shoulders stopped quivering. She sniffed and blew her nose with the handkerchief she clutched in her hands. She wiped her eyes and struggled with the last few tears. Her lower lip trembled. "You should be outside playing."

With a smile, Marilyn said, "I'll leave in just a minute."

The stern look Hannah tried to muster was ruined by the hiccups.

At last she managed a weak smile. "It's really going well, isn't it?"

"You know pride is a sin, Miss Cartwright." Marilyn straightened and showed no sign of leaving.

Since she was caught anyway, Hannah decided she was glad for the company to interrupt her foolish tears of joy. She dabbed at her eyes. "And why do you mention pride?"

"Because you're so proud of yourself for the way things went this morning." Marilyn's smiled broadened, her blue eyes flashing with pleasure as she gently teased. "I don't think it's a sin for *me* to be proud of you, though."

"Are you proud of me?" Hannah leaned forward. "Did it go as well as I think?"

Marilyn nodded. "I've just come to live with Grant recently. Before that, well, there was never much time for schooling, but I did manage to do some learning. I think you have a rare gift for working with children. I'd say you've done it before a lot, haven't you."

"I've never taught a school before. This is my first time."

"There are other ways to work with children, other ways to teach besides in front of a classroom." Marilyn sighed. "I've done some teaching myself in the orphanage where I lived before I ran off."

Needing to get on with preparing for the rest of the morning classes, Hannah said, "You'd better go on out. Charlie isn't one to let anyone push him around. Maybe you can keep the peace."

"I'll go. I just thought you looked a little wobbly, and I wanted to make sure you were all right."

"I am now. I'll come out and watch recess in just a minute."

"No hurry." Marilyn pulled a sandwich wrapped in a square of fabric out of her coat pocket. "Pa sent way too much food with us today. He must have packed it thinking Joshua was still going to school. Sadie and I pack the lunches, but he came in after chores and threw a few more things in. I can't possibly eat three sandwiches, two apples, and six cookies. I don't want Pa to feel bad if I don't finish it though." Marilyn laid the sandwich on Hannah's desk.

Hannah felt her stomach growl. She'd had no breakfast. She wouldn't have money to eat until her first pay came. It frightened her when she dared to think of it, because that might be a month away. The only food she'd had since she arrived at Sour Springs had come from eating at Grant's. But Hannah would never take food out of a child's mouth. And Marilyn was thin already. "Uh. . .I don't think I should."

"It'd help me out if you took it."

Hannah realized that part of the reason she'd broken into tears was because she felt so shaky from hunger. Marilyn set the food on her desk, holding Hannah's gaze. Hannah didn't look at the sandwich because she was sure Marilyn would see hunger. Marilyn no doubt had plenty of experience with the feeling.

"Take it. There's plenty more for me. I wouldn't lie to you, Miss Cartwright."

"Thank you." Hannah noticed the faint trembling of her hand as she reached for the sandwich. "That's really generous of you."

"I can handle whatever trouble comes up outside. You should eat your lunch early. You'll need the energy for class. You look like you skipped breakfast this morning."

Hannah couldn't even control her hunger long enough to let Marilyn leave the classroom. She bit into the hearty roast beef sandwich and chewed slowly to make it last. She didn't know where her next meal might come from.

As soon as her hunger eased, Hannah reflected on the morning. She had worried that Grant's children might be well behind others their ages, but all of them were quite well educated. The older girls, Marilyn and Sadie, stepped in so willingly and helped with the younger ones—all of them, not just their own brothers and sisters—Hannah nearly had two other teachers in the room.

Sadie had a voice that would stop a naughty little boy in his tracks. She must have had considerable practice making little brothers and sisters mind. Hannah was distracted by envy every time Sadie verbally cracked the whip.

Marilyn had a comforting touch that made children turn to her like flowers turning toward the sun. If anyone cried, whether from hurt feelings or a scratch, Marilyn went to the child before Hannah could so much as move.

She had thirty-two students; many had to sit three to a desk so everybody would fit. But they shared with good spirits, listened when she taught, and studied quietly when she worked with others. She'd spent the morning quickly dividing them into classes and starting their lessons.

Learning was the important thing. If only she could educate them so they'd never be forced into mill work or, because of illiteracy, have no prospects of any jobs. She believed giving them an education could be the difference between life and death for some of them. It might be the difference between keeping their own children or sending them off to orphanages. With a kind of desperate urgency, Hannah taught them words and numbers to put them one step further from the awful fate that could await the uneducated.

The morning had gone wonderfully. Once her sandwich was finished, she went out and observed the playground. There was lots of running and shouting, but everything looked peaceful.

Emory Harrison, a first-grader in the same class as Benny, sidled over to Sadie and, wide-eyed with curiosity, asked, "Why do you have black skin?"

Hannah froze, afraid that this could bloom into trouble.

Sadie pointed to a big, dark freckle on Emory's arm. "I've got that kinda skin all over."

The boy stared at his arm a moment then nodded and went back to playing.

Hannah found an apple on her desk when she came in from watching the children during the noon recess. She found two cookies after the afternoon recess. She knew Marilyn had left them, except once she caught a gleam in Sadie's eyes that made her wonder about the apple. And Libby grinned at her impishly when Hannah asked about the cookies. No one would admit to leaving the food. Not knowing what to do, Hannah slipped the treats into her desk drawer for later.

The rest of the day went well, and Hannah went back to her cold room. There'd be no supper, but her stomach wasn't painfully empty as she'd expected.

The sun set early in the Texas January, and with no time wasted preparing an evening meal, and no light from a lantern because she had no oil, she looked out the single narrow window overlooking Sour Springs. She saw again the window in the living quarters of Prudence's sewing shop. And again she saw a second figure, just as she had on the night of the blizzard. Of course it wasn't late. Anyone could have dropped by for a visit. Anyone. . .including Grant.

Even after such a brief acquaintance, Hannah had a hard time believing Grant would go out on a date the day after Joshua was so badly hurt.

The curtains were drawn, but they weren't heavy enough to block out the pair of silhouettes. Hannah turned her back on the sight and on her roiling emotions.

SEVENTEEN

Hannah got to school early the next morning. She had a complex arithmetic problem she needed to explain to her older students and she wanted to review.

Hannah was distracted from her studying when four ladies and two men, looking grim, stormed into the schoolhouse.

"Can I help you?" Hannah smiled, rising from behind her desk, but her stomach sank as she studied the somber crowd. She recognized Quincy Harrison from the interview for her job. The others were familiar faces from around town, but she didn't know them by name.

The six people approached her desk and stood without speaking for a moment, until one particularly sour-faced woman poked the man beside her. "Get on with it, Quincy."

Hannah braced herself.

Quincy looked uncomfortable, but he stepped forward. "We need to discuss the trouble here at school yesterday. We're concerned that the children won't be able to learn in these conditions."

Mystified, Hannah asked, "What trouble? The children all worked hard, and they seemed—each one of them—bright and eager to learn."

"Of course they're bright," the woman who'd poked Quincy said. "Did you expect our children to be stupid?"

Another woman interrupted, "Let Quincy speak for us, Gladys. We agreed."

Hannah opened her mouth to apologize. Of course she hadn't expected her students to be stupid, but caution kept her silent. Instead of talking she began to pray. She waited to hear what the problem really was, terribly afraid she knew already.

"It's not that our children didn't learn." Quincy looked from his toes to Hannah and back. "It's just. . .we don't like the idea of them uh. . .uh. . ."

Gladys lifted her nose even higher in the air. "Mixing with the wrong sorts."

Hannah remained silent. Her empty stomach twisted with dread. This was what Grant had been talking about. These people had made it impossible for the children at the Rocking C to attend school. Her prayers flowed to God as she wondered how she was going to feed herself. Because if these people insisted she send the black children home, or for that matter the orphan children home, she was quitting.

Gladys elbowed Quincy in a way that made Hannah guess he was her husband. "Get on with it."

"It's just that. . .that. . ." Quincy fell silent.

The other man was thin and nervous looking. "I'm Theodore Mackey, Miss Cartwright. We got together last night and decided we needed to meet with you. We all just want what's best for our children."

Hannah finally had control of herself enough to speak calmly. "School went very well yesterday. I don't see the need to change a thing."

"We saw that older girl. . . ," Theodore said.

"Which older girl?" Although Hannah knew which quite well. Sadie.

"The Negro." Gladys said it as if she were spitting.

"Well," Quincy said, "she was playing with the other children and sitting right with the other girls."

Another woman spoke up. "They're all part of the orphanage that man runs on his ranch."

"His name is Grant, Agnes. And well you know it. I'm Ella Johnson," the third woman said. She looked at Hannah while she introduced herself then turned back to the crowd she'd come in with. "Now being orphans doesn't make those children bad. They had no say in how they came into this world."

Hannah immediately focused on Ella Johnson, hoping she'd found an ally.

"You're just saying that because your sister married one of Grant's brood," Gladys said.

"That's right, Gladys, that's exactly why I'm saying this. I know what a decent man Will is, and Grant raised him. It's not right to deny those children a place in this school just because they came out here on a train."

"It's more than that," Gladys snapped.

"Then it's about that girl being black?" Ella stood her ground

Gladys turned toward her. "It's about more than their skin color."

Ella might be better able to absorb any cruel words Gladys jabbed at her, but this was Hannah's fight. "Ella, if you don't mind, I'll handle this."

Ella looked at her then with a nod said, "Yes, ma'am."

"What's going on here?" Grant's voice, far harder than usual, broke into the conversation.

All of the people confronting Hannah turned to the back of the schoolroom.

"Glad you're here, Grant," Ella said. "I'm planning to see that your children get the education they've got coming."

At Ella's announcement, dead silence fell over the group.

"Obliged, Ella." Grant stayed near the back of the room, looking over the rows of desks at his neighbors. "But this is my fight."

Ella fidgeted but didn't say anything.

"No, it's not, Grant. It's mine." Hannah rested her hands on her waist. "I'm the teacher of this school, and I'll be the one to talk with parents who have a problem with the way I run things."

"This isn't about you, Hannah. It's about my children." Grant pulled his hat off his head in a reflex show of manners. But there was nothing polite in his expression. Grant stared at the group for a long awkward minute, then he turned from them to Hannah. "I most always accompany the children to school the second day and come in ahead of them so I can attend this meeting. It waited until the third day this year because my young'uns didn't come in on Monday. Three whole days in school." Grant laughed bitterly. "A new record. 'Course they missed the first and are being kicked out before the third begins."

"This happens every time?" Hannah fought to control her temper. If the angry words that pressed to get out escaped, she'd say things that, no matter the provocation, she shouldn't say.

"I'm here, aren't I?" Grant went back to staring at the group. "And they're here. As dependable as the rising sun."

He opened his mouth, then clamped it shut and shook his head. "What's the use? I'll just take them home," he said to Hannah, as if the others weren't there. "They really liked school. They really liked you for a teacher, Hannah. But I won't subject them to this treatment."

"They were treated well." Hannah pushed past the crowd and ran to catch hold of Grant's arm as he turned to leave.

"So I heard. And they really felt like they could learn things from you that I'm missing. Marilyn talked about becoming a teacher. She said you let her help, and she really enjoyed it. Maybe if you recommended the right books for them, I can do better."

She refused to let go of his wrist. "They're not quitting school!"

Grant looked at Hannah, and she felt his kindness and the regret he had over taking his family out of school. But she could see how fiercely he wanted to protect them.

Whispering for only Grant to hear, she said, "I don't know how I could have looked in your eyes a single time and doubted that you'd take good care of your children."

Grant's eyes lost some of their wintry sadness. "Thanks, Hannah. I'd best be going."

Hannah held on tight. "I'm not letting you go anywhere." Still latched on to him, she turned to the group of complainers. She knew if she said what needed saying, she'd be fired. She didn't have a spare penny to feed herself. Still, she couldn't stand by and let Grant's children be cast out while she stayed safely employed. "If you don't allow orphans in this school as students, then I'm sure you wouldn't want one as a teacher," she said politely. "I'm afraid you'll have to fire me. I'm an orphan myself."

Fear, disgust, and surprise crossed the faces of the people in front of her, all but Ella. Then Grant tugged on the hand she had latched onto him, dragging her attention back.

"Why didn't you tell me?" he whispered.

She couldn't meet his eyes, and she spoke low to keep their conversation private. "I don't like to talk about it. It. . . M—my childhood. . . was awful."

"That's why you were so worried about the children. That's why you expected the worst." Grant fell silent for a second. "That's how you got those marks on your back."

Hannah nodded.

"That's why you care so much."

Hannah lifted her chin and almost fell forward into the understanding in Grant's eyes. He'd know how it was. She'd spent all her life being strong for her little sisters and Grace, never adding her misery to the weight anyone else had to bear. But Grant was strong. He could bear a lot. He'd lived much like her. Like a yawning chasm, the dangers of sharing everything about herself opened at her feet. Tempting her to take that step.

"My years as an orphan weren't pleasant. Too much work, too little food, not enough love. Then I got adopted and things got worse. I escaped from the man who adopted me, and I have been looking over my shoulder since I left, wondering if he's searching. He's the type to want revenge."

Grant rested a strong hand on her arm, as if could take all of the bad memories away. . .or at least replace them with new ones that would outshine the bad. Hannah wanted to tell him more, tell him everything.

"There was certainly no mention of you being an orphan when you applied for the job of teacher." Gladys scowled, striding toward the back of the classroom. "You have lied to us, Miss Cartwright."

Applied? Hannah remembered her interview and almost smiled. She turned away from the offer Grant made with a kind touch and understanding eyes and faced the lynch mob. She'd just handed them all the rope they needed to hang her. "I didn't lie. I'm a twenty-year-old woman." Hannah wasn't all that sure, but it was a fair guess. "And how I was raised had nothing to do with whether I could do this job."

Furious, she ruthlessly suppressed her temper, knowing they would chalk up any bad behavior on her part to dreaded orphanhood. "I just didn't tell you everything about my childhood. The full truth is I've been teaching children all my life. When I was adopted, I was taken to a home where the man pressed all of us into work at a carpet weaving factory. I was six when I started working sixteen-hour days. I and my older sister taught my younger sisters how to read and write and cipher late at night when my father wouldn't catch us and punish us for it."

"Still, you should have been more forthcoming, Miss Cartwright." Gladys sniffed and began pulling on her gloves as if the meeting were over.

Hannah suspected it was. "The only lie I told you was my name." Hannah glanced up at Grant and tears filled her eyes. "I made up the name Cartwright. I don't know what my last name is."

"Orphans can't be trusted," Gladys went on. "And I believe your lies have proved that to us."

"They learn bad ways that have to be taught out of them," Agnes said. "Maybe Grant does all right when he has them for a long time to train them, but he keeps getting new ones and—"

"You can fire me if you want, but I will not listen to you speak ill of Grant's children. They are good, hardworking children who were a wonderful addition to this classroom."

Ella shoved herself between Hannah and Gladys. "Hannah is not fired, and Grant's children are welcome in this school. You do not make the decisions here, Gladys. I've already talked with the parson and Harold at the general store. They both heard good things about the school and want Miss Cartwright to stay."

Gladys's lip curled. "You went behind my back to talk to them?"

Grant stepped in front of Ella. "Stay out of this, Ella. You've got to live in town with these folks. I don't want trouble stirred up that's going to bother you, or your sister and Will."

What Hannah heard in Grant's voice humbled her. He was worried about someone else. Nothing she'd felt had come close to the depth of Grant's kindness. How many times had Hannah longed for a father to care this much?

It inspired her to be kind herself, when her temper wanted free rein. She walked around Grant and Ella and faced Gladys. "I know how much you love your children, Mrs. Harrison. I know you only want what's best for them."

Gladys's mouth clicked shut.

"Did any of your children come home upset about school?" Hannah looked right at Gladys, but her question was for everyone.

Quincy said, "It was just the opposite. I've never had my young'uns so excited about learning. Why, my littlest one even read a few words out of the family Bible and he wrote his name, after only one day of school."

"That's Emory," Hannah said. "He was so good yesterday. So eager to learn. He's a really special little boy, Mr. Harrison. I'll have to work hard to keep ahead of him."

Quincy fairly glowed with pride.

Even Gladys's dour expression softened. "He's always been quick. He keeps the two older boys working on their studies, afraid their little brother will catch up and pass them."

Hannah laughed, and several of the group who had been so disapproving before smiled. "And your twins, Agnes, they are so pretty. They tried to fool me about their names once yesterday, but I had them figured out from the first."

"You could tell Samantha and Emily apart?" Agnes shook her head. "Are you sure? They even manage to trick me and their pa part of the time."

"I counted the freckles on their noses the first minute I saw them."

"Their freckles?" the twin's father exclaimed. "I'd never thought of that."

"I knew a set of twins when I was young, in the orphanage, and they liked to play twin tricks, but I could tell it meant the world to them if someone could tell them apart. So I suspected your girls would feel the same. Samantha has ten freckles and Emily only has eight. Emily and eight, both start with E. It was easy after I figured that out, if they just gave me a second to count."

Agnes and her husband smiled.

Grant said to the parents, "Miss Cartwright, having so much experience with children, knew a way to touch your daughters' hearts. Being an orphan is the reason she's as good at teaching as she is."

Gladys looked long and hard at Hannah.

Ella's hand rested on Hannah's shoulder. "Say all you want about this being someone else's fight, Grant's or Miss Cartwright's, but I've got the backing of the school board. Two against one, Quincy. You'll have to persuade them to change their minds in order to fire Hannah."

Hannah wanted to weep at Ella's generous courage. Hannah hadn't planned it, but she had come to be standing between Grant and Ella as if they were guarding her.

The parents had come in here with their minds made up, and it didn't sit well, especially with Gladys, to change. But Gladys was proud of her boy, Emory.

Finally Gladys relented, relaxing her shoulders. The rest of the group took their cue from her and exhaled silently.

"It's true that you did a good job here yesterday, Miss Cartwright. And it's true that Ella's brother-in-law is a good man. I can see that with my own eyes. And Grant, your son Ian is a good blacksmith, honest and hardworking. I'm just. . ." Gladys hesitated.

"You want your three boys to grow up to be decent men." Hannah nodded as she spoke. "You're watching out for them and trying to protect them from being hurt or being led astray. That's what any mother would do. You were right to come in here and get your questions answered. You come back in any time you are concerned about the school, Gladys. I will work with you to give your boys the best education I can."

Gladys seized on Hannah's offer as if she'd gotten exactly what she'd come in for. "I'll just do that, Miss Cartwright. You won't be doing anything in this school of which I disapprove."

Hannah had a sudden inspiration. "You know what would be really good? If you would take control of part of the Easter pageant I'm planning."

Gladys's eyes gleamed. Hannah thought the use of the word "control" was inspired. It looked like Gladys thought she should control the whole world.

"I'm going to teach them songs, and there'll be a speaking part for every child. There'll be songs and Bible readings. I've written it to be appropriate for children. We'll need simple costumes, and I'd like the parson to say a few words and maybe the parents could bring in cookies so we could have refreshments afterwards." Hannah heard the enthusiasm in her voice, and she thought she saw a corresponding reaction of interest from the parents.

"Gladys, you could be in charge of organizing the whole thing. The children will need help learning the songs and their parts. I think we should insist that they memorize everything."

Now Gladys was really excited. Hannah surmised that she was a woman who was all for "insisting."

"Why, I'd be happy to take charge, Miss Cartwright," Gladys said.

"I'll help," Ella offered. The other parents chorused their willingness to get involved, although Hannah noticed Grant stayed silent. Hannah wondered if they realized yet that they'd just agreed to let her keep her job until spring and had quit trying to get Grant's children expelled. She didn't point it out.

"We haven't ever had an Easter pageant in Sour Springs. I think it's a great idea." Quincy turned to his wife. "Now, we'd better let Miss Cartwright get on with her preparations for school."

The angry little mob of parents disbursed in a flurry of cheer.

Ella patted Grant on the shoulder. "Will wanted to come, but I thought he might make things worse."

Grant nodded silently and Ella left.

Hannah heaved a sigh of relief.

EIGHTEEN

G rant heaved a sigh of despair.

"They'll never leave my family alone." He turned to face Hannah. "They were this mad after yesterday, and yesterday there was no trouble. Just wait until one of your students goes home crying because Sadie beat him in a spelling bee. That bunch will be back."

Grant noticed Hannah's hands were trembling as she crossed her arms.

"I can't believe they let me off as easily as they did. I thought I was done for from the minute they showed up because I was going to quit before I let them drive your children out of the school."

"Don't sacrifice your job, Hannah." Grant put his hat on with a rough jerk of the brim and turned to go. "I don't expect you to do that for me."

"I wouldn't cross the street for you, you idiot." She grabbed his arm and spun him around.

She only managed to manhandle him because he was turning back toward her anyway in surprise. Grant had one split second after she exploded to marvel at how well she'd kept her cool with that posse of orphan haters. Then she attacked.

"If you think I'd side with that mean-spirited, selfish bunch of vigilantes over your children, you don't—"

Grant held up both hands to ward her off. "Look, Hannah, I didn't mean—"

Hannah grabbed the lapels of his flannel shirt. "—have any idea who I am. Why, if you think—"

"It's not that. I didn't say—" Grant backed up a step.

Hannah followed him all the way to the wall. "—I'll stand by and let Sadie get thrown out of school because of the color of her skin—"

"I'm sorry. Really, Hannah. I wasn't suggesting—" Grant caught her hands where they were shaking his collar. She seemed determined to strangle him to death.

She tightened her grip. "—or slam the door in the face—"

Grant stopped trying to placate her and leaned over her, "Listen, I didn't mean to imply you had anything against orphans. If you'll—"

"—of any child—"

All his tension uncoiled like a striking rattler. "—just shut up for a second—" He pulled her hands off his throat.

She yanked away from his grip. "—orphan or not, who wants to learn—"

He just needed her to shut up for a minute so he could tell her how much he appreciated her standing by him, and how sorry he was she had to face down a mob, and how annoying she was, and how pretty, and sweet— He turned her around and trapped her against the wall. "—and let me apologize, I'll—"

She turned her face up, her eyes flashing with fire and spirit, her cheeks flushed. "—then you're the most insulting man I've ever—"

He couldn't think of any other way to close her yapping mouth.

He kissed her.

It worked.

She shut up.

He jumped back so fast he tripped over a desk. "I shouldn't have done that."

"You shouldn't have done that." Hannah covered her mouth with her hand, her eyes wide, watching him like he'd grown rattles and fangs and attacked her.

Grant shook his head and felt his brain rattle, so maybe he *was* close to growing the fangs, and he was very much afraid he might attack her again.

Hannah ran her tongue over her lips as if she wanted to wash the taste of him away. "That can't ever happen again!"

"That can *never* happen again." Grant couldn't back farther because of the desk. That's the only possible reason he went forward instead. And kissed her again.

"Let go of me!" Hannah wrenched away from Grant, which was hard with her arms wrapped around his neck. But she managed, with Grant helping, to pry her hands loose where they'd gripped the hair curling down the nape of his neck.

Grant looked aghast. "That never should have happened."

"Never, not ever."

"It's never going to happen again." Grant turned his back on Hannah and figured out that if he moved sideways he could get away from her. Why hadn't he thought of that before? "We don't even know each other," Grant added.

Hannah smoothed her hair, which Grant noticed was messy.

He remembered running his fingers through it. How long had he spent kissing her? Her lips were pink and a bit swollen. He looked closer. He moved closer.

Those lying pink lips said, "We don't even like each other."

Shaking his head to break the spell Hannah had cast over him, Grant pushed his hat firmly on his head and looked straight at her out from under the low brim. "Oh, maybe we like each other a little."

"Some." Hannah's eyes found his. . .and held.

"But it was wrong." Grant turned away to prove he could.

"Oh yes, it was."

"Very, very wrong," Grant agreed, suddenly furious with her for being so certain, because in his whole life he'd *never* felt anything so right.

At that moment, three dozen children flooded into the room.

Grant saw Hannah's knees give out, and she caught herself before she fell by leaning against the wall. It was a good thing she saved herself from collapsing because Grant wasn't capable of moving.

If they'd been a few seconds earlier, the whole school would have walked in on them. By nightfall, all of Sour Springs would know he'd kissed the new schoolmarm in front of all her students. Something like that had to be followed immediately with a wedding, or Hannah would immediately be fired. And if they announced an engagement, Hannah would be fired with everyone's best wishes for happiness, and Grant would be saddled with a wife—a meddling, potato-burning wife. He looked sideways at her, leaning against the wall, both hands clapped over her bright pink cheeks. An annoying, nosy, beautiful, kindhearted wife who'd offered to sacrifice her job to fight for his children.

That wasn't going to happen since Grant had promised himself and God a long time ago, on a cold Texas morning in Houston, that he'd never marry. The day he took six children home with him, he dedicated his life to caring for children nobody wanted rather than having even one speckled-eyed child of his own.

Besides, he didn't have room for her. He'd have to put her on the kitchen floor.

Next to him.

"Gotta go." Grant ran out of the building like a man being chased by a pack of hungry wolves, or worse yet, one pretty little woman.

Hannah wanted to send him on his way with a swift kick.

And she might have if she could get her knees to stop wobbling.

Suddenly her spine stiffened, if not her knees. What if he'd kissed her knowing a kiss would make her stay away from him? And by staying away from him, she'd naturally stay away from the Rocking C, which meant she'd never know for sure what went on out there.

She thought of the few times she'd seen Parrish in action. The man had a masterful front he'd put on for others who questioned whether he should be allowed to adopt children with no mother in the home. Her skin still crawled when she thought of the times Parrish had rested a loving hand on her shoulder while he spoke of his devotion and wanting to help those less fortunate. She'd known full well that the same so-called loving hand would punish her brutally if she didn't smile and call him daddy for the onlookers.

Grant wasn't like that. Her heart knew he wasn't. But what if her heart was reacting to a handsome man who made a public display of his affection for his children? He'd said he never let them go to school. He made it sound like he was protecting them. But what it amounted to was the children were cut off almost all the time. Had Hannah's intervention stopped him from doing exactly what he wanted to do? Getting his children back home and putting them back to work?

Hannah couldn't trust her instincts about Grant. And she couldn't face him.

Hannah closed her eyes and prayed for wisdom. Her prayers kept being interrupted by the memory of Grant's strong arms and how wonderful it felt to be held.

Stirring restlessly, she knew she couldn't go out to the Rocking C to inspect again. She didn't trust herself. Chewing one stubby thumbnail, Hannah decided that as long as he left the children in school she'd know they were released from any hard labor for a few hours every day. So she'd stay away from the Rocking C as long as the children were here. But if Grant pulled them out, she'd have to go back.

She thought of Grant's head lowering toward her, pulling her close, and something very sweet and rather desperate turned over in her chest. She'd shared lots of hugs with her sisters in her life. But she'd never been held by a man.

She'd seen moths fluttering toward a burning lantern. They'd fly straight into the flame and be burned, sometimes to death. The moths never learned, or maybe as they burned to death they finally did. Until it hurt that badly, the pull of the warmth and light was too powerful. Even if Grant had done it to keep her from finding out his secrets, mesmerized by the heat of his arms and his kiss, she still felt the pull.

How humiliating!

Even more humiliating, what if he tried to kiss her again? She knew deep in her heart that she might well kiss him back.

While the children settled in their desks, she headed for the outdoors, hoping the sharp cold would ease the burning in her cheeks and cool her crazy thoughts about Grant and how badly he needed a mother in that house of his.

She wanted to—had to—avoid Grant, and to do that she had to keep his children in this school.

NINETEEN

He had to get his children out of that school!

He practically fell down the steps of the schoolhouse in his hurry to escape whatever had happened in there.

He slammed into something soft. His attention abandoned the disaster that was Hannah, and he saw that he held Shirt Lady in his arms. She leaned toward him; her lips seemed to be pursed. She might be going to kiss him.

A door opened behind Grant and he turned, knowing it had to be the schoolhouse door. Grant looked straight into Hannah's eyes. She was just a couple of yards away at the top of the three steps. She was flushed, her lips still shiny and swollen, looking as bothered as a woman could be. He knew it was about that kiss. He was mighty bothered himself.

Hannah saw him and her expression turned to horror. He read every bit of what she was thinking. Grant, holding someone else, another woman, seconds after he'd been kissing the daylights out of Hannah.

Lips came at him, and he saw them just in time to dodge. Shirt Lady missed his lips and grazed his neck ever so slightly. He shuddered. Her lips were soggy and flabby and. . .

Hannah made a sound that distracted him from his revulsion. A wounded wildcat growl, part pain, part fury, all dangerous. She was in a good position up there to pounce, too.

Grant braced himself to be buried under two women.

Hannah's expression of horror and fury changed to utter contempt. She whirled around, her tattered skirt flying, and stormed back into the schoolhouse, slamming the door so hard the whole building shook.

Sick to imagine what Hannah thought about what she'd witnessed, Grant turned back and saw Shirt Lady zeroing in on him again with those disgusting lips. He'd rather kiss one of his longhorns, one who'd just sucked up a river full of brackish water. He ducked before he could commit his third act of stupidity concerning a woman's lips in less than a minute.

Shirt Lady almost fell, for the second time, because of his clumsiness. Then she staggered and cried out with pain. Her hands tightened around his neck.

He reached up to free himself.

"No, please, be careful. My ankle. I think I sprained it. If I let go, I'll fall."

Grant stopped in his headlong effort to free himself from these poison ivy arms. He shook his head to clear it, knowing he was still reacting to Hannah—to what had happened inside the school and out. There was no sense knocking Shirt Lady over just because he was upset with the schoolmarm.

"Sorry. Here, let me get my arm around your waist."

Hannah wanted to get her hands around Grant's neck.

She should have gone all the way inside, but that window, right by the door, was too handy, and she looked out at that lowdown, stinking polecat as he slipped his arm around his girlfriend, seconds after the skunk kissed Hannah!

She should have moved on, but it was like she wanted the pain. Hannah watched Grant practically sweeping the horrible seamstress off her feet. Standing, staring, Hannah knew it was a good thing to see. Let it burn her eyeballs to cinders so she'd remember.

She'd always been afraid of men. Her father had taught her well. But for some awful, ridiculous reason her common sense had deserted her with Grant. Even when he was scowling and snarling like a smelly old ogre, she'd never been scared. That just proved that not only was she right to be afraid of men, her instincts were also never to be trusted.

Boiled down to its simplest form. . .she was an idiot.

Prudence smiled and leaned close. Grant slid his hands up her arms. Hannah couldn't see his face, shadowed by his hat, but she could see that nasty Prudence, batting her eyes like a Texas dust devil just blew straight in her face.

Hannah finally had all she could take. She forced herself to turn from the window.

School!

She was a teacher. She had students and responsibilities and a life that had nothing in the world to do with that awful, lowdown Grant or his appalling mistreatment of both Hannah and that dreadful Prudence.

Hannah smoothed her hair and forced her breath to come more evenly. She wished her heart would stop thudding. More than thudding, it seemed to be breaking, but she couldn't imagine why. She'd barely had one kind thought about Grant in all their brief, unpleasant acquaintance.

Well, there'd been a few kind thoughts. More than a few in all honesty. And a few pleasant moments. Extremely pleasant.

Then she decided, despite her firm belief that God wished her to be honest in all things at all times, this once she'd go ahead and lie to herself about those kind thoughts and pleasant moments and dwell on the bad ones. She'd pick them apart, see that even worse things lay beneath Grant's disgusting behavior.

She squared her shoulders as she imagined shoving him off that train platform the first day. She'd have saved herself a lot of time and trouble if only she'd known.

Feeling marginally cheered by the image, or at least capable of not bursting into tears in front of her class, she marched into her true calling. Working with children. . .only children. . .no man ever!

Grant firmly unfastened Shirt Lady's clinging hands. He controlled the urge to gag as he peeled her loose. "Should I help you to the doctor's office?" Doc Morgan was nearby. That'd get rid of her right away.

"No, I don't think that's necessary."

Grant stifled a groan.

Prudence smiled. "I don't think it's broken. I just need some help getting home." She looked up at him, and she must have had something in her eye. Her lashes flapped as if she was trying to dislodge a dirt clod.

"I'll help you then." What choice did he have? His natural inclination, which was to shake her off him like a slimy leech, would leave the woman lying in the dust. He didn't know much about women, unless they were his children, but he was sure dropping Shirt Lady in the dirt wasn't right.

He slid his arm around her back. His head cleared enough that he realized the woman was almost letting him carry her. Her ankle must really hurt. Grant walked the length of the meager Sour Springs Main Street with Shirt Lady clinging to him.

Mabel came to the door of the general store, wiping her hands on her apron. "Howdy, Grant, Prudence."

Grant controlled a flinch. Prudence. He thought of her as Shirt Lady, and he wasn't going to stop now. He was determined to never know this woman well enough to learn her name.

"Good morning, Mabel."

Expecting Shirt Lady to say something about her injury, Grant hesitated. Then it seemed like it was too late somehow. Oh well. Surely Mabel could see the woman limping.

"Tell Harold thanks again for coming out to help yesterday." Grant reached up and tipped his hat.

Harold appeared in the door behind Mabel with a big grin on his face. "Mornin', you two."

You two? Like they were a couple or something? Grant had to fix that misconception.

"Can we hurry along, Grant, honey? I'm anxious to get home."

Honey? Grant was suddenly almost pulled along. Prudence didn't seem to be favoring her ankle as much. That was a good sign.

"So, when are you going to keep our next date?" Prudence's voice had a piercing quality that carried up and down the street. Grant was sure Mabel and Harold could hear. He saw Doc Morgan grinning at him as the man unlocked his office.

"What date?" Heart sinking, Grant knew these fine citizens of Sour Springs were drawing the wrong conclusion. And he hadn't cleared a bit of it up by the time they'd reached the shirt shop.

"You said you were too busy to come for supper the other night, remember? Come on in now and have a bite of my seed cake and some coffee."

Prudence kept dragging him, but Grant drew the line at actually going into her store. He didn't want to be alone with the little ivy plant for even a second. He dug his heels into the wooden sidewalk. "Gotta go. No time for cake." Wasn't that pretty much what he'd said last time, and look how much trouble that had gotten him into.

"Then when, Grant?"

It came to Grant in a flash that instead of fighting he should go along with her. Better the town folks knew there was nothing going on between him and Hannah. Of course nothing could ever come of a date with Shirt Lady. His skin crawled when he thought of that almost-kiss he'd dodged.

The woman had definitely set her cap for him, and he couldn't let her go along believing they might be suited. But one date would solve a lot of problems between him and Hannah. He made a promise to himself not to be alone with Prudence for a second. He'd just come to her door, take her for a nice public ride so Hannah and everyone would see them but nothing improper could be even whispered, then he'd drop her off and run like a scared rabbit.

"Um, how about we go for a ride some evening?"

"I'd be proud to make dinner for you. I'm an excellent cook." Prudence must have that dirt back in her eyes again. With her ankle hurting and her eyes all stinging from the dirt, it was a wonder the woman didn't want to go on inside and get some rest.

"It wouldn't be proper for us to be alone in your room, Prudence. But we can take a quick ride. Just this once. You know"—Grant felt he had to be honest. The woman needed the truth—"I'm not planning on taking a wife. I've got a house too small for a gnat to find a place to settle in. I'm running all day every day to keep up with the children, and I'm planning on taking in more when the need arises. There's no room for a wife in that."

Shirt Lady's eyelids stopped flailing and her smile went kind of hard around the edges, but Grant was impressed that she held onto it at all. The mention of the children bothered her. And hearing that they couldn't do more than just take a single ride had to pinch her feelings.

Half expecting the door to slam in his face, instead she said, "I'd enjoy your company, Grant. Even if it's not a wife you're looking for, we could be good friends."

Somehow, Grant sincerely doubted he could ever be friends with a woman who didn't like children. He decided he'd said enough for now though. "I'll come for you on. . ." He hated to do it of an evening; he was too tired. He didn't want to give up Saturday; he got a lot done on Saturday with the children home. It didn't seem proper to do something he was dreading as much as this on the Lord's Day, so Sunday was out.

"Come Friday night, please. Not too late, so the dark doesn't catch us out riding."

Well, the woman had beaten him to the asking again. It didn't suit him a bit, but at least he'd be getting it over with soon, except... "Uh...can we wait a little longer?" He had to be sure Josh was well. Like maybe a year or two?

"How about a week from Friday then?"

Grant couldn't think of a single excuse. He wasn't prepared. If he'd known this was coming, he'd have practiced excuses. But who could predict a thing like this? His shoulders slumped. "A week from Friday sounds fine. I'll be here...before the supper hour. We'll take a short ride, but I want to get home to my young'uns for the evening meal. Don't want them alone at night."

Her smile hardened again. It was a purely frightening expression. But most things about women frightened Grant, so he didn't know if he could trust his reaction.

"Fine. I'll see you next Friday then." She closed the door with a sharp click that didn't sound near as friendly as her words.

Grant turned and almost ran to his wagon. Women were a mystery to him, and he'd had two mysteries fetched down on him in a single morning. Then he saw Mabel, still wiping hands that had to be bone dry by now, and she gave him a smug smile that he had no idea what it meant.

Three mysteries.

He leapt to the wagon seat. Tossing the brake free with a thump of wood and iron, he yelled.

The horses cooperated nicely and took off as if Shirt Lady chased them, flying on her broomstick.

Finally, Grant found someone who understood him—his horses.

"Why couldn't you get him in here?" Horace emerged from the back room.

"All you'd have needed to do was get the door closed then rip your dress and start screaming loud enough to draw a crowd. He'd have been forced to marry you and the land would be ours."

Prudence scowled at the filthy man. "He's coming by next Friday night. We'll finish this then. I think you should be here to knock him in the head. Then after he's been in here a good long time and comes around, I can act out the whole scene. As soon as he's conscious, I'll get the preacher in here breathing fire and brimstone, and he'll force the marriage."

Prudence went and made sure the window curtains were drawn shut. "I know just how to do it, too. I was hiding behind the school, waiting for my chance to get Grant in here, and I watched in the window at that crowd who came to toss Grant's kids out of school. Those folks will believe the worst of him because he's an orphan."

"People are always suspicious of orphans." Horace headed for the back room. "I remember how we got treated, like we was dirt. Trash under their feet. We deserve some payback for growin' up that way."

Purdence's temper flared, and there was only one person handy to take it out on. "Why'd you sleep so late? Now you can't get out to the dig all day because someone might see you." Prudence noticed Horace's steps falter. "What? You're hiding something."

Horace turned slowly, his eyes narrow and shifting.

Prudence braced for him to solve this with fists.

"I went to LaMont and didn't get back until late last night. I overslept."

"I know and spent half of what we should have made in the saloon." Prudence jammed her fists on her hips and felt the thrill of daring him to shut her mouth.

He stalked toward her. "There's more. Monday morning early, one of those riffraff kids from the Rocking C came on me. I had to shut his mouth for good."

"You killed him?" Prudence's mouth watered. She loved a man

strong enough to take what he wanted. Horace was the strongest man Prudence had ever known.

"Yep. I'm surprised you didn't hear about it in town."

"There was a fuss yesterday. I heard Grant's son fell. I reckon that's what it was about. It must not have bothered anyone too bad. Things were normal with Grant and his get this morning." Prudence walked back to the window and peeked through the burlap curtains to stare at the school building.

"No one's gonna make much ruckus about one dead orphan." Horace came up and shouldered her aside. "And he was one'a them black-skinned ones, too. No loss all the way around."

"Stay back from the window!" Prudence shoved his hand away from the curtain.

Horace wheeled and grabbed the front of her dress in one fist and shoved her against the wall so hard the shop shook.

Her head slammed against wood. She saw stars.

"I'll go where I want to go."

Her knees buckled, but he held her up.

"Do what I want to do." Horace clamped one massive stinking hand around her throat. "And you'll keep your mouth shut about it." With a vicious laugh, his yellow teeth broken and bared, he tightened his stranglehold. "You hear me, Prudence?"

"Yes." She could barely whisper.

"Good girl." He kissed her.

When she kissed him back, he let her breathe.

TWENTY

Grant forked fresh clean straw into the last horse stall, tossing around ideas and horse bedding with equal abandon.

He'd always taken the kids out of school for their own good. Only now, when there was no reason to take them out, Grant realized how much he liked having them around. Joshua was here, but right now the boy was sleeping, and he was a quick healer. He'd be in school in a couple of days. Grant hadn't been alone like this since those painful few months after his pa and ma died.

He hated it!

He worked hard just like always, but now, all day long, he heard no childish chatter from Benny, no thoughtful questions from Joshua. Marilyn never called out that the noon meal was ready. Sadie never giggled and whispered secrets to her sisters. He even missed Charlie, and the boy had yet to speak a kind word.

With the children here, Grant was always needed for something.

Had he taken his kids out of school on the least excuse all these years because he missed them? That meant Grant had sacrificed his children's education so he wouldn't have to be home alone.

Stabbing his pitchfork into the last of the straw, Grant refused to admit it was all his fault. The Brewsters had made it impossible. Breathing a sigh of relief, Grant remembered Festus Brewster. That thug had driven them away. If he'd have been in that posse this morning, there'd have been no going home without his children.

Looking around his tidy barn, Grant saw a few spots that could use attention and attacked them. The hours of the day crept by.

"Pa, what are you doing?"

Grant yelped, so lost in thought he almost jumped out of his skin. He jerked away from his bucket of water and looked at Joshua. Up and around. Grant smiled, so relieved he was speechless. "You look better."

"Is something wrong?" Joshua moved carefully, but he came on into the barn.

Grant realized what the boy had said the first time. "I'm...uh...just..." *acting like a madman.* Grant couldn't say that because Joshua would ask why and Grant wasn't about to admit that, if he *was* a madman, it was Hannah who had driven him crazy.

"I'm cleaning the barn floor is all."

"Are you planning to sleep out here?"

Good idea. No, bad idea. Grant didn't want to sleep in the barn. The barn was cold. But good excuse. "Maybe. Thought I'd see how it cleaned up." So that meant he wasn't a lunatic for scrubbing the barn floor on his hands and knees. Or at least Josh wouldn't realize he *was* one.

"We probably ought to all move out here and move the animals inside." Joshua grinned. "They have a better house than we do."

More cheerful now that his son was here, Grant got up from the ridiculous scrubbing. "Dumb idea anyway. I just had some spare time." Then Grant realized that it wasn't just Hannah-induced insanity. It was also boredom. That he could admit.

"It's so quiet around here with the young'uns all in school. I hate it. How can the father of six be so lonely?"

"I was bored, too. That's what made me come out here."

"You're looking good, Josh. Real good. Give yourself time to heal though." In other words, please don't go back to school and leave me.

"I think I can go back to school tomorrow."

Grant kept his smile in place by pure force of will. He didn't want the boy to stay sick after all. "How about your memory? Do you remember any more about what happened?"

Josh rubbed his head with his good arm, avoiding the spot with the stitches. He favored the arm that'd been knocked out of its socket. But he didn't have the sling on today, and his eyes seemed clear.

"I can't remember anything after I set out hunting that cow." Worry cut creases into Josh's forehead.

Grant was sorry he'd brought it up.

"I don't know what happened at all. I can't believe I fell off that cliff. I've been playing on that slope since I first moved here."

"The doc said it's normal to lose your memory around an accident. It may never come back." Grant didn't want to say the next words, but he felt like he had to warn the boy. "I scouted up that hill. It looks to me. . ."

Josh's eyes narrowed when Grant hesitated. He came farther into the barn. "What?"

"I think. . ." Grant hated saying the words, but the boy had to be warned. "I think you were hit on the head by someone." It looked to Grant like Josh's knees wobbled. He stood and rushed toward his son. "Let's sit down a minute."

Sheaves of straw, bound tight and set ready to bed the horses, were stacked close at hand. Grant helped Josh ease down on one and took the next one over. A person with black skin wouldn't go pale, but Grant had a feeling that all of the blood had flowed out of Josh's head.

"I'm sorry. Maybe I shouldn't have said anything." Grant clenched his hands between his knees and stared sideways at his son. "But you and all the young'uns need to be on your guard."

Josh steadied after he sat down and gave Grant a man-to-man look. "I'd rather know, Pa. We're all raised rough, except maybe Benny. We can handle bad news and we don't scare easy. I know I'd rather hear what I'm up against than have trouble sneak up on my flank. Do you have any idea who it was?"

Grant shook his head. "Tracks were wiped clear if there ever were any on that stony ground. The back side of that hill is that stinking spring. We never go anywhere near there and the cattle avoid it. They want no part of that foul, oily water or that black tar seeping out of the ground. I've got no idea who it was, but that's a good overlook for this property." Grant looked around his ridiculously clean barn. "What have I got anyone would want?"

Josh stared into the distance, thinking. "I've heard there's a way to get lamp oil out of a seep like that. I suppose someone might be sneaking in there to fill a lamp."

"You can't fill a lamp with that kind of sulfuric sludge. I know men who have tried it."

"No, you have to refine it. I read of such a thing in a newspaper once. But I don't know if I've ever heard of a refinery around these parts."

"Besides, if someone does think they can do it, all they'd need to do is to ask permission, I'd just say they could have it. There's nothing there to try and kill a man over."

"If I could just remember what happened!" Josh's fists clenched together between his splayed knees.

"Don't fret on it. It'll only give you a headache. Doc says your memory will either come back or it won't. Nothing we can do to force it."

"I know, but it's frustrating." Josh shrugged then winced at the shoulder movement.

"You should stay home a good week, Josh." Grant's spirits lifted at the thought. But he didn't want the boy to stay hurting. That was pure evil. Nothing wrong with a little coddling though. Of course the boy was as tall as Grant and took care of himself with adult confidence. But still, a father could fuss over his son.

Grant sighed and said a quick prayer for the boy's aches and pains to heal. He threw in a plea for forgiveness for the selfish wish to have his family back. And while he was at it, he asked God to take his loneliness away.

Hannah flashed into his thoughts, and Grant quit praying and focused on his son.

"I'll take things a day at a time. If I'm up to the ride to town tomorrow, I'll go. Any time I get to hurting, I'll stop and laze around awhile." Josh grinned, his smile broad and white against his black skin. "You're in need of a few more children, I'd say, Pa."

Grant smiled back even though he saw no humor in it. He *did* need more children.

Joshua stood slowly, protecting his shoulder, aching head, and tightly wrapped ribs from any sudden moves. "I was lonely in the house, but coming out here was more effort than I expected. I'd better go on back in and rest."

The instant Josh wasn't there to witness it, Grant's smile faded away. Just imagining Josh leaving made Grant's ears echo with the silence of his barn and his house and his life.

Hannah crept back into his thoughts. Thinking of her made the loneliness a thousand times worse.

Grant tried to think of something more constructive to do, but the barn was pure clean to the bone. The horses were brushed. The stock cattle were fat and healthy. The chickens had given up their day's supply of eggs and been fed.

Grant sighed and went back to his bucket. A madman scrubbing the barn floor.

Joshua went back to school, and Grant had a new problem.

As much as he missed his kids, he started dreading them coming home, because then, instead of thinking about Hannah to fill the silence, he had to hear about her. They came home full of excitement about their lessons, news about the Easter pageant, and endless tales about how much they adored Miss Cartwright.

Something else to drive him crazy!

To prove he was crazy, he noticed all the cobwebs on the barn ceiling. He started knocking them down—as if spiders didn't have a right to live outside. But he needed something to do!

Once the spiderwebs were gone, Grant hunted for any spot he couldn't eat off. He'd already cut a winter's supply of firewood, splitting it down to toothpick size.

He enjoyed the weekend with his children more than he ever had. They went to church together. Grant noticed Hannah never even looked his way. He'd have liked a chance to apologize for kissing her. But he saw Prudence bearing down on him after services and ran for home.

He worked and played side-by-side with his family all weekend. And then they left again.

He spent the next week working himself to death, moving his longhorns from the high pasture of his rugged ranch to the valley. A five-man job that could have been handled in a half day if he'd waited until Saturday with the children helping. He'd done it by himself.

The meaner and more feisty those half-wild cattle had been, the more Grant liked it, because only when he straddled the line between life and death did he forget about how much he'd enjoyed kissing Hannah.

By midday Wednesday, the winter term of school was near two weeks old, and he could count the hours since he'd put his hands on Hannah. His rough, work-reddened hands wrapped around her slender waist.

He kept thinking about that ride he'd promised Prudence, too—his stupid plan to make Hannah mad enough to never get close to him again. But to make the plan work, he had to survive an evening with that child-hating battleaxe. Shuddering with dread, Grant tried to figure out why he'd thought that was a good idea.

Looking around frantically for something to occupy his mind, there was nothing left outside so he started on the inside. He scrubbed the kitchen floor and baked bread and a couple of pumpkin pies. When the kids got home, the young'uns ran outside to play and do their chores as they always did. No reason for them to spend time in this dinky house if they didn't have to.

Sadie and Marilyn stayed behind to start supper and saw the baking Grant had done.

"Don't you like how we've been cooking, Pa?" Marilyn asked, her blue eyes downcast.

"You've been doing fine, honey." A lot better than him.

He looked at the blackened pies. "I just. . .uh. . .had some spare time today. I used to cook a lot, but since I've started having grown-up daughters, I haven't kept my hand in. The bread didn't rise like it should've, and I burnt one of the pies and forgot to add eggs to the other one. I guess that's why it's kinda flat-like."

"Then why'd you do it?" Sadie frowned at him. "I mean, if you have extra time, a lot of parents are coming in to work on the pageant. Easter is early this year, and it's already the end of January. Maybe Miss Cartwright could find something for you to do."

Grant flinched at that woman's name. She seemed to be all the children talked about.

"Almost every other parent has helped, especially the mothers. And since we don't have a ma, maybe we aren't doing our share." Marilyn looked at Sadie. "Shouldn't he come in and work with Miss Cartwright? Don't you think that'd make her happy?"

"Does she seem unhappy?" Grant bit his tongue too late to stop the words.

Sadie turned away from the mess he'd made of supper and studied him like he was some kind of bug she'd caught crawling out of the cornmeal. "Does it matter to you if Miss Cartwright is unhappy, Pa? Are you worried about her?"

Marilyn caught the overly interested tone in Sadie's voice, and the two of them exchanged a quick glance. His daughters, full-grown women and as stubborn as the rest of the female breed, snagged his arms and pulled him onto a bench. They sat down beside him.

"What's going on, Pa?" Sadie asked, her eyes shining. "Are you sweet on Miss Cartwright?"

Grant surged to his feet. His daughters held on tight and plunked him right back on the bench between them. Marilyn got up and stood so close he couldn't escape without knocking her over—which he hated to do, but still he seriously considered it and saved the idea in case it came to that.

"What kind of question is that to ask your pa?" Grant tried out his best I'm-the-Head-of-This-House voice. He'd never used that voice much, mostly because it didn't work worth a lick. "You girls behave yourselves now. I'm sorry I messed up supper, but you can see clear as day I needed the practice."

"We've been trying something fierce to get Miss Cartwright to come out again." Marilyn leaned down, her eyes narrowed as she studied him. "She seemed to want to learn how to sew a riding skirt, and she asked a lot of questions about cooking. I was sure she'd be back, worrying about orphans the way she does."

Grant had never been one to turn a child over his knee. He'd just never found it necessary. Most of his children were so happy to live with him—sometimes after a rocky start of course—that he'd never had to resort to such as giving a whoopin'. He reckoned Marilyn and Sadie were a little old now for him to start in. But still—

"Now she won't come." Sadie leaned in from the side. "Pa, did you do something to hurt her feelings? Did you try and steal a kiss or—"

Grant erupted off the bench. "Now, you girls just stop that."

Marilyn didn't get knocked clear over, but that was only because Grant caught her and set her aside on his way past.

"We're not havin' that kind of talk around here." Grant grabbed his hat as he ran out the door.

The girls were giggling. One glance over his shoulder, just before he hid in his immaculate barn, showed the two of them standing in the doorway of his crooked little house with their heads together, chattering like a couple of pea-brained magpies.

"All right, children. You're dismissed for morning recess."

As the classroom emptied amid shouts of joy, Hannah held two slates together on her desk, studying Charlie's handwriting. Charlie's was so beautiful, full of loops and swirls, it made Hannah think of an ancient Bible handwritten by monks.

Benny's wasn't so good. He'd have been all right except he'd taken to copying Charlie's style. All he'd done is end up with words Hannah couldn't read. She mulled over how to redirect Benny's attempt at beauty without hurting his feelings.

Maybe she should talk to Charlie, get him to tone it down. But it was a shame to stifle such creativity.

"Miss Cartwright?" Marilyn's voice broke her concentration.

Hannah glanced up, surprised to see Marilyn and Sadie still in the room. The children usually all stormed out for recess. "What is it?"

Sadie held up a small bundle, wrapped in brown paper. "This is some extra fabric we had at home. People give us things like this all the time, and we can't begin to use it all. We've been wanting you to come out and learn to sew. But since you haven't, Marilyn and I thought maybe we could work on it here."

Hannah thought of her worn dress. Heavily patched, faded until it was colorless, nearly torn to shreds when she'd fallen off Rufus that day at Grant's, only wearable because of Sadie and Marilyn's talented needles.

Looking down at her frayed cuffs and the drab gray color that had once been blue gingham, she remembered stealing it off a clothesline when she was still in Chicago, over four years ago. The way she'd gotten it was a disgrace even more so than the way it looked. She'd never had the money to spare for a new one, but it didn't matter because she wore it now as penance. A reminder of the depths to which she'd sunk to survive. The rags of a street urchin because a thief didn't deserve better.

"Girls, I can't take that fabric." Hannah shook her head. "You might need it for yourselves. No, absolutely not. Thank you, though. I should get paid soon. Then I'll buy some cloth. I would be very grateful for your help then." Getting paid would be wonderful. Right now she was eating each day solely because of the generosity of Grant's children. A situation that had to end.

Marilyn kept coming. "Now Miss Cartwright, I'm afraid we can't let you wear this dress anymore. It's indecent and...and..."

Sadie pushed past her sister. "You're shaming us, miss. Why, anyone who sees you thinks you aren't paid enough and this town doesn't care about you, and it's just plain hurting the honor of the good town of Sour Springs, Texas."

One corner of Hannah's mouth turned up. *Oh yes, the highly developed skill of all orphans—the ability to manipulate.*

Marilyn stepped past Sadie, and the gleam in Marilyn's eyes sent a little thrill of fear through Hannah. "The plain facts are, Miss Cartwright, people in this town are generous to Pa with things like fabric. You saw the pile of it in our kitchen when we were digging around for a patch for your dress, now didn't you?"

Hannah remembered the little mountain. It was a fact that the family had more cloth than they'd ever use. "I saw it."

"Well, this is how it's gonna be." Marilyn arched her eyebrows at Hannah, and Hannah remembered that the girl was a big help with the teaching. She was old enough and strict enough to do it better than Hannah ever could.

"Marilyn, don't take that tone—"

"We're going to make you a new dress," Marilyn cut her off. "You can help us and learn something or you can stay out of our way."

"You can make it, Marilyn, but you can't make me wear it." Hannah didn't like the direction of this conversation. It put her on an equal footing with these girls when she was supposed to be in charge.

"We will make it and you will wear it, even if we have to 'accidentally' rip a big hole in that dress, which would take about two seconds and next to no effort."

Hannah gasped. "Marilyn, you wouldn't!"

Sadie's eyes got wide with what could only be admiration. She stepped up beside her sister. "The honest truth is that even if we don't do it, it's going to happen someday. You'll snag it on a nail or a rough corner of a wooden chair or have another run-in like you did with Rufus, and your dress is thin as paper."

"And when that happens," Marilyn went on, "you won't have anything to put on. You'll be standing here with your dress hanging in tatters with nothing to change into because you don't have another dress. You need this dress now, made of good sturdy cloth so something *disgraceful* doesn't happen. Or at least you need to have it so, when something disgraceful *does* happen, you're ready."

Sadie jerked her chin in a way that seemed to say everything was settled. "So we are going to make this dress, with or without your help. And if you don't want to wear it, we'll just stuff it in a corner of the classroom to be used in the event of a disaster. Then you'll be happy enough to have it."

Hannah glared at the girls. Then she glanced down at the patches Grant's girls had sewn on the sleeve of her dress. There was another big one on the back and the cloth didn't come close to matching. When the girls had sewn her dress back together, they'd commented on the tissue-thin cloth. She knew she needed to replace it soon for the sake of decency. But her pay hadn't come yet, and Hannah didn't know how to sew when she could afford fabric. And she'd die before she let that dreadful Prudence sew for her. . .as if Hannah could afford to pay someone for a job Hannah was ashamed she couldn't do for herself. And now, here stood these generous, blackmailing children offering her fabric.

She knew Grant hadn't been consulted, although in fairness to him, she admitted he'd have probably let her have the cloth. But the girls hadn't asked. And that probably made her a thief yet again. At the very least she was a beggar. The only food she had was a share of the children's lunch every day, something they'd also manipulated her into without Grant's knowledge, since their excuse for each one sneaking her bits of their food was that they didn't want to hurt their pa's feelings by not eating every bite of the mountain of food he sent.

Between Grant unknowingly feeding her, his daughters offering her fabric to dress herself, and the knowledge that what she wore was stolen, she could hardly look the girls in the eye. She couldn't have looked them in the eye anyway. They walked past her.

Turning, she watched them clear her desk, spread dark green wool out, and begin talking about what to do next. With a huff of disgust, she went up to stand beside them. "Oh, all right, you little monsters. Tell me what you're doing and go slow."

The girls started giggling, and before long Hannah took up the giggling and was in the middle of her first sewing lesson.

Sadie pulled a tape measure out of her pocket. "Stand up straight, Miss Cartwright. You're so slender I'm afraid we'll make it too big."

As they worked, the girls chattered pleasantly. Hannah learned far more than she wanted to about Marilyn's affection for Wilbur Svendsen.

"We need to find a man for Miss Cartwright before she's too old to have children," Sadie announced.

Marilyn gave Hannah a quick glance then started giggling. She covered her mouth as she laughed louder. Through gasps for air, she said, "Miss Cartwright could use a beau for sure."

Sadie ran the tape from Hannah's shoulder to the tips of her fingers. "That is unless you already have someone sparking you, Miss Cartwright."

"I most certainly do *not* have anyone sparking me. It's not proper for you to ask me such a question, Sadie."

Sadie and Marilyn exchanged a strange, satisfied look.

"And anyway, I can't cook or sew." Doing her best to sound falsely forlorn, Hannah said, "Why, any poor husband of mine would most likely not survive. I think I'll just keep teaching if you don't mind. I believe God has given me a gift for teaching, and I plan to devote my life to it."

Sadie said, "Well, husband or not, it won't hurt you any to learn to sew."

Grant's girls told her what each measurement was for and how to lay out the fabric to cut. In the end they made her do most of it herself, just like any good teachers.

When the time came, they wanted her to cut, but she refused. Sadie took over, and Hannah flinched every time the scissors snipped for fear the precious piece of cloth would be ruined. But Sadie cut and chatted as if she did it every day.

TWENTY-ONE

Grant went through the whole mending basket.

He even darned some socks, although he was afraid his uneven stitches might cause a blister or two. But it wasn't a bad job all in all. He hadn't had grown daughters to do for him at the first, and he'd learned some things. He ran like a scared rabbit when the children came home so there was no way Sadie and Marilyn could ask about it.

But when he came in to supper, Marilyn next-thing-to-attacked him with a bolt of cloth. "Pa, I've been thinking. Since Wilbur's been sparking me, I need to get some experience making clothes for a man. It's all your fault I don't know how to do that."

Grant backed away from her, looking between her and that length of brown cloth in her hands. "Why's it my fault?"

Sadie came up behind him and blocked the door so he couldn't escape. "Because you never let us make you any clothes."

"I don't need any new clothes."

"Yes, you do, Pa." Joshua sat leaning against the wall, reading a schoolbook, with his long legs drawn up to his chest so he wouldn't stretch across the whole floor and trip everyone who came by. "Sadie already made a whole new outfit for me just this year, but that was before Marilyn came. I don't need anything. Marilyn is sure enough right that she doesn't have much practice."

"You don't want me to be a failure as a wife, do you, Pa?" Marilyn wheedled.

"I don't need clothes." Grant grabbed the fabric out of Marilyn's hands with too much force, feeling an almost desperate need to stop her.

The gleam of mischief faded out of Marilyn's eyes. Grant hadn't noticed it was there until it was gone.

Grant held her stare for as long as he could stand it. "What?"

"When's the last time you let us make you something?"

Grant folded the fabric clumsily as he went and set it on a teetering pile of cloth that he'd been given by kind ladies over the years. There was quite a heap of it, enough to keep his children in clothes for a long while.

"We're not wasting cloth on me."

The touch on his shoulder turned him around. Sadie smiled at him. "Now calm down."

Grant fought the pull of her sweet charm. Sadie, his youngest daughter in that first group of children he'd adopted, had always held a special place in his heart—of course *all* his children held special places in his heart. Still, he knew how he responded to Sadie. He had a hard time denying her anything. His stomach twisted for fear he'd calm down. He didn't *dare* calm down. He'd end up doing something he didn't want to do.

"You're trying to store up everything for us, aren't you?" Marilyn's voice pulled him back to look at her.

Grant frowned. "You kids are growing. There's no call to waste good fabric and time on me when you boys will tear the knees out of your pants by tomorrow night and need new. There isn't always fabric to be had."

"You've got quite a few dollars in the bank these days, don't you, Pa?" Joshua waited in silence. The kind of silence that made a man talk, even when he didn't want to say a word, just to end that silence. And how did Joshua know what he had in the bank? That wasn't anything proper to speak of with children. Grant had certainly never told him.

"Even if I do, there are hard times in ranching. We've got some cash money built up for now, but a hard winter might cost us a crop of calves and we could be in trouble. You kids need things. Your shoes wear out and your arms and legs sprout. I spend what needs spending and save the rest for a rainy day."

Grant noticed Charlie looking down at his outfit. Everything the boy had on was new. Grant remembered the shame of having clothes come to him secondhand. Not that his children didn't wear hand-me-downs; they did. But when they first came to the family, they got one set new, right down to socks and boots, made just for them.

Charlie, settled on the floor on the far side of the fireplace, raised his eyes. Those hostile eyes, so suspicious, carrying a world of anger around on his thin shoulders. Grant saw the war in the boy. He wanted to get mad about the clothes because he reacted to everything with anger. But what was there to get riled up about with clean, freshly made, nicely fitting shirts and pants?

Grant also noticed something sticking out of Charlie's pocket. The little corner he could see had the look and shape of a pocketknife. Charlie didn't own a pocketknife. Grant knew that for a fact. And how could the boy have any money? With a sinking stomach, Grant knew it had most likely gotten into Charlie's pocket in a dishonest way. Charlie wouldn't be the first orphan to have a knack for thieving. Just because a boy had enough food and a warm bed didn't always stop things from sticking to his fingers. Sighing, Grant knew he had something else to deal with. He said a silent prayer for his troubled son.

Looking at his children, Grant's eyes landed on Libby with her new dress. After Grant had fixed her worn little shoes, he got her new ones at the mercantile and fixed the soles on those. Now she had a pair for good and another for home.

The little angel was settling in well, but Grant had to clear up this fuss about clothes and go for a walk with Charlie.

"I think we've got enough cloth to spare to make you a pair of pants and a shirt." Sadie stepped to Grant's side as Charlie rose to his feet. The two of them exchanged a glance then turned to face Grant. Grant noticed Charlie tuck that knife deeper in his pocket.

"And you need new boots, Pa." Sadie crossed her arms. "Yours are worn clear through on the bottom. They have to be cold."

Grant studied his boots. They were the ones his ma and pa had gotten for him when he was sixteen, just a couple of months before they died. They'd seen to it he had a new pair the two years he lived with them. But that was when his feet were growing as fast as summer grass. His feet hadn't grown since then. Why buy new? Two leather thongs held the soles on, and his toes peeked out in half a dozen places. He'd slipped new pieces of leather on the inside because the bottoms were worn thin as paper, and he'd sewn buckskin on over the heels a couple of times. "I'm fine."

Sadie reached past him and snagged the piece of fabric off the pile. "Please, Pa. It makes me feel selfish to have nice things and see you go without."

Marilyn stepped up behind Sadie, her blond head nodding. "We're not going to make one more new thing for anyone in this house until we get you out of these rags."

Benny dodged in front of Sadie with his wide, loving eyes. "Are we selfish, Pa? Do you think we are?"

"No, son. Not a one of you kids has a selfish bone in your body."

"You must think we are, or you'd have something nice for yourself once in a while," Sadie said. "You gave up your room, and now you sleep on the floor without complaining."

"I didn't even think of that when I was so mad at Benny. You don't even have a room." Charlie's hand slid deep in his pocket to hold the knife. The boy looked up and Grant caught his eye. A faint flush of red that screamed guilt rose on Charlie's fair cheeks.

"Now, you guys stop it. The kitchen is a room. No one's using it at night. It's a waste not to have someone sleeping in it. I'm closest to the fire. Why, I'm the selfish one. If you kids'd just think about it, you'd be fighting me for the kitchen floor."

He scanned all those worried young faces. None of them was buying it for a second.

"You never have anything nice for yourself." Sadie held up the yards of brown cloth. "And we never even noticed till now. We really *are* greedy and selfish."

This had started out differently. Grant had seen the teasing light in Marilyn's and Sadie's eyes. He'd known they were up to something that had only a little to do with clothes. But they weren't teasing anymore. Somehow he'd made them feel bad. The last thing he ever wanted to do was hurt a child.

"You young'uns are the most generous people I've ever known. There's nothing greedy about any of you. It's not that. It's just. . ." Grant looked at all of them. "You're such fine young people."

Charlie dropped his chin to rest on his chest and studied the floor as if it held the meaning of life.

"I'm pure lucky to have gotten you. We've all lived through hard times. What if there's not enough? What if we run short of something? Yes, we may have fabric we'll never use, but if times got hard, we could maybe sell it. There's always a day coming when there might be a need for us."

"It makes no sense for you to dress in rags," Marilyn said. "Using up three or four yards of fabric that came to us as a free gift will not change a thing if hard times come. I want you to let Sadie and me make you some new clothes. If you love us at all, you'll let us share with you one tiny bit as much as you share with us."

Grant tightened his jaw. An almost desperate fear twisted around inside him when he thought of wasting anything on himself.

A tug on his hand pulled his attention away from Marilyn's stubborn eyes. Libby held his hand. She looked at him then lowered her eyes to study a patch in his flannel shirt torn away from the nearly rotten fabric. She reached one tiny finger into the hole in his shirt, stuck her finger on in through the hole behind that in his union suit, and poked him in the belly.

She wiggled her finger back and forth and tickled him. With a little laugh he jerked away, surprised to find out he was ticklish. She smiled up at him and reached her twitching finger toward him again.

Grant jumped back and glanced up to see all of his kids with their eyes focused straight at him.

"You're ticklish," Benny said.

"Pa's ticklish." Sadie's dark eyes almost caught fire as she came toward him, her fingers raised in front of her, wriggling around like ten worms.

"You're gonna get some new clothes, Pa." Sadie gave him a diabolical smile. "We're not going to leave you alone until you say yes."

With a scream, Benny jumped on him, tickling his belly. Libby latched onto one of Grant's legs, and that tripped him as he tried to get away from Benny while laughing. Marilyn, Sadie, and Charlie stepped back to watch him go down under them, but Grant saw a gleam in Charlie's eyes like he wished he could be part of the wrestling match. Sadie looked like she'd be willing to attack if need be. Joshua laughed from his spot on the floor.

"Okay, okay, okay!" Grant laughed as he tried to escape his tormenting children. They quit attacking as quickly as they'd begun. Grant dumped them off him, pretending to be rough but very careful not to hurt either of them. Through laughter, he said, "Make the blasted clothes. Just don't tickle me anymore."

"New boots, too?" Sadie said with an arch of her eyebrows and a twitch of her fingers.

Grant collapsed flat on the floor. Gasping for breath, he said, "Yes, fine, new boots, too, you little monsters."

Sadie and Marilyn exchanged satisfied nods that made Grant

wonder what they were up to. But he'd never known how ticklish he was, and he didn't want to go through it again. He stood patiently while the girls measured him.

He tried Joshua's boots on and when they were too tight, the young'uns wouldn't be satisfied to let Joshua guess at a fit. Under threat of another attack, he promised he'd go to town the next day and let Zeb at the livery measure him for new boots. With that, his cantankerous household settled down to do their studies.

As he sat with Benny, going over his lessons, Grant wondered what he'd ever do with fancy clothes. Then he wondered if Hannah would like the way he looked in them, and if it weren't for the tickling, he might have gone back to refusing. It didn't matter anyway. It was too late to stop 'em. Once the girls had gotten him to go along, they'd been cutting quick as lightning, most likely afraid he'd weasel out of his bargain somehow.

"Pa, you remember when you first brought me and Sadie home?" Joshua drew Grant's attention, and Grant realized Joshua had been watching the sewing just as he had. "You sewed all six of us a new outfit of clothes."

Grant laughed. "Yeah, I really made a mess of 'em, didn't I?"

Joshua shook his head. "We should have saved 'em just as a bad example. Even then Sadie was better at it than you. And she was only five."

Sadie nodded over her needle and thread. "And you made me a dress."

Sadie and Marilyn looked up from their fine, neat stitches.

"Pa sewed you a dress?" Marilyn looked at Sadie as if she'd grown another head.

"I'd seen my ma do some sewing. Even threaded a needle for her. I didn't really know anything. But Pa's hands were so clumsy." Sadie started giggling until she had to set her needle aside. "He made Joshua a pair of pants so big, Joshua and Will could've both fit inside them."

All the children snickered. Even silent little Libby giggled behind her fingers.

"They weren't that bad," Grant said between his own chuckles. "It beat what you were wearing."

"We were all in rags, even worse'n what you've got on now." Joshua nodded. "When you made Sadie try on her new dress, it dragged on the floor in back and her knees showed in front. Plus there was no hole for her head, so you just hacked an opening with your knife."

"And then you cut the back off so it wouldn't drag, and then it was too short so you cut the front off." Sadie quit talking so she could laugh full time.

"Good thing it was about four times too big around for Sadie," Joshua said, leaning his head back against the wall, his shoulders shaking with laughter. "Will ended up wearing it as a shirt as I recall."

"Sadie got better at it quicker'n I did." Grant shook his head.

"Sadie taught me most of what I know." Marilyn grinned at her little sister.

"You picked it up fast enough." Sadie picked up her needle.

"And Cassie was ten," Joshua added. "And she knew a few things that helped us along. And you boys pitched right in to help on the ranch."

Grant remembered that little gang of orphans. Joshua, Sadie, Will, Cassie, Eli, and Sidney. They'd all been starving. It was a cold morning, and they didn't have a single coat between 'em. Will had tried to pick his pocket. Grant had caught him and known right away he was dealing with a street urchin just like he'd been near all his life.

He'd convinced Will to trust him, and before long he'd been carrying out food from a diner. . .a diner that wouldn't't'a allowed black children inside. He fed six little kids breakfast while he fretted over how to take care of them forever.

Grant could see people in a huge city like New York ignoring hordes of children. The problem was just too huge for a lot of people to deal with. But it made him furious to think of the citizens of a good

Texas town like Houston letting those children scurry around in alleys without taking them in.

He'd been riding his horse, planning to sign up for the Confederacy if he could ever hunt up the War. He'd seen those children, banded together, Will acting as the father, ten-year-old Cassie mothering the littler ones, Joshua and Sadie, black, but accepted as members of the family without a question. Grant had been planning to fight for the Confederacy, just because that's what a good Texan did, but after seeing Joshua and Sadie, and knowing what danger they were in running around loose in the South, he couldn't have taken part in any fighting that supported slavery.

With no paperwork and no permission, he'd claimed them as his adopted children and taken them home. He'd found his calling in life.

Soon after the War, the first orphan train came through Sour Springs.

"Cassie and I both learned a sight quicker than you, Pa." Sadie basted a sleeve onto the shirt she was making for him.

"A fractious longhorn would'a learned quicker'n me."

The family laughed again.

Sadie looked up from her work. "Now Cassie's sewing for her little ones, just like Megan and all your other grown-up daughters. You would have made everything easier if you'd have rounded yourself up a wife before you started collecting children. That's the proper way of things."

"I was too young to get married." Grant flinched when Sadie and Marilyn exchanged a quick glance. "I'm still too young to get married."

Marilyn said quietly, "But not too young to have children, right?"

That set the whole bunch of them off in a fit of laughing again, and Grant felt his cheeks warm up even as he laughed along. He'd never explained to his children about the vow he'd made to care for young'uns. He'd told some of them when they'd grown up, after they'd left his home, but the ones who lived with him would never know. He didn't want them to think he was sacrificing anything for them, because he wasn't. He got so much more than he ever gave. But talk of marriage led to thoughts of Hannah, and kissing her, and how she'd stood shoulder-to-shoulder with him and offered to sacrifice her job for his children.

And that made him desperate to think of something else. He couldn't think of a way to talk to Charlie about that knife without embarrassing him in front of the family, so Grant left that for later and settled in beside Benny to help him wrestle with the words in his reading book.

Maybe it was time he polished up his skills for working inside the house. It'd keep him busy and keep his mind off Hannah if he'd do the sewing. He could stab himself a few times with a needle anytime she bloomed inside his head.

The girls could teach him fine stitchery and dressmaking. As Benny droned out the words of a psalm, Grant stared down at his callused hands and wondered if it was hard to crochet lace.

"Pa." Marilyn came up behind him while he leaned over Benny's book. "The fabric's cut now and the basting done, so while Sadie is busy sewing, I think I oughta cut your hair."

"Cut my hair?" Grant whirled around to face his daughter. The gleam in her eyes near to set him running out of the house.

"I need to practice on a man, since I'm getting married soon and all. Just turn around and sit still." She opened and closed the scissors with an ominous snip.

Grant glared at the little troublemaker.

She glared right back.

Finally, rolling his eyes, he turned around and ignored her to the best of his ability. . .while she scalped him.

TWENTY-TWO

Grant had put up with the new clothes and a haircut, but now it was eating him alive.

He ran his hands through his stumpy hair, wishing he could sleep. Lying on the kitchen floor, listening to the sound of his children breathing, living, fed and warm and safe, there was no way to explain to them the desperate burden he felt for unwanted children. He'd had Parson Babbitt tell him once that he needed to trust God to care for His sheep. That Grant, try as he might, couldn't care for them all.

Grant wrestled with the worry. He could feel those children, cold and hungry, out there, begging for a coin, just enough to keep the front of their stomachs from rubbing against the backs. The hard wood of his floor was a reminder of the hard life of a child who had no one to care if he or she lived or died.

He could still remember little Sadie when he first laid eyes on her. Her body shivered so hard in the cold, the skirt of her thin little dress waved back and forth. It haunted him to think of all Sadie had suffered before she'd come to him.

As he lay there, the clothes the girls were making started to bother him more and more. That cloth was wasted being cut and sewn into something for him. Anger burned low in his belly until he was furious thinking of it. But the children were right. It was a kind of foolishness to wear rags, thinking it would feed one hungry child.

"Trust," the parson had said. "God is in control."

If God was in control, then why had He given Grant a tiny glimpse of family? If God was in control, why had Grant's parents died? If God was worthy of trust, then Grant had to accept that He wanted children like Libby to be frightened beyond their ability to speak.

Sadie, cold and shivering. Grant opened his eyes and ruffled his short hair. He stared at the dark ceiling, the nightmarish image of his freezing daughter. Her skinny little bare knees shaking beneath a skirt that she'd grown out of years before. Rolling onto his stomach, he wondered how many nights in his life he'd been left sleepless with this torment.

God, why would You make a world where children lived, hungry and cold, in an alley? How can I believe You're in control when the innocent suffer like this?

It was a sin to spend money on himself for new clothes. And new boots were a foolish waste while children froze.

He listened to the wind whip around his ramshackle cabin and knew it was so much better in here than out there. There were more children out in the cold. He couldn't go to New York and get them without abandoning his family, but what if some were close to hand? He'd found Joshua and Sadie in Houston. It was a long trip, but Grant should be looking for them, bringing them home. He had six, but there was room beside him on the floor. He could squeeze in six more if he tried.

He rolled back to stare at the ceiling, and his heart cried out to God for sleep and peace and for a chance to take care of all the cold, hungry children who needed a home.

A creak on the ladder to the loft pulled him out of his worry. He saw Charlie backing down the steps, as silently as possible. "What are you doing?"

Charlie froze and looked down. Even in the barely existent light from the fire, Grant saw Charlie's guilt. What was going on? Grant was afraid he knew.

Charlie's rigid muscles relaxed and he climbed on down. "Just. . . uh. . .couldn't sleep."

He was running away. Grant had seen the guilt in Charlie's eyes when he'd realized Grant didn't have a room. Between the anger the little boy carried around and the desire to leave before he got left, the boy would use this as an excuse to move on. Probably planning to steal a sack of food on his way out the door.

"Pa?"

Grant sat up and leaned forward. He turned so his back leaned against the table leg. "Yeah, what is it?"

"I'm just restless is all. The wind is keeping me up, I suppose. A cold wind makes me think of bad times I had before I came here."

Pa pushed his bedroll aside. He rolled to his knees and grabbed a couple of logs and threw them onto the fire. Charlie dropped down in front of the licking flames, and the two of them watched as a friendly, reassuring crackle lit up the room.

"Did I wake you?" Charlie asked.

"I wasn't asleep."

"Are you sure?

Grant shrugged. "I don't think so. Maybe I dozed off. The night can trick a man."

Grant rested his palm on Charlie's shoulder, and Charlie flinched like a child might who'd been treated harshly by a man's hand.

"It sure enough can." The boy sat frozen under the touch.

"It can trick a man into thinking only dark thoughts. It can trick a man into making some small thing into something large without the light of day to shine on his worries." Grant felt Charlie's fear and tension and let go of him. Turning around, Grant rested his back on the stones that framed the fire. Charlie visibly relaxed and leaned closer to the warmth of the crackling fire.

Grant decided the boy wasn't going to say anything more. "I was awake because. . .I don't. . .need new clothes. I want to be ready in case there are children who come along. I shouldn't have let Sadie talk me into those duds. I should leave Joshua in charge and go see if there have been any children abandoned nearby."

"And leave the family alone?"

"No, I can't do that."

A silence stretched between them as the smell and warmth of the fire soothed and eased the knots tying up Grant's thoughts.

"Pa, it's not the new clothes that are bothering you. It's not even thinking about children who might need you."

"Yes, it is."

"It's the devil."

"What?" Grant sat forward. He hadn't expected to hear that from the boy.

Charlie, crossing his ankles, propped his elbows on his knees and rested his chin in both hands. "The devil is who torments good folks in the night. He whispers doubt in your ear. He stirs up anger. He picks at any little mistake you've made, or thinks you've made, and blows it up big. That's Satan, stirring and stirring trouble, like a pot he's trying to boil over, hoping he can spill sin through your soul and slop it all over the people around you."

Grant's eyes narrowed as he considered that. "I reckon you're right, son. When I'm up and about, busy with you kids and life, I know I'm doing God's work. But if you could have seen Sadie when I found her. . ." Grant couldn't go on for a minute. He scrubbed his hands over his face and combed his fingers through his short hair.

When he was sure his voice wouldn't break, Grant continued. "I remember other little children when I ran the streets of New York. I saw them die, run down by carriages. I saw older children beating on them. I saw them dead from the cold. They beat on me, too." Grant paused. "I saw the younger ones grow up and turn mean and get in trouble. I was right along with them. I'd spend time in an orphanage, then I'd run off, then the police would catch me doing something and send me back. I felt my own innocence die, replaced with anger and cruelty. As I got older, I saw new little ones show up. I knew what was ahead of them. I couldn't do anything for them then when I was young. But now I can."

Grant leaned toward his troubled son. "I want you here, Charlie. If I found others in need, I'd bring in ten more. I'd find the room for 'em. Maybe I should build a great big house and, who knows, maybe find room for a hundred. They could stay here until they're grown and. . ."

"You can't be a real father to a hundred children at once, Pa. You couldn't even feed them. And you could never give them a father's love, not enough to change their lives."

"Maybe I could. I'm glad I've had each one of you kids."

"Even if we've done bad?"

Charlie was talking about the knife. And maybe some other things Grant hadn't caught the boy at. "The funny thing is I seem to love the one who's going through the hardest time the most."

Charlie sat up straight. He and Grant studied each other. Grant didn't want to force a confession out of the boy. Instead, to make it easier, Grant said, "I saw the knife. If you give it to me and tell me where you got it, I'll slip it back. No one needs to know it was stolen."

Charlie sat silently for a long time. Grant gave him as long as he needed.

Finally the boy fished into his pocket and handed the knife to Grant, then reached in again and brought out a handful of coins. "I took it from the Stroben's Mercantile. Some money, too."

Grant nodded. "Things stuck to my fingers when I was young. It's not right. But when you live like we lived, sin starts to look like the only way to survive."

Grant patted the boy on the back, careful to be gentle. "I look back now at the food I took and the clothes and other things and I know it was wrong, but I know I'd do it again to live."

This time Charlie allowed the touch.

"But you don't need to do that anymore, Charlie. I don't have a lot of money for a knife and to give you young'uns spending money. But you'll never go hungry. You'll never be cold. And I think, if you asked, they sometimes hire help at the mercantile, delivering supplies in town. You could earn the money for this knife if you really want it."

Charlie slouched again. "No one's gonna give me a job. I've tried that before."

"You might be surprised. Harold's a good man. He'd make you work hard, but he'd pay you fair."

Charlie's eyes lit up in the flickering fire. "You think so?"

"I could ask him for you. Or, if you felt brave enough, you could take this knife back to him, tell him what you did, and ask permission to work off the cost. I think Harold would respect that. I know God would."

"Why do you suppose God lets children live on the streets? Cold, hungry, hurt?"

Grant sighed. The exact question he had been wrestling with for years. He knew the truth. It just wasn't easy to accept. "I think, Charlie, that God doesn't really care that much about our bodies."

"What?" Charlie seemed upset.

Grant tried to explain himself. "Oh, He does care. He loves every one of us so much. He knows the numbers of hairs on our heads. But I think God sees inside us, and what's in there is more important than food or clothes or good health. God cares about souls. He cares about us, one soul at a time. If a child dies, cold on the street, but he knows the Lord, then there is rejoicing in heaven. And a lot of street kids do have a beautiful, childlike faith in God."

"A lot don't."

"A lot of warm, well-fed people don't, either. God loves people one soul at a time. And His truth is written in all their hearts so every child has a chance to believe." Then Grant added, as much to himself as to Charlie, "I can only help the children God puts in my path, and I've done that. If God wants me to have more children, He'll send them. All those years ago, Will didn't try to pick my pocket by accident. He and his friends were sent into my path by God. It wasn't an accident that little Benny got put on an orphan train at such a young age. He was mine and God got him here. Marilyn didn't just happen to show herself at the exact instant I took a shortcut through an alley. It's not a coincidence Mrs. Norris broke all the rules for Libby by letting her join the other orphans. I know each of you children was meant to be mine. That includes you."

"And any other children that are meant to be yours will be sent here." Charlie was clearly visible by the now-roaring firelight. The crackling wood, the comforting smell, and the soft whoosh of heat coming from the hearth seemed to mute the howling wind outside, or maybe the wind had died. Or, Grant thought, maybe Satan had been vanquished, at least for tonight.

Charlie yawned.

"You'd better get yourself to bed, boy. Morning comes almighty early around this house."

Charlie nodded. "It's long past time for rest, and that's a fact. Uh. . .Pa?"

"Yes?"

"I think God wants you to let the girls dress you up. I think this is something you should do for them and not fight it. Your reasons not to spend money on yourself. . .I understand them, but now and then it's okay to have a new pair of boots if your feet are really cold."

Grant nodded. "I reckon that's a fact."

"If you'll give me back the knife and money, I'll go have a talk with Mr. Stroben tomorrow after school."

"I'll come with you if you want."

Charlie was silent for a long time. Grant though he saw the boy's shoulders trembling. At last he said, "Yeah, I guess you'd better, in case he calls the sheriff."

Grant gave Charlie a gentle squeeze on the back of his neck. "He won't. I'll come by the school and walk over with you."

"Thanks." Charlie climbed back up the ladder.

Grant lay awake until he heard soft snoring coming from overhead.

Sadie braced him about the boots first thing in the morning.

Grant promised he'd go in and order a pair from Zeb. He meant to ride in along with his family when they were heading to school, but a cow had delivered her baby out of season and needed to be driven into the barn before the calf ended up as food for the coyotes.

Grant told the children to go on ahead.

"Pa, you're just trying to get out of buying new boots." Marilyn crossed her arms and refused to get in the buckboard.

"No, I'll order 'em. I promise."

"Today?" Sadie asked, standing shoulder-to-shoulder with Marilyn.

"Yes, today."

His older daughters, suddenly a bossy pair of mother hens, climbed into the wagon. After she was perched on the wagon seat next to Joshua, Sadie hollered, "Make sure and wear your new clothes to town. You're shamin' the whole family wearing those rags."

Grant would have felt worse about shaming them if Sadie had been able to keep the smile off her face. "Scat, all of you. Get down the road to school, or I'm turning you all over my knee."

He could hear them laughing until they were out of sight. Handing out punishment had never been his strong suit.

Grant rode out to round up the cow and her calf. The cow seemed bent on killing Grant for messing with her baby. And the calf, wobbly and shivering, needed tending. Grant's shorn neck froze him the whole time. With one thing and another, he didn't get back to the cabin until well past noon.

When he came in, he saw his new shirt and pants all folded neat as a pin on the kitchen table. Resting on top was Joshua's new Stetson. Grant wondered if this was a hint for him to buy a new one, or if Joshua was offering Grant the hat.

Too tired to worry about it, Grant shed his only pair of pants and noticed his old clothes were not only rags, they were filthy rags. Oh, the girls kept other things washed up nice and tidy, but Grant only had one pair of clothes. How was he supposed to have his clothes washed if he was wearing them? Once in a great while, he'd shed his things and get along in an even older pair he'd kept, but those had holes that were next-thing-to-indecent, so he usually just hung on to his pants and shirt and shooed the girls away to clean someone else up. After a morning dodging slashing horns and flailing hooves, he was coated in dirt and sweat. He'd also ripped a couple of new holes in his rags.

Maybe God had stepped in last night, knowing what a fierce mama cow could do to fabric so rotten sharp words could shred it. Grant thought about his talk with Charlie last night. The talk had brought a considerable new peace in Grant's heart. He accepted that God had sent children who needed him into his path. How had that orphan train picked the little town of Sour Springs as the last stop?

For that matter, how had he happened to be in Houston all those years ago? He was hunting for the War. Why had he thought he'd find it in Houston? It'd made sense to him at the time. And if Grant was honest with himself, he knew Houston wasn't a huge impersonal city like New York. The good folks there wouldn't leave six children on the street. People would have stepped in and found them homes—well, maybe not Sadie and Joshua. There could have been trouble there. Grant's heart rebelled at the thought that Sadie and Joshua would have been turned over to some slaver for the remaining years of the War. It didn't sit well to trust God to bring children to him, but Grant knew it was right.

Grant turned his attention to the wreckage of his old clothes.

Imagining how the girls would fuss if he dirtied up his new clothes the first time he wore 'em, he took a quick bath, even washing what was left of his hair—a blamed nuisance in the middle of the day.

He found a nasty bruise on his stomach where the cow had landed a hoof. A scrape ran from his hip to his knee where she'd hooked him with her spread of horns. He'd worn his chaps or that cranky old cow would've poked a hole right into his leg. Shaking his head at his battered body, he dried off and dressed. Then he noticed his old clothes, piled beside the tub. They really were rags. Not even fit to save for scrubbing the floor. He knew Sadie was teasing him some, but he probably *was* shaming his young'uns by wearing them.

With a resigned sigh, he did what he had to do. He tossed his old rags onto the fire and grinned to think of telling the girls he wanted another set of clothes right away so he'd have one for good and one for work.

It was midafternoon before he headed for town. He brought along an extra horse so Charlie could stay in town with him.

Stopping first at Zeb's, he found out it'd take a week to get his boots. With some grumbling about highway robbery, Grant paid for them. Then he went to the mercantile and warned Harold and Mabel about the coming talk with Charlie, just to give them a little time to decide how they wanted things handled. Grant bought himself a new hat while he was there and went to pick up his light-fingered son. His children came flooding out the schoolhouse door and embarrassed him half to death with their fussing over his clothes and hat.

They went together to Ian's blacksmith shop, and Grant visited with his grown-up son while the two of them hitched up Grant's team that boarded at Ian's during the school day. Before he was done, Joshua, even with his tender ribs and gimpy arm, was beside them helping out.

"Pa, most of the other parents have been in to school helping with little things." Joshua glanced uncertainly at Ian, one of Joshua's many older brothers.

"True enough," Ian said. "Megan did some sewing for costumes. I like her staying close to home, with the baby on the way, but if I bring her the material she's able to sew."

"Yeah," Josh went on. "And Ella Johnson and Agnes Mackey, along with a lot of other mothers, are bringing cookies and cider for a party afterward. Mr. Mackey fashioned a cross. He and Mr. Harrison brought it in and we're using it for the play. Almost everyone has come by and offered to help."

"Well, it sounds like she's got everything handled already. Don't reckon she needs me underfoot." Grant buckled the leathers across the broad backs of his horses.

"Ian donated some lumber so she can knock together a little set of steps for us to stand on." Joshua passed a strap under one of the horses, and Grant caught it and fastened it. "But I don't think she's got anyone to help her build 'em."

"I'll go do it for her." Ian started leading the team outside to hook it up to the buckboard. A horse shifted and snorted in a back stall of Ian's shop. It drew all their attention. "No, I've got to finish shoeing a horse. I told Zeb I'd have it ready tomorrow morning. Well, I'll shoe the horse now, and maybe I can get Miss Cartwright's carpentering done tonight."

"You shouldn't leave Megan alone, not with the baby so close." Grant fell silent, knowing what he needed to do.

Joshua looked Grant straight on. "I can do it, Pa. I still ache some but I'm up to it. But since you haven't done anything, and you've got the most kids of anyone in the school, and the main reason she has to build the steps—she calls 'em risers—is because there are so many of us, I think it's the right thing for you to offer."

Grant's temper started heating up to hear his son reminding him of his responsibilities. Grant was a fair enough man to know he wasn't really mad at Joshua. He was embarrassed not to have helped. But that didn't stop him from doing a slow burn. And mixed up with his mad was a sharp ache to see Hannah. She could hurt herself trying to build things. For heaven's sake, she'd near burned herself to death trying to pour coffee. Anything could happen if she was turned loose with a hammer. Grant knew for sure the little woman didn't have the skills a body needed to build risers, whatever they were.

Grabbing the crown of his hat to clamp it as firm as iron on his head, he said, "I'll do it. First, Charlie and I need to go to Stroben's Mercantile. Then I'll send him on home. He won't be long, Josh, so travel slow so he can catch you. I don't like any of you on the trail alone these days. You leave the evening chores for me. I don't want you reinjuring yourself."

Harold arranged for Charlie to work for him after school for the next month to earn the knife. Grant sent Charlie home and headed for the schoolhouse like it was his own doom.

When he got inside, he found the priggish little teacher eyeball-deep in a mess. . .as usual. She knelt at the front of the classroom, wrestling with a long piece of board. Several nails were clamped tight between her lips, and she had a hammer tucked under her arm.

Joshua's polite scolding burned in his ears as he strode to the front of the room. She turned, a pleasant smile on her nail-holding lips as she heard him approach. And then she saw him, and that smile shrank off her face like wool washed in boiling hot water.

"Let me do that." Grant pulled the board out of her hand.

She stared at him, acting as mute as Libby.

He held out his hand. "And get those nails out'a your mouth before you stab yourself to death with 'em."

She removed the nails and laid them in his hand.

Now that her mouth wasn't occupied, Grant moved to stop her before she could start yapping at him. "Joshua said you needed help. What do you want me to do in here?"

Twenty-Three

W hat was he doing in here?

Feeling a little like she'd swallowed the nails, she tore her gaze from Grant and looked at the pile of wood in front of her.

"Hannah?" Grant's sharp voice jerked her out of her daze.

She looked at him. His face was red as a beet, his jaw clenched until he bared his teeth when he talked. He looked furious.

"What did I do now?"

Grant blinked. Startled into relaxing his jaw a bit, he said, "You didn't do anything."

"Then why are you so mad at me?"

"I'm not mad. I'm here to help build this riser Joshua said you needed for your pageant. What is it, anyway?"

"Well, you look mad clear to the bone, Grant Cooper. And if you're going to come in here and be unpleasant, I'd just as soon do it myself."

Grant's eyes narrowed. She felt like she stared straight at a gunslinger at high noon. "My name isn't Grant Cooper."

Hannah stood and walked straight up to his cranky face. "Your name *is* Grant Cooper, and I've listed all your children, except for Sadie, with the last name of Cooper, and listed Grant Cooper, you"—she jabbed him in his chest with her index finger—"as their father. Since you're too stubborn to name yourself, I did it for you."

The red in Grant's face turned an alarming shade of purple.

"*Fine.*" He could have dissolved the nails with the acid in his voice.

Hannah was glad he didn't have them in his mouth because she needed them.

With a choppy slash of his hand, he said, "Call 'em whatever you want."

"I will." Hannah gave her chin a little jerk.

"But just remember, I came in here offering to help and you started right in calling me names."

"What names?"

"Stubborn and unpleasant."

"I wasn't insulting you."

"Yes, you were."

"I was asking you why you were being so stubborn and unpleasant."

"I'm *not* stubborn and unpleasant."

"Well, that's my point exactly. If you *were* stubborn and unpleasant, and you came in here acting like this, I'd just think, 'There goes Grant being himself.' But since you *aren't* those things, I had to wonder what set you off."

Grant dragged his hat off his head as if he had to keep his hands busy so he wouldn't strangle her.

Hannah was distracted from his temper by his haircut. The man looked purely civilized.

"So, the thanks I get for offering to help is to be braced with more of your insults?"

Hannah clapped her mouth shut from defending herself. She'd give him this one point to end the quarrel he'd started. Besides, just because something was true didn't mean it wasn't insulting to point it out. And anyway, she did need help with the risers.

Inhaling long and slow to get her pounding heart to settle into a normal rhythm, she said, "You're right. I just thought after last time you were here, you might..." She stopped. What crazy impulse had made her bring up his last visit? Maybe the same impulse that kept her remembering, day and night, how much she'd enjoyed kissing him. And how badly she'd wanted to do him violence when she'd seen him holding Prudence in his arms. She'd heard the gossip, too. Grant was definitely sparking the seamstress. They'd walked arm-in-arm down the street. Behaving that way in public was nearly an engagement announcement.

Trying to move on, she said, "I'd be grateful for your help. Here's what I planned to do." She described her idea for risers. She'd seen such a thing at a church in Omaha one time and heard them called such, but she couldn't figure out how they'd made them.

From her description, he began hammering, knocking together sturdy risers so quickly she could barely follow his flashing hands. He made two sets without speaking to her beyond grunting.

Hannah stood off to the side the whole time, doing little more than giving directions, and precious few of those.

After setting them in place, he turned to go.

"Grant?" When she said his name she looked down to avoid making eye contact and noticed she'd twisted the frill around the middle of her new green dress into a knot. She released her death grip on the fabric and tried to smooth away the wrinkles.

She glanced up to see Grant freeze. Then his shoulders slumped, and he turned around to face her. Hannah saw a look of pain on his face. She forgot what in the world she wanted to say to him as she closed the distance between them.

He looked at her, long and quiet. "New dress?"

Hannah kept swiping at the mess of wrinkles she'd made. This fabric had come from Grant. She'd thank him if she wasn't afraid he knew nothing about it.

"Sadie and Marilyn helped me make it." Distracted by the knowledge that she could get the girls in trouble by telling the truth, Hannah forgot about how awkward things were with Grant. True, the dress she was wearing now had come from him, but she'd been paid since then and gotten enough cloth for a riding skirt. She and the girls were already done with it.

"I got my first pay. I earned ten dollars for the first two weeks of school. I wasn't supposed to get paid until I'd worked a month, but Sadie encouraged me to tell the school board I needed the money. She said they would understand, and they did. I bought fabric for. . .uh. . . for myself." Hannah went back to twisting her skirt. "And my students turned the tables on me and became teachers. With your girls working together, I had this dress done in no time."

"Money," Grant said with the first relaxed smile Hannah had seen on his face today. "I remember the first time I earned an honest dollar. It's about the sweetest feeling on this earth."

Hannah smiled and set aside the story about the girls bringing her fabric. There was always time to tell him later. "I've never spent much on myself. Before I came here, even if I did find some work, there was. . ."

Hannah almost said Libby's name, thinking of how her injured little foot had taken up every spare penny. Catching herself in time, Hannah wondered what Grant would say about all the lies. Libby was doing well from what Hannah could see. She still never spoke, but her limp was barely noticeable these days, thanks to the shoes Grant had fashioned for her. Libby smiled easily and ran around with the other children in school. Emory Harrison, Gladys's youngest son, enjoyed quieter play than the roughhousing big boys, and he and Benny had become Libby's champions around the playground. There was no reason to bring up her relationship with Libby to Grant. Silent Libby certainly wasn't going to spill the beans

"There was what?" Grant asked.

Hannah drew a blank for a few seconds. "There was. . .uh. . .oh, just always something more pressing to spend it on."

"The girls forced me to get some new clothes." Grant looked at himself. "They sewed them up for me, the whole outfit just last night."

Hannah had noticed how tidy he looked. "And you got a haircut?"

"Marilyn sheared me like a sheep. My girls set on me like a pack of wolves. Told me I was shaming them with my old clothes. When they were done, I looked like this." Grant held his arms out and looked down at himself, shaking his head. "Kids."

"You look really nice." Hannah almost choked when those words slipped out.

"So do you." Grant closed his mouth so quick Hannah heard his teeth click together.

They stared at each other. Hannah knew what he had on his mind—the same thing she had on hers. Hannah felt as if a team of Clydesdales had just galloped into the schoolroom between them and they were pretending not to notice.

Forcing herself to do the right thing, she said, "We never should have. . ."

"Hannah, I owe you. . ."

Speaking on top of each other, they both fell silent.

Into the silence, Grant said, "I want to apologize for the other morning. I took. . .uh. . .that is. . .improper familiarities passed between us. I. . .I don't. . .it won't. . .we can't let that happen again."

Hannah thought of Prudence. He was getting ready to confess that he had betrayed his intended with that kiss. She had to stop him before he cut her heart completely out. "You're right. We can't. I was as wrong as you. I'm here to teach school and nothing else. And you've got someone else, I know. Thank you for your help with—"

Grant kissed her again, quick as a striking rattlesnake, only way, way nicer.

He practically jumped away from her. Shaking his head, he turned and rushed out of the building, muttering something Hannah couldn't hear.

It was a good thing the risers he'd made were well-built because Hannah barely managed to stumble over to them before her knees gave out. She sank onto them hard enough that if they'd been rickety, she'd have squashed them flat to the floor.

TWENTY-FOUR

Grant did the chores the next morning so fast he was finished before the wagon rattled down the lane, taking his family to school.

Charlie rode his own horse so he could stay in town to work. Grant planned to ride out to meet the boy when he returned.

Jamming the pitchfork into the haystack, he headed to the immense pile of split wood, wondering if he should make each piece a little smaller. He had to find something, anything, to keep his mind off Hannah.

Worse yet, he was facing a ride with that child-hating Shirt Lady. He shuddered every time he thought of that awkward hour he'd have to spend with the fool woman.

He stared at his tiny, ramshackle house. He looked at the looming mountain that rose up behind it, covered with trees that clung to the sheer slope.

Most of the woodlands surrounding the Rocking C were either scrub or older trees that wouldn't work for a log cabin. Three small stands held trees the right size. He'd considered chopping down these trees a hundred times and rejected the idea because it was so dangerous. Even in the summer he'd avoided them. Now, in the bitter winter with its short, dreary days, it was a nightmare.

Perfect!

It beat his other plan—holding his head under a bucket of ice water until his thoughts cleared of confounded women making his life a living nightmare.

He jogged to the woodpile, snatched up his axe, and headed for the stand of young trees. Sure it might kill him, but if he died, Joshua, Marilyn, and Sadie could manage. And until it did kill him, he'd be clinging to the side of a mountain for dear life, which would keep him from saddling up his horse and riding to town to see for himself if Hannah's hair was as thick and soft as he remembered. It had come to mind around a thousand times that, as long as he kissed her anyway yesterday, he might as well have touched her hair just once, to check and see if—

With a near howl to stop his wayward thoughts, he charged the mountain. Gripping the axe handle as if holding onto his last shred of sanity, he headed up that slope.

He fell halfway off the mountain a dozen times that morning. He tossed the axe away and grabbed a tree as he slid past and always scrambled right back up to work. The pile of trees at the base of the mountain grew fast, and Grant thought he was getting the knack of being a mountain goat. It's not like he was falling off a cliff or anything. He'd just slide along, sometimes get to rolling a little, and catch himself as soon as possible. He slammed into a couple of trees and that hurt. But thanks to the peril, it definitely took his mind off Hannah.

Mostly.

With no notion of time passing, he sidled along the treacherous bluff, chopping even while he knew he was acting like a maniac. The hillside was slippery with half-melted snow and so steep that, when he cut a tree, if it didn't snag, it fell most of the way to the house.

He came close to forgetting how much he wanted to see Hannah again toward the middle of the afternoon when he was so exhausted he couldn't see straight. Cutting down a whole forest was a stroke of genius.

Joshua came home driving the wagon.

The young'uns saw the load of lumber that had tumbled to within a hundred feet of the cabin.

"What are you up to, Pa?" Josh yelled from below.

"We're building on. You go ahead and start chores. I'm almost done here." It wasn't exactly true, because Grant intended to keep chopping down trees for the rest of his life if it helped keep his unruly thoughts in order. But it was true enough, because he had nearly enough for the two extra rooms he had in mind. For now, he was almost done.

With cries of excitement, the children ignored his wish to be left completely alone and immediately jumped in to help.

Grant thought of Charlie riding home alone from Harold's and the lowdown polecat who had attacked Joshua still running loose. Grant had to quit and go ride his son home, then go back to face Shirt Lady. He was out of time.

The children were so excited, begging to help, Grant almost quit going crazy with his wayward thoughts. "You young'uns can't go up that hill. It's too steep. And I don't want any of you working the axe. Josh, you could be chopping, but you're too beat-up and you girls haven't had enough practice."

"We could hitch up the horse and drag the logs into place. Just tell us where you want them." Marilyn's eyes flashed with excitement.

Sadie looked like she wanted to jump up and down just from thinking of the new rooms.

Grant didn't want them to do a thing. This was his project. Meant to keep him busy working himself near to death for the rest of his life. "Leave it. There's plenty to do with chores."

"But you'll be back with him in just a few minutes, Pa." Benny started climbing around on the teetering mound of tree trunks, risking his life.

Grant's stomach clenched when he realized his children might be in danger and he shouldn't leave them. Then his heart lifted. He'd tell Shirt Lady the ride was off and blame it on his children.

She'd hate it.

She'd hate him.

She'd never come near him again.

Grant smiled for the first time all day.

But he had to ride in and do it. That'd still take awhile because she'd no doubt nag him near to death. He'd better make sure the young'uns didn't worry.

"Uh. . .after I get back with Charlie, I have to ride back to town for. . .for. . ."

"For what, Pa?" Sadie asked.

"I'm supposed to go out riding with. . .with. . ."

Sadie and Marilyn whirled to face him, their eyes blazing with excitement.

His throat dried up and ached as if he'd swallowed a cactus thorn.

"With. . .who?" Marilyn clutched her hands under her neck.

Sadie took a step closer. Grant noticed Josh grinning and wondered what the boy had in his head.

"With that. . ."The thorn grew into a whole prickly pear, and Grant cleared his throat and wished for a drink of water. "That. . .seamstress woman. . .Prudence." Confound it, he'd gone and learned her name. He'd have his hands full forgetting it now that he'd actually said it out loud.

Marilyn's hands dropped to her side in fists. Sadie gasped. Josh's grin shrank away. Benny straightened from his wild scramble and rolled off the pile of lumber.

Grant snagged him in midair, glad for the distraction. "Now, you quit your climbing. While I'm gone, I want you to—"

"Prudence?" Sadie screeched like to break a man's eardrums. "You're going out riding with *that* nasty woman? Why, she won't so much as look at any of us. Last week at church. . ."

"How did you get mixed up with her?" Marilyn talked over the top of Sadie. Both of them tore into him in a way no child should ever speak to a father. As a matter of fact, the way no person should ever speak to another.

"I can't stand her, Pa." Benny squirmed to get loose of Grant's hold. "I ran into her once in the store. I mean ran hard into her. But it weren't on purpose. It was an accident. And she got so mad I thought she was going to take a swing at me. She doesn't like. . ."

Josh started in, too. "One time we just passed on the street and she made a face like I smelled bad. She held her skirt off to the side like she was afraid my skin would stain her. . . ."

Grant took a moment to thank God for Libby's muteness and Charlie's absence. Sure Grant hated being alone. But when his children were here, it didn't mean it was okay for them to yell at him.

The noise went on until Grant was afraid Charlie would be home on his own. "Okay! Enough!" Grant took a long route around the mob his children had become. "I told the woman I'd take her for a ride and a promise is a promise." One he intended to weasel out of, but he'd do it face to face, like a man. A weasely man, but still. . .

"I'm going!" Grant was madder at himself than his children were, so their yelling barely vexed him. They tagged him to the barn, yapping and nagging to beat all, which at least got Benny away from that log pile.

Grant's ears were ringing by the time he hitched up the wagon and rode out of the yard. Spending time with that nasty, child-hating Shirt Lady wasn't going to be that much different than home. He planned to talk fast while he told her there'd be no ride then run for home.

He sat up straighter. He'd ask Charlie to wait at work rather than ride the boy home and go back. With that as an excuse, Grant wouldn't even be much delayed. He remembered that determined look she'd had while cornering him into the ride. If he couldn't head her off, he'd pick up Charlie and take the boy along for the ride. Make sure Charlie sat between them on the buckboard. Better yet, maybe he and Charlie could sit on the seat and they'd stick Shirt Lady in the back by herself. Bringing a surly child along on their date ought to put the perfect finishing touch on any ideas Shirt Lady might be hatching in her brain.

For the first time, Grant worried that Charlie might be settling in and cheering up. A good-natured child wouldn't get under Shirt Lady's skin nearly as much as a sullen, sly child. Sorely hoping Charlie hadn't turned happy on him, Grant hurried the horse toward Sour Springs.

"Tonight's the night." Prudence looked at Horace. This was it. Tonight they'd get it done.

She'd be married to Grant by sundown and his property would be hers within days. The man would then take an unfortunate fall off his horse. She'd inherit, sell to someone who recognized the value of that seeping oil, then head for California with Horace. A man who was too dumb to know he had an oil field in his backyard deserved to have it taken away.

"I know what to do." Horace slurped the last of his coffee and slapped the tin cup on the table. "Get this table cleaned up. He'll be here soon enough. You don't want him seeing there's two people living here."

"I'll get him inside somehow. The sprained ankle worked last time, except he left me at the door. This time I'll force him to bring me in. Collapse if I have to."

"All we need is to get him one step inside. I'll be behind the door and knock him cold. By the time he comes around, the whole town will know he's been in here too long. Won't matter what he says, they'll believe you." Horace rubbed his hands together. Prudence could see he was already counting the money.

Prudence tried her best not to let the greed shine in her own eyes. "Stop talking about it. I'm afraid he'll see it in my face how much I'm looking forward to our marriage." Prudence laughed.

Horace put his hands on her. Money always brought out the animal in him. He pulled her hard against him.

"Stop it. It's almost time for him to get here. Don't mess me up."

Their eyes locked. "This is the big score, Prudy. The one we've been waiting for."

The light in Horace's eyes made Prudence's heart bound with excitement. He lowered his head to mess her up good just as they heard the clatter of wagon wheels pull to a stop by the shop door.

"He's early. Maybe he's lookin' forward to his big date." Horace let her go with a crude laugh.

Prudence's living quarters were in the back of her shop. She hurried ahead of Horace to let Grant in. Horace followed, and as Prudence brushed the wrinkles out of her prettiest gingham dress and straightened her hair, Horace slipped behind the door, his eyes hot and excited.

Prudence knew he wanted to finish this now. So did she. If she could just get Grant to take a single step inside. . . She inhaled slowly, concentrating on replacing the hungry look of greed with one of adoration for the stupid fool now knocking on her door.

She reached for the knob.

Grant pulled his hat off his head as Shirt Lady swung the door open. "I don't have much—"

"Grant, you're here at last." Prudence threw her arms around his neck and came at his lips again.

Grant ducked and he accidentally kinda butted her in the lips with his head.

"Oww." She pressed one hand to her mouth and clung to him with the other.

He pulled loose quick while she was distracted. "Uh, sorry about that. I'm a clumsy one, for a fact. Listen Shirt. . .uh. . .I mean. . .uh. . ." Grant had to think for a second, but he remembered—much to his dismay. "Prudence. I've got a...uh...the thing is..."

Her eyes met his, something sharp and knowing in them. She glanced down at his feet as he backed away. She could tell he was canceling their ride most likely.

"I left this dangerous pile of logs...."

"My fault entirely, Grant, honey. Don't worry a speck about that little bump." She slipped past him and practically ran to the wagon.

"Now, Prudence, the thing is..."

She climbed up that wagon quick as a squirrel scaling a tree trunk. Grant sighed. Now he was going to have to get her down. He'd told Harold he had to run an errand and to keep Charlie working for another few minutes. But Harold wanted to close up shop, so there just wasn't going to be time for a ride. He slumped as he followed after.

"Let's go, Grant. You promised." She shined those wide eyes on him, and he thought he saw tears getting set to fall. Well, he'd been a father to girls for a long, long time. A few tears didn't matter a bit to him. Women went with waterworks just like a beaver and buckteeth.

"I can't take you riding." Grant choked on her name. The woman made him feel as awkward as an ox trying to sled down a hill on a toboggan, and there was no denying it.

He thought of Hannah at that moment. Of course he thought of Hannah most moments, so that came as no surprise. No ox on a toboggan with Hannah. He hadn't put a foot wrong there when he'd kissed her. Except he shouldn't have done it at all. But he'd never come within a mile of knocking her in the head. Probably a shame. A good head butt might have ended all of Grant's troubles. But no, everything had gone just right. In fact, it was so right he'd...

"Hi, Harold." Shirt Lady's overly loud voice drew him back to the present. "Grant and I are going for a little ride."

"No, I'm not!" Grant decided. Since the woman was determined to have her way, he'd have to be doubly determined to get rid of her. "If you'd have let me finish, I was trying to tell you I've got a problem out at the ranch and I can't take time for a ride. Plus, I've got to get Charlie home. With Joshua hurt and. . ."

"Joshua hurt?" She stopped her babbling to Harold and turned on him.

Grant got the impression that he'd said something important, but he couldn't think what.

"Yes, with him hurt, I don't like leaving the children alone."

"I heard he died." The little witch's eyes narrowed into something that made a shiver run down Grant's backbone.

"Where'd you hear that?"

A long silence stretched between them. Then, talking too fast, she said, "I heard he fell off. . .off. . .I mean I heard he fell. I heard it was a long fall, and I guess I assumed he'd died."

Grant suddenly didn't give two hoots and a holler whether he hurt Shirt Lady's feelings. "You thought I'd have a son die and just go on as if it were nothing? I talked to you in town the day after it happened. You think I'd send the rest of the children to school the next day? You thought I'd agree to go riding with you a day after my son died?"

The longer he talked the more furious he got. It was all true. The woman really did believe all of that. "You didn't notice in this little town that there wasn't a funeral? Or what'd you think I'd do? Just toss him in a dirt hole and pay it no mind?"

The nasty hag's face turned stony, and she didn't answer his questions. Well, what she'd said before was all the answer he'd ever need. "Get down from the wagon. Now! I've got to get home. There'll be no ride now. . .nor ever."

Prudence held the spot and Grant crossed his arms. At last she moved, swinging down, slipping and tumbling toward the ground.

Instinctively, Grant moved to catch her.

She cried out in fear and pain. And instead of guilt or regret, all her caterwauling made Grant's stomach turn to be this close to the battleaxe.

His children had been right. Of course, he'd already known it. He wanted to kick himself for thinking this was a good idea, all because he wanted to make sure Hannah didn't have any crazy ideas about him just because. . .just because he. . .he had. . . crazy ideas about her.

Shirt Lady said in a tearful voice, her arms clinging around his neck, "Just help me inside. The ankle you hurt storming out of the school and colliding with me is acting up again."

Grant practically lifted her off her feet in his hurry to get shed of the woman. "Fine."

"I didn't mean to offend you with my comment about Joshua. I just heard he had a terrible fall. I thought terrible meant that he'd died. I didn't think about funerals and such. Please don't be angry with me, Grant. Please!" Her voice rose to a screech and tears now flowed freely from her eyes.

"Okay, I misunderstood." Grant didn't think so, but he'd do about anything to get her to quit squalling. Anything but go on a ride with her. He hustled her the few steps to her door while she seemed determined to drag along like a freight wagon with the brake on. "But I've got children. And you don't like children. That's as clear as the Texas sky. That makes us a bad match, and there's no point in wasting time denying it. We won't be going on any rides, ever." He swung her door inward and stepped back, letting loose of her waist.

She gasped in pain and caught at him. "Just please, get me to the chair."

He let her grab his arm but kept it extended, holding his body well away from her. For some reason the woman had a knack for ending up hanging from his neck. Her clinging arms gave him chills. Like ice cold chains were wrapping around him.

Grant saw a straight-backed chair only a few feet into the murky store. How could the woman see to do any sewing? "Okay, but the door stays wide open." He took a step in.

"Pa, you need any help?"

Grant turned and saw Charlie just a step behind him.

"Yeah, reckon I could use some help. She fell off the wagon and hurt her ankle and now she needs me to help her inside."

"Miss Cartwright, could you help, too, please?" Charlie said, turning to look back.

Lifting his eyes, Grant looked over Charlie's shoulder.

And there stood Hannah, her lips pursed, her arms crossed. Ready to start in nagging him, too, most likely.

Grant wished mightily for a chance to climb back up that mountain and tangle with cliffs and trees and a razor-sharp axe. His life made sense when he was doing things like that.

"I'll be glad to help, Charlie." Her eyes were as bright and burning hot as the blue at the heart of a flame. "What exactly is the problem, Prudence?"

"Uh...I...my ankle is..." Shirt Lady straightened and took her arm off Grant's neck, favoring her leg but standing well enough.

"I thought you were limping on your right leg when you first fell. Now it's your left. Did you injure both of them then?" Hannah's chin lifted, defiant and strong, but Grant saw the hurt in her eyes.

And why wouldn't she be hurt? He'd kissed her twice now. The woman had a right to believe, if Grant was an honorable man, that he wouldn't do such a thing unless he had feelings for her.

Grant let the child-hating Shirt Lady go to stand or fall on her own and had his hands full not reaching for Hannah and that pert chin and sassy...

"Good night, then, Grant." Shirt Lady stepped back and closed the door with a hard snap.

"Pa, what were you doing with that mean old hag?" Charlie said it plenty loud for Shirt Lady to hear. Grant didn't even consider shushing the boy. "Why, she told me after church the other day that I smelled like a—"

"I'll see you tomorrow at school, Charlie." Hannah spared Grant one last look, contempt laced with pain. Then she whirled away and headed for the diner straight across the street. Her ankles were working just fine. Why couldn't Hannah ever collapse in his arms?

Unable to stop himself, Grant rushed after her. "Hannah, wait." He caught her arm just as she stepped into the alley, where she'd go around to the back to climb the stairs.

She jerked free and turned on him. "Wait for what, Grant? For you to start yelling at me? Or maybe parade your girl around in front of me and the whole town? And would that be before or after you try and steal another kiss?"

"She's not my girl. I just. . .I just wanted. . .you to know there wasn't going to be anything between us. The woman's been pestering me for a carriage ride and I thought. . ." Grant's voice faded away.

"You thought you'd make it clear that you were just dallying with me when you. . .when you. . ." Her eyes brimmed with tears

Grant would have done anything to make it up to her. He could feel his control slipping. "Hannah?" He suddenly loomed over her. He hadn't meant to get this close or be this angry or feel so out of control.

"What?" Those fire-blue eyes faded to warm instead of burning. Instead of hurt there was longing. He suspected she could see that longing reflected back at her in his speckled eyes.

"Get upstairs right now."

"But I. . ."

"Right now, Hannah, before I give you one more reason to hate me." The eyes held. The moment stretched.

Grant took rigid control of himself and waited and hoped she'd go away and stay away. He clenched his hands to keep from reaching for her. He clamped his teeth to keep from asking her to come see what he had planned for his house. He locked his neck to keep from lowering his mouth to hers. He prayed to God for the self-control not to break all of his promises.

Neither of them moved. It was as if a cord bound them and stretched taut between them. Suddenly the cord snapped. Hannah whirled and ran down the alley and around the corner.

Grant held himself still as he heard her door open then slam shut. "Good for you, Hannah."

Then he turned to see Charlie sitting on the wagon seat with a weird, satisfied look on his face. He'd ridden a horse to school, and now it stood tethered to the back of the buckboard. Even the horse looked smug.

Feeling beset, Grant practically leapt into the wagon and headed his horses toward home.

Being a father was the only thing Grant had one bit of talent for. Although he was discovering he had a gift for making women cry. With a stifled groan, he knew the addition he had planned for his house wasn't going to be enough.

He pulled his Stetson low on his brow. "How'd you like your own room, son?"

"You wrecked it! I remember the day all you had to do was smile at a man, but you're getting old and tired and ugly." Horace had followed her into the back part of the store.

Prudence kept her eyes on Horace's fists and moved to the far side of the table in her back room. She was leery of him, but she was also thinking. "We're not beat yet."

"How'd'ya figure that?" Horace's eyes, cold and watchful as a rattlesnake, could have cut her flesh.

"So he won't come in here by himself. Not willingly. Well, we'll just bring him here unwillingly. You're out and about his place working."

"Digging in that stinking black tar, filling buckets, breakin' my back!" Horace picked up a chair in front of him and heaved it across the room, snapping its legs.

Prudence swallowed and talked fast. "You sneak out there next time, wait until all those brats leave for school, and you knock him senseless. Tie him up and hide him away, then keep him until dark and sneak him in here. We'll keep him overnight. Maybe we can even force some liquor down his throat while he's out. The next morning he'll have to come out, and I'll make sure there's a lot of ruckus. I'll stage a scene right in front of the whole town, crying and saying he promised to marry me, that he spent the night. He'll be forced to marry me on the spot."

Prudence went to close the door that separated the living quarters from the store. The heavily curtained front window had a slim opening, and through it she saw that snippy schoolteacher stalking away from Grant. Prudence knew human nature enough to recognize the light in Grant's eyes as he watched her go. If Prudence didn't move fast, she'd lose Grant to Hannah. She didn't have much time to stake her claim.

Grant followed the schoolmarm into the alley, and they disappeared from sight.

Seeing the teacher reminded her of all the fuss Sour Springs was making over this stupid passion play at the school. Her mind, always sharp, focused on that now.

"Wait, I've got another idea, an idea that'll catch him good, right in front of the whole town. We'll try that before you dry gulch him and drag him in here. He's a tough one. I can see it in his eyes. Catching him won't be that easy. But he's soft in the head on collecting children." She leaned forward and outlined her plan.

Horace's fists relaxed.

A floorboard creaked in the front of the building, and Prudence's eyes went to the closed door. She swung a hand at Horace. "Someone's out there. Get behind that curtain."

Horace concealed himself quickly. The fat old coot could move fast enough when he was swinging a fist or hiding out. Too bad he was so slow with his digging. She wouldn't have to put up with the nuisance of people wanting sewing done. She was sick of working for pennies.

She smoothed her skirt, plastered a smile on her face, and went out to the front. No one was there. She looked around the room then strode to the door. She pulled it open and noticed it squeaked. If someone had come in, she'd have heard for sure.

Shutting the door again, she scanned the room then shook her head as she studied every shadowy corner of her dumpy little business. Her eyes caught a crack of light coming from beneath the window that opened onto the alley between her store and the mercantile. She went to it and raised it a bit. She didn't remember ever opening it, so why hadn't it been closed?

Maybe Horace had wanted a breath of fresh air? And maybe if she asked him, he'd use those fists of his this time.

She slid the window open and closed and noticed it moved silently.

A rattle of a wagon drew her attention and she saw Grant drive away with that blond boy that had ruined her plans. She'd delight in seeing that child be sent down the road.

After they drove away, she stayed in the front, piddling with her fabric and a shirt she was overdue to deliver, giving Horace plenty of time to calm down.

TWENTY-FIVE

Grant got home to a warm supper and cold shoulders. The girls slapped food on like they were trying to give the table a good beating. Even Joshua, Charlie, and Benny were mad at him. Libby seemed a little huffy in her silent way, too.

Well fine! He'd managed to head-butt Shirt Lady. Hannah hated him. His children were furious. And he might as well admit he was good and sick of himself. He ought to form a club for people who hated him and charge membership. He'd be a wealthy man.

The only sound besides pottery on wood and the clink of silverware was chewing.

Grant wolfed down his food as fast as he could swallow to keep them from burning him to a cinder with their glaring eyes. He got done eating long before they did and practically ran out of the house toward the barn. Once there, he found the chores were done perfectly, and when he came out, he saw the young'uns had managed to get two rooms' worth of logs stacked and ready for building while Grant had been in town making enemies. He grumbled over all the help. He'd intended for this job to take him years.

He stepped into the kitchen to overhear his children settled down to their dinners, speaking at last. "Miss Cartwright has the pageant planned for the Saturday night before Easter. We'll have to drive into town at night." Benny spoke around a mouthful of roast beef.

Grant resisted the urge to hammer his head good and hard on the door. If he could only get through one night without hearing Miss Cartwright this and Miss Cartwright that. He saw a look pass between Charlie and Sadie and decided Charlie had told what went on in town, and since his dealings with Shirt Lady had turned into a disaster, they seemed ready to talk to him again.

Sadie wiped Libby's mouth with gentle hands and tucked the napkin more firmly under Libby's dimpled chin. "I've been asking and asking for Miss Cartwright to come out after school or on a Saturday or Sunday to work on her sewing. She needs a lot more practice. But she is really busy with the pageant."

Grant gripped the doorknob until it seemed likely to snap off.

"You're doing a wonderful job as Mary," Marilyn told Sadie as she served Benny more mashed potatoes. "There's a little nativity scene included as part of the Easter story. Miss Cartwright calls it a passion play."

"We've all been given really good parts, Pa." Charlie sat next to Benny. Charlie's shoulders were straighter, and he barely resembled the hostile, defiant boy who had moved in here such a short time ago.

"I get to sing a solo," Sadie added.

"Thanks for going in to help Miss Cartwright the other day." Joshua reached his long arms halfway down the length of the table and snagged the meat away from in front of Benny. "The risers are going to be great for the singing. All of us can get in rows and nobody's head is lost behind the person in front."

Grant sighed as the children chattered happily. Libby still remained silent, but she smiled and had a good appetite. He heard Gladys Harrison's name several times. It seemed that Hannah's chief critic had become her right hand. Everything was going fine at school. More than fine. Fantastic.

Grant wanted to scream!

He had no excuse to take his family out, and that meant he had to listen to All-Hannah, All-the-Time. And that meant he could never forget about her or how much he wanted to spend more time with her. If he did, sure as shooting he'd end up kissing her. He'd already proved he wasn't equal to the task of behaving himself in that area. And someone would catch them, and he'd end up married to her, which meant, in a world full of children, they'd add a few more.

Stirring restlessly, Grant forced his thoughts away from the stunning temptation of having children with Hannah and thought of all the unwanted children who needed him. He'd promised himself and God long ago that he'd devote his life to helping these lost little ones. He was *not* bringing more children into the world.

So that left marriage out. That left Hannah out. That left Grant with a lot of unruly thoughts and feelings that he had no idea what to do with. And that left him with some rooms to build.

"I know it's late, but I think I can level the ground and lay the first few logs for the foundation of the new rooms while you young'uns are doing your studies."

A mighty cold night, he'd rather be out building than listening to his children talk about Hannah.

"I don't have any homework, Pa." Joshua had always been an exceptional student. Right now, Grant wished the boy was dumb as a fencepost because he didn't need this house addition to go up any faster.

"I don't have any either." Charlie stood from the table.

"Maybe you two should stay in and help Benny and Libby with whatever homework they have." Grant pulled on his coat and listened to a rising wind whip around the cabin. Good, this oughta about kill him—which should keep his mind occupied.

"No need, Pa," Sadie said as she cleared the table off. "I'll wash up, and Marilyn can watch over the studies. As soon as we're done, we'll be out, too."

Marilyn began settling the little ones at the end of the kitchen table

Sadie had already cleared. "Miss Cartwright and Mrs. Harrison both say I'm old enough right now to be a schoolteacher. If it wasn't for Wilbur, I might consider it. I could probably take a term somewhere while Wilbur is making up his mind about building a cabin. Mrs. Harrison is going to ask around and see if there are any openings in the county. I could even teach a spring term."

Grant flinched to hear of one of his children growing up so soon. "I think this spring is too early, Marilyn. You're just sixteen."

"I'll be seventeen in a month, Pa. We've had teachers younger than that at school and there's a real need."

Grant looked at his daughter and thought of how well she did running his house and caring for her little brothers and sisters. He knew she could handle a school. "I don't want you out on your own just yet."

"I could help a lot of children who might not get an education otherwise. Besides, I'm almost through all the books. Miss Cartwright says I'll graduate this spring. And the schools are real careful to find a good place for the teacher to live."

"All except Sour Springs," Charlie said. "Working at the mercantile is kinda fun. I run all over town, carrying packages. I'm getting to know a lot of people. When I made some deliveries to the diner, I peeked in Miss Cartwright's room to see where she lives."

"Charlie, you shouldn't be sneaking around." Grant spoke sternly then ruined it by adding, "What's it like?"

"It's hardly bigger than our loft."

Grant looked up at the tiny triangle of space over his head. "That small?"

"Well, she can stand up straight in the middle, but it's not much bigger. Her room is cold, too. There's no heat except what comes up from the diner, and they shut that all down at night. I saw half a loaf of bread and no other food. I don't think she had enough money to feed herself at all until her first pay came in. Now, it's barely enough to make do. Most schools let a teacher live with a family, and then they can have their meals and a warm house. It's no wonder this town can't hang on to a teacher."

"Hannah's cold and hungry?" Grant's heart started beating too hard. He hadn't known. She'd never said a word. Of course, when had they exchanged normal words? They were either fighting or. . .

"I'm sure she'll be okay. Warmer weather is coming. She'll only have to be cold a little while longer." Sadie smiled at him, but it wasn't a friendly kind of smile. "And after all, she's an orphan. I'm sure she's *used* to being cold and hungry. I'll bet she doesn't even mind suffering anymore."

Grant's eyes narrowed. Sadie and Marilyn exchanged another one of those confounded female glances.

Joshua pulled on his coat. "Miss Cartwright said I'm going to graduate this spring, too, Pa. Ian offered me a job at his blacksmith shop."

Grant thought of his son Ian, who'd gone out on his own blacksmithing after living with Grant for only a year. As soon as he was set up in business, he'd come back and scooped up Megan, one of Grant's daughters, to marry. That had been a first. Ian and Megan had two children and one on the way. The blacksmith shop was a success, and Ian hustled to keep up with all the work. It was a fact Ian could use the help.

Joshua's dark eyes flashed with excitement. "I'm thinking I can work for him and file on a homestead. I've already got my eye on a good spot out near Will's ranch."

"You have to be twenty-one to do that." If Joshua and Marilyn left, he'd be down to four kids. He wouldn't even need to add on to the house.

"Who's to say how old I am, Pa?" Joshua buttoned his coat up to the neck. "You always make us pick a birthday for ourselves so we can have birthday cake, and all I know about my age is what I guessed at. I don't have any record of being born. If I say I'm a full-grown man and do the work of a full-grown man, then I don't see why the people filing homestead claims should disagree."

Grant saw Joshua slip a quick look at Sadie and Sadie looked back. Grant was shocked. Sadie did know her birthday. She'd be sixteen in a few months, the same age as Megan when Ian married her. Sadie'd been with Joshua since before Grant found them in Houston. She'd have her birthday about the time Joshua graduated from high school, got a job, and had his house built. If Sadie hauled off and married Joshua, Grant would be down to three kids.

"When we're done here we can start building a cabin for Josh." Charlie went out the door following Joshua.

The boys disappeared, closing Grant inside with the girls and Benny. If he wasn't careful, they'd build on to the blasted house without any help from him at all!

Sadie, Joshua, and Marilyn all growing up right in front of his eyes. Grant pulled his old Stetson on tight against the cold wind, saving his new one for going to town, and went outside to add on a room before his whole confounded family moved out on him.

There wasn't another orphan train due for two years.

Jogging to catch up with his boys, he thought desperately that he was getting plumb short of children!

Twenty-Six

The day Gladys Harrison dropped in unexpectedly at school and caught Hannah handing out the award for champion speller to Emory, Hannah knew her position as teacher was secure for life

Gladys seemed to have completely forgotten which children were orphans and which weren't. Emory, Libby, and Benny were best friends, and Gladys was as kind to them as if they were her own. Blessed with a beautiful singing voice, Gladys worked tirelessly helping the children learn songs for the pageant.

The day three new students showed up at the school, along with their burly father and browbeaten mother, Hannah doubted she'd last until the end of the week.

Mrs. Brewster stood slightly behind her husband and studied her clutched hands. Mr. Brewster spoke rudely to Hannah, scowled at Joshua and Sadie, and left after making a few veiled threats.

The three students, two boys and a girl, managed to disrupt the whole school.

Hannah would never have made it to morning recess if it hadn't been for Joshua, Marilyn, and Sadie.

Joshua kept interfering when Wally, the older boy, would get too disruptive. He stepped in when the boy, nearly as big as Joshua but in Charlie's grade, tried to pick a fight with Charlie.

Sadie spent all morning diverting the little girl, Celia, who was about Sadie's age and pulled hair and tattled with every breath.

Hannah had her hands full with Cubby, a first-grader who was as big as two of Libby, his classmate, and didn't seem able to sit still for a minute.

Marilyn taught the rest of the school by herself.

At one point, Joshua came to the front of the room to ask a question. Since Joshua had yet to need a moment's help with his lessons, Hannah wasn't surprised when he whispered, "This is the family that made Pa pull us out'a school every year. They joined a wagon train to head west, but something must have happened to bring 'em back. No way will we get through the first recess, let alone the whole day, without Wally knocking someone down."

Hannah shared a worried look with Joshua. "We have to keep that from happening."

Hannah saw Cubby get up from his desk and go to the window.

Marilyn came up to the two of them. "No matter what we do, these boys will still hit someone, and Celia will run crying to her father to tell lies. She's always hated Sadie especially."

Hannah couldn't stay and plot strategy for another second. When the window wouldn't open, Cubby had pulled a length of firewood out of the woodbin and approached the glass.

Just before it was time for recess, Charlie stood from his desk and said loud enough for everyone to hear, "I'd like to stay in from recess today and practice the pageant. I want to know my part a little better."

Charlie knew his part, letter perfect.

Hannah caught on instantly. "Let's all stay in from recess. It's a really cold day anyway."

The howl from the Brewsters was deafening.

Hannah did her best to act surprised. "You children don't have a part in the pageant, do you? Would you like a part? We've got plenty of time to work you in. Or, if you'd like, you can go on out and play while we keep working."

Hannah saw smiles break out on every face in the room but three. The Brewsters didn't confine their cruel mischief to orphans.

"I was thinking Ma should be here for practice," Emory suggested.

Gladys lived over a mile from town, but maybe tomorrow. Her heart lifted as she thought how much help Gladys would be, even if only as a witness.

"Ma was going to stop for coffee at Mabel's," Emory said. "She always lingers when she does that. I'll bet she's still there, just across the street. She'd be glad to come over."

"Emory, why don't you run over right now and see if she can come."

"And if she's gone, maybe Mabel will come back with me." Emory nodded and dashed out of the room.

Wally Brewster reached out his leg to trip the little boy as he ran past, but somehow Joshua was there, not saying or doing anything except being in the way. Emory had to slow down and make a wide detour around Joshua, and that kept him away from Wally. Emory escaped unscathed.

"Why does he get to go out and we don't?" Cubby started banging his fist on the desk.

"Why, you can go out, Cubby," Hannah said brightly then kept talking to slow them down so Emory could make a clean getaway. "It's time for recess all right. I'll work on a part in the play for all three of you tonight. Tomorrow you can stay in at recess and practice with us." Hannah looked out the window and saw Emory disappear into the mercantile. "But for now you might as well go play."

Wally got up, shoving his desk out of line with the others. Celia pinched Sadie so hard Sadie jumped out of her desk with a squeal of pain. Cubby kicked Libby as he passed her. Hannah caught Libby because the little girl looked inclined toward revenge. The three Brewsters stormed out of the schoolhouse door.

"Joshua, watch to make sure Emory gets back inside without trouble," Hannah ordered.

Joshua headed for the window.

The minute the Brewsters were gone silence reigned. Hannah breathed a huge sigh of relief until she remembered that the recess couldn't go on forever. And it wasn't fair for the rest of the school to go without a recess so they could hide from the Brewsters. This was no time for relief.

Hannah didn't feel it was appropriate to discuss the naughty children with her students. Instead she began working on the pageant just as Charlie had suggested.

Gladys and Emory showed up almost immediately, and Hannah could tell from Gladys's disheveled appearance that she had hurried over. Hannah wondered how bleak a picture Emory had painted. Gladys gave Hannah a commiserating look then dove into working on the play.

Gladys stayed for the rest of the day. Hannah even allowed a short outside recess after the children ate their dinner. She and Gladys stayed on the playground the whole time. Despite the Brewsters' best efforts, the school day passed and some learning even went on, mostly thanks to Marilyn.

Hannah excused the children after school, but none of them left. They usually exploded out of the building. Instead they sat quietly until the Brewsters were long gone. A few, whose parents arrived in wagons to drive them home, left.

"Cubby'll be waiting for me after school cuz I made him look bad in reading," redheaded Gordy O'Reilly said. "Can I just sleep here, Miss Cartwright?"

Gladys ended up escorting the children who lived in town, including taking Charlie to work. She got Zeb at the livery to hitch up his team and take the children home who lived close enough to town that they were expected to walk.

In the end, only Grant's family, who brought their own team, was left. Just when Hannah had decided she'd have to rent a horse and ride along with them to see they got home all right, Charlie came into the schoolhouse with a wild, nervous look on his face about a half hour after school had let out. Wally Brewster had slowly begun to focus most of his considerable angry mischief on Charlie, who wasn't inclined to be pushed around.

"They were hanging around awhile, but their pa called them home." Charlie started handing out his family's coats. "I explained things to Mr. Stroben, and he let me off work early. If we head out now, we'll be fine."

They all loaded into the wagon and hustled away.

Hannah went to her room and collapsed. She ached in every muscle of her body from the hard work and tension of the day. She was never going to survive teaching school with the Brewsters in residence.

Grace couldn't survive one more minute in this canyon! She waited until no one was watching.

Daniel had been eagle-eyed ever since she'd made her first break for the high trail out of the canyon. She'd only made it out three more times. Each time he'd caught up to her, let her have her visit with Tillie, then, contented, he let him drag her home.

But now, he'd been lulled into a false sense of security with the coming warm weather. He didn't realize she could almost hear the snow melting, one flake at a time. Spring had long come to the valley of their canyon, but winter would not let up its hold on the gap.

Matthew had given up his nap at fourteen months of age. Grace sighed when she thought of how lively her little boy was. Nowadays, Matthew went out to work with Daniel for long stretches and never came back with more than bumps and bruises—he was a sturdy little thing. So, when Daniel climbed the hill behind the house to start chopping down trees to add onto the house so the baby could have a room right next to her and Daniel's, and all of the boys followed him, Grace saw her chance.

This time it wasn't about seeing Tillie or Sophie. She had much more in mind.

Grace put on sturdy hiking boots, sneaked out the front door, slipped past the barn, and headed up the canyon wall. She thought as she climbed that she might possibly have a fever. Or maybe she just felt a feverish need to escape. Whatever it was, she couldn't help making a break for it from time to time. And this time she was going all the way. She was going to see Hannah.

She was nearly to the steepest part of the trail when Mark caught up to her. "Runnin' off again, Ma?"

Grace scowled down at the little imp. Only not so little anymore. He was nine now, and as wily as ever. "Did you tell Pa?"

"Nope, I decided just to trail along in case you needed help. I don't mind a visit outside every once in a while."

"Well, why don't you convince Pa to go along with me then? It's a plumb nuisance having to escape when he's not looking."

"Maybe he'll come around. I heard him say he's going to turn his attention to the high pass trail as soon as the new room is done."

"Well, good. That'd make this a lot easier."

"So, you think you're gonna die havin' this baby, Ma?"

"Ma's not gonna die, Mark. You take that back!"

Grace stopped and turned.

John was just a few yards behind him. Luke tagged along a few yards farther back.

"What are you boys doing?"

"We're coming, too." Luke grinned. "Busting out of the canyon is fun."

"Pa says Ma's gonna most likely die havin' this baby." Mark started up the trail toward the canyon wall. "I just don't think it's a good idea to get our hearts all set on her surviving. I think it'll be better if we plan for the worst."

"Mark!" Grace turned and walked faster toward Sophie's.

"Could we have two or three this time, Ma?" Ike appeared on the trail just a few paces behind Luke.

Grace stopped to see her fourth son. She threw her hands wide in exasperation. "Your pa cannot have helped but notice you're all gone."

"You're not gettin' the hang of sneakin' like you had oughta, Ma." Mark came back to her side and took her hand.

Grace held on as she plodded toward the most treacherous part of the trail. She'd have to let go of Mark and use her hands and feet and cling like a scared cat to the little handholds. But it was only a hundred feet of sheer rock face, with the occasional perfectly good handholds. Then she'd go over the peak. There were some touchy spots on the other side, and then things eased off some. "Well, I'm still practicing. I haven't been at it as long as you have."

Grace came to the base of what she thought of as The Spike. The trees quit growing and the canyon wall turned to pure rock. It reached upward at an almost vertical angle, came to a point, and dropped on the other side just the same way, with only a few outcroppings of rock on the other side that were big enough for a person to sit and rest. Daniel had cut handholds and footholds in it, because he worried about getting out in case of an accident. It used to be a life and death matter to scale this cliff. But now it was just hard work. He'd been complaining about her abusing all his efforts for something as frivolous as having tea with Tillie or Sophie. The man had no idea where she really wanted to go. She touched her pocket and wondered if she'd brought enough money for train fare for eight.

She gritted her teeth and took a step toward the first grip, but Mark beat her to it. He raced up the sheer wall like a scampering mountain goat. John headed up right behind him and Luke was next.

Ike paused as he drew alongside her. "Go ahead. I can catch you if you fall."

"No, that's fine. I'll slow you down. When you boys get to Adam and Tillie's, have them send a horse back for me."

Ike nodded and went straight up. She envied him his youth and strength then remembered she wasn't that much older than he was.

As she reached for the first handhold, she heard footsteps. She knew they'd come. She turned around just as Abe emerged from the treeline with Matthew on his back. She tapped her toe as she waited. Honestly, if they were all going out, she was tempted to stay in.

Abe nodded to her and began his climb. She noticed Matthew wasn't just clinging for a piggy back ride. He'd been strapped like a papoose on Abe's back. He faced backward.

"Hi, Ma!" Matt waved as Abe ascended. Grace waited until they'd gone a ways. She wasn't in any mood to have Matt's drool dripping down on her head.

The only reason she didn't go home now was because they'd figure it out and come on back. Then she thought she felt the baby kick, which was impossible. She couldn't be more than two or three months along. But it reminded her of this claustrophobic canyon. That kick was like a kick up the mountain.

She reached for the handhold again, knowing the only one left was Daniel, but the boys were good at sneaking. If she'd gotten away with only them noticing, he might be awhile coming. He'd come along soon enough though. He knew she liked having him along on the way home.

She was a dozen feet up the cliff when a handhold crumbled and she began sliding backward. She didn't even scream. She'd learned to flatten herself against the rock and slide to the bottom. A few scrapes were all she'd get.

She'd only gone a few feet when Daniel caught her by the back of her dress. "I didn't hear you coming." She turned, smiling, her feet back on solid ground. "Thanks." She held her breath, afraid he'd haul her home.

He pinned her between himself and the cliff and scowled. "Grace, you are determined to die one way or another, aren't you."

"I just want to have a little visit." Let him assume it was with Sophie. "I don't mind a few scrapes on my hands."

"A few scrapes?" Daniel loomed over her, looking down, disgusted. "How am I supposed to go gallivanting all the time and still get my chores done?"

"You're going to get cranky wrinkles if you don't stop looking at me like that."

"Well, good. If my face is set in permanent wrinkles, it'll save me using my frown muscles."

Grace ran one finger down the corner of his mouth, tracing the deep furrow. "I'm sorry I make you frown. But Daniel, I just have to go for a visit once in a while."

"You've never had to before."

"That is the honest truth. I don't know what's changed, but this year I just have to." Her finger rose, and she ran it down the lines that were working themselves in between Daniel's blond eyebrows.

Daniel shook his head to escape her finger, but his scowl eased some. "Can this be the last time, please? The gap has to thaw pretty soon. I'll take you and we'll have a visit, but then we come home and stay home. I've got to get that room built, and I've got cow and chicken chores. Having to run to the neighbors so often is a strange quirk that I don't like to see you developing, Grace. You're strange enough as it is."

Grace nodded. She didn't bother to tell him that she was going to see Hannah. She'd only be gone a week. . .or two. By then, surely she could hold herself to home until the thaw. "I can't seem to stop being strange though, Daniel. You know, I've wondered before if maybe I'm not all that strange. Maybe women and men are just different."

Daniel shook his head. "You're not going to get away with this by blaming it on being a woman."

"Why not?" Her finger lowered to his frown again.

His eyes dropped to her lips. "Quit distracting me."

"I'm not." Grace smiled, hoping to distract the dickens out of him so he'd be a good sport about it when she headed for town.

"Oh yes, you are. And you know it."

"Is it working?"

"I'll say it's working." Daniel kissed her right there on the mountainside.

The boys had been pestering the McClellens for a long, long time before Grace and Daniel caught up.

Hannah trudged home after surviving another day.

Grant still hadn't taken his children out of school, and that surprised her. Was it possible they weren't telling him about the Brewsters? Once Grant found out about the Brewsters' return and how awful they treated his children, he was bound to take his young ones out.

Hannah, slumped exhausted in her single chair, wished Grant was here so she could tell him it wasn't just orphans. The Brewsters were nasty to everyone. Gladys and the other townspeople had learned to trust Grant's children.

She stood up, her spirit renewed. If Grant took his children home, he'd be quitting on the school, quitting on the town, and worst of all, quitting on his children. He'd be making them feel like they were being picked on when they weren't—well, they were, but no more so than anyone else.

"I'm not going to put up with it." Hannah paced in her tiny, sloped-ceiling room as she focused her anger on Grant—the quitter! "You're going to keep your children right here in my school, and when things get tough, you're just going to have to get tougher."

She declared to the empty room, "I'm not going to let him run away!"

TWENTY-SEVEN

Hannah wanted to run away.

The school became a daily struggle. Hannah knew that only sheer stubbornness, combined with the need to feed herself, plus endless prayer kept her going back.

She wrote parts for the Brewsters. One minute she'd try and teach them their parts, and they'd refuse to join in the pageant. The next minute Hannah would excuse them from being in the play and let them quit practicing, and they'd complained about being left out.

The Brewsters were allowed to go outside for every recess, and the rest of the students mostly stayed in. Hannah let them all out for a few minutes, but the second the Brewsters started trouble, Hannah would announce play practice, and the students, except for the Brewsters, would run for the schoolhouse like they were running for their lives. Even though it was well into March, a cold spell had settled in and shortened recesses weren't a great hardship, except her students needed to run off steam. The whole school fairly buzzed with pent-up energy, and Hannah began to have discipline problems in addition to the Brewsters.

Marilyn was good at teaching the school. Charlie was always right at Wally's side, diverting the big boy's flair for cruel mischief onto himself. Hannah watched Charlie like a hawk in case she needed to step in, but Charlie always seemed to be one jump ahead of Wally. In fact, Charlie seemed to enjoy the chance to taunt Wally and attract the boy's wrath.

All of the parents had taken to meeting their children and seeing them home from school. Ian now rode out with Grant's family until he was sure they were in the clear.

Hannah found herself spending all her time protecting Sadie from Celia and Benny and Emory and Sally from Cubby. Through it all she never gave up trying to force a little learning into the Brewsters' stubborn heads.

Hannah collapsed after another stressful day, grateful to have survived. It was two days before the pageant. All of the children had already headed home. She sat in her desk chair and prayed fervently to live through tomorrow. It was too much energy to pray for more than strength sufficient for the day.

The pageant was getting closer.

The Brewsters were getting more unruly.

The winter was dragging on.

And Hannah was considering applying for a job at the diner.

Before she was anywhere near done catching her breath, a red-haired woman, very pregnant, carrying a toddler, came in the classroom. "Miss Cartwright, I've wanted to come in and introduce myself any number of times."

Hannah couldn't resist returning the warm smile. "You have to be Gordy's mother." Hannah thought of the vivid curls and the abundance of freckles on one of Benny's classmates.

The young mother laughed, as the toddler squirmed in her arms. "Yes, I'm Megan O'Reilly. You wouldn't say Gordy looks like me if you could see his pa."

Hannah heard a soft Irish lilt in Megan's voice. "Your husband's a redhead, too?"

Megan smiled, running her hand over the red curls on the little girl bouncing and patting her mama's mouth with pudgy hands. "We're a matched pair and that's a fact. Ian is Sour Springs's only blacksmith."

"I'm glad you found time to come in." Hannah stood and waved Megan into the only adult chair in the classroom. It was a cinch the young woman wouldn't fit behind a student's desk. "Sit down. Please, you look like you've got your hands full."

Megan lowered herself gratefully into the chair with a soft groan.

Hannah perched on her clean desktop. "I wanted to get around and visit all of the children in their homes, but I've been slow getting it done. I had no idea teaching and putting on the pageant would be so demanding."

The little cherub in Megan's arms blew spit bubbles and squealed as she tried to get down. Megan wrestled with her like she'd done it a thousand times before. "I wanted to help you, but Ian hasn't been letting me get far from his sight these last few weeks, not even for church. My time is close, and our babies come fast. He's afraid I'll get caught out and have the little one along the trail."

Hannah was tempted to get the woman out of the school right now for fear she'd give birth on the spot. She didn't say that of course. "I understand. I appreciate that you wanted to help."

"The main reason I came in wasn't because of the children but because I wanted to talk to you about Grant."

Hannah's heart sank. Had word finally gotten out about what went on between her and Grant in the school, not once but twice? Maybe one of the other children saw the two of them through a window. Hannah opened her mouth to ask for forgiveness.

"Grant is my father."

Hannah's mouth dropped closed. "Your. . .your. . ."

"I know." Megan laughed. "I'm only about five years younger than he is. He's only two years older than Ian, and he's Ian's father, too. It makes me laugh to think of him as our pa, but I called him that for the years I lived with him. I wasn't the first child he adopted, but I was mostly grown so I had a bunch of little brothers and sisters from the minute he plucked me off the train."

Suddenly Hannah was intensely curious. She'd heard about the twenty children, and it made sense that some of them were still around, but she'd never wanted to ask who was an orphan and who wasn't, partly because the question could be hurtful but mainly because she'd been avoiding the whole subject of Grant like he was a full-blown plague.

"Do many of Grant's children live around Sour Springs?"

"There are six of us still around, plus the six still living with him. My husband lived with Grant for a year before he was out on his own. Ian never should have been put on an orphan train. He was near seventeen and no one wanted to adopt a boy that old, which meant he was a leftover."

"A leftover?" Hannah asked, masking her horror at a person being called such a thing. Megan had said it almost affectionately.

"Yes, we had no more scheduled stops before we turned around and headed back to New York. So Sour Springs is the end of the line. Any children who get this far aren't going to be adopted. Grant found that out and started showing up at the train station when an orphan train pulled in. He takes any children that are leftover."

Hannah saw it now. Crystal clear. Leftovers. "I heard Grant talking with the lady who rode with the children."

Megan's face lit up in a smile. "Martha. She's a saint. She and her husband took in more than a dozen leftover children themselves when they were younger."

Hannah knew her instincts that Grant couldn't be trusted had been born from her own awful experience. She still resisted believing in him fully, but she knew her lack of trust was her own problem, not his.

"The real reason I wanted to talk to you about Grant is that I wanted to thank you for whatever you've done to keep my family in this school. We've been afraid, Ian and I, that whatever resentment people in this town feel toward orphans might spill over onto our children. We were half expecting to end up teaching Gordy at home, too. But he loves coming to school, and he's found good friends and is welcome in people's homes."

Hannah stood, her jaw tense, her fists jammed against her slender waist. "Well, for heaven's sake, why wouldn't a sweet little boy like Gordy be welcome in anyone's home? What is wrong with this town that you'd even worry about such a thing?"

With a quiet smile, Megan said, "We heard that you are an orphan, too."

Hannah said rigidly, "That's right."

"And that you didn't have a very nice time of it with your adoptive father."

Hannah didn't respond.

"So you know what's wrong with people. You know what it can be like. You know how much an orphan longs for a family. I reckon that's why I've had so many little ones so quick, having a family just means so much to me. It's the same reason Grant has promised God to give his life to orphans. He's vowed to have no babies of his own when there's a world full of children who need a home. And to Pa, that promise includes never getting married because married folks"—Megan patted her substantial belly—"tend to have children."

"Never have children of his own?" Hannah felt a little lightheaded. "He promised God?"

"He just can't bear the thought of bringing more children into the world when there are so many now who need love. He told me that, once I was grown and gone, when I was pestering him about finding a wife. He never tells his children about it. He doesn't want them to think he's giving up anything. He's committed his life to children. He's a wonderful man." Megan heaved a sigh then hoisted herself and two babies—one inside, one out—to her feet. "I didn't mean to go on so long. Ian will be hunting me if I don't get on. But I wanted to meet you and thank you for your kindness to my son and my little brothers and sisters."

Hannah didn't want to let her go. She had more questions that needed answers. But she didn't dare ask any of them since the basis of all of them was, "What is a man who never wants to get married doing kissing me?" and, "How can I get him to do it again?" And maybe she'd ask, "Is wishing a man would break his promise to God an unforgivable sin?"

TWENTY-EIGHT

On the night of the pageant, Prudence waited with the patience of a stalking cougar for Grant's wagon to pull up to the schoolhouse.

She'd watched him at church long enough to know he'd be late. Always last in, first out. Those worthless orphans were the cause of his living like that. Her mouth watered when she thought of how she'd rid this town of that trash. The fact that she'd been an orphan didn't matter. She'd made a life for herself. She'd left the horror of her childhood behind when she teamed up with Horace. The fists of one man were easier to take than the hands of many that she'd had to endure to earn coins on the streets of Boston.

The milling around of the crowd settled down as everyone got inside.

Horace came up behind her and slid his arm around her waist. "Tonight's the night."

Prudence nodded. "If this doesn't work, tomorrow we take what's ours by force. But we won't need to. I've got it all planned."

Horace kissed her neck and laughed. She hated the stench of him. It never went away since he'd been working Sour Spring. But they'd get their land, they'd get their money, and they'd leave this stench behind. She hugged his hand tight and leaned back against him, laughing as she counted the money and saw their lives stretched out ahead of them. No more cold weather. No more working that sharp needle. No more hard

250

times. Grant was their way up, for good this time.

She saw his wagon pull into town and straightened. "This is it."

Horace turned her around and kissed her soundly. "Do it without messing up."

Prudence nodded and slipped away from him, then pulled on her cloak. She peered through the window in the front door. She had to time it just right.

Guilt alone got Grant to his children's pageant.

To avoid the sin of skipping the Easter program, he had to break his promise—given only to himself but a promise just the same—to avoid Hannah. His avoidance plan was all he could come up with to keep from kissing her again.

His children's excitement defeated self-preservation. Here he stood unloading the children from his wagon when he should have been home adding more rooms onto his house. He was up to six new bedrooms, and he had one more stand of trees he could attack.

As he jumped down, he noticed that Joshua looked him square in the eye. Charlie had picked a birthday and declared himself thirteen. The boy was probably closer to eleven, but Grant didn't care, unless the boy decided to haul off and build a house and get married, too.

Grant sighed, shoved his hands in his pockets, and let the children go ahead as he secured the team to a hitching post. He trailed glumly behind the others to the brightly lit school as he considered the grand nest he was building that might well be empty soon. He'd deliberately come late, hoping to have only a few minutes to get the kids inside and pick out a spot for himself in the back.

The children ran ahead and he was alone as he stepped into the small entry area. The last in, he stood gathering his courage, holding the door open like an escape route he didn't dare take. He pulled on the knob to close himself in with Hannah. Sure the whole rest of the town was here, but Hannah was the only one who was haunting him.

Prudence slipped in. His arm stretched out holding the doorknob in such a way that she stepped into what was nearly a hug. She had that look in her eye that she'd used a few times, right before she attacked him with her lips.

He abandoned the door and backed away. He got just far enough that she could get some real speed up when she swung at him. So unexpected was it, Grant stood and took the full force of the slap without even ducking. The sound echoed in the hallway. She hit him so hard he staggered back into the wall, dazed and barely registering Shirt Lady's words.

"You promised," she yelled so loud a little dust sifted down from the rafters. "You lied to me."

Trying to make sense of her words, Grant shook his head as she launched herself into his arms. A thundering sound that Grant thought at first was from the blow he'd taken was a room full of people rushing into the little entry all at once.

"You said you loved me."

Grant looked down, trying to figure out what was going on. She caught him in a near stranglehold, and this time he wasn't quick enough. She landed her fishy lips right square on his. He tried to lift his head, but her grip was like iron. He did look up though. Straight into Hannah's horrified eyes.

Grant pulled at Shirt Lady's arms and tore her loose. Freeing her lying lips only gave her back the ability to speak her awful words. "You said we'd be married, or I'd have never let you be with me as only a married couple should be. I might even now be carrying your child."

The crowd gasped. Hannah's face went pure white.

Grant saw Marilyn and Sadie cover their mouths, but their expressions were of shock, aimed at Shirt Lady. They didn't have a single spark of doubt in their eyes.

Joshua pushed into the room and shook his head, scowling. "Pa wouldn't do that."

Shirt Lady broke into desperate sobs.

Grant saw the trust of his children solid in their expressions. He knew they believed him. But the rest of the town—the folks who barely tolerated him and his family to begin with—looked shocked.

He tugged on the little leech still clinging to him but without being rough with her, not wanting to be seen abusing a woman on top of everything else. He couldn't get her loose.

Gladys Harrison's eyes grew stone cold as she crossed her arms. "What's the meaning of this?" Gladys said. "If you made this poor girl promises, then you'll stand by them."

Quincy shook his head, thinly veiled contempt on his face.

Then Grant saw Hannah. The color had faded from her face until Grant thought she might faint. And it wasn't contempt or shock or anger he saw there. It was pain. He'd hurt her. Again.

"This isn't true." Grant nearly choked on the words. The humiliation made his face heat up until his ears burned. "I don't know what she's talking about."

The crowd kept filling up the little entry.

People he respected, people he thought respected him, glared at him. Harold, Mabel, Doc Morgan, the parson. Mixed in were others who looked at Shirt Lady with disgust. Will, Ian, and Megan. His own younger children looked confused. It couldn't get any worse.

Then Festus Brewster shouldered his way into the entry. "Startin' a whole new generation of orphans, huh?" Brewster's pockmarked face, wrinkled from years of grim anger, settled into creases of derision.

"No, I've never told her I was interested in marriage."

"Just playing around?" Brewster shoved Grant's shoulder, pushing him hard against the outside door. Shirt Lady held tight and staggered back with Grant. "Foolin' with a woman just like the trash you came from and all the rest of this riffraff."

"Don't deny our love, Grant." The crying rose to a wail. "Anything but that."

Parson Babbitt stepped just behind Brewster. He didn't shout, but that only gave his words more power. "This can't be allowed, Grant. You know you've got to do right by this woman."

"But I didn't do this."

The parson shook his head, his eyes burning.

Grant felt guilty even though he'd done nothing. Nothing except possibly lead her on by agreeing to that ride. He'd known she was interested in him. Would she disgrace herself in front of the whole town like this because she was so desperate to marry him? What woman would behave like this? Could she really love him this much?

His guilt must have shown on his face, and everyone interpreted it as an admission that the liar's words were true because he saw the doubt on many faces shift to anger.

"You'll do right by that girl, or I'll see you run out of this whole county," Gladys said.

"You and your young'uns should *never* have been allowed in this school." Festus's hand came down hard on Grant's shoulder until Grant had to lock his knees to keep from being pushed to the ground. "You're like a disease this whole town'll catch if we let you get close."

Gladys and Quincy Harrison nodded; Agnes and others joined in. Muttering voices rose to a low roar.

The parson looked tired, but his voice was firm. "You will do the right thing by this girl, Grant."

"No, I. . ."

"I love you, Grant. Don't leave me in shame. I'm ruined if you don't marry me. Ruined!" She looked up, her eyes swollen nearly shut with tears. Her nose ran. Her skin was mottled red and white. Grant couldn't remember ever seeing a more repulsive sight.

"You'll ruin every good woman in this town, you and the rubbish you've taken in." Festus was three inches shorter but twice as wide, and he outweighed Grant by fifty pounds. Festus had been harassing him ever since Grant was a teenage boy, taken off an orphan train here in Sour Springs by the Coopers. Festus, sixteen at the time, had made school a nightmare for Grant. And Festus's children had tormented Grant's children from the beginning. He knew the Brewsters'd come back to town and he'd been expecting trouble. The trouble had never come.

Until now.

"My young'uns come home from this school every day wearing a stench from sittin' next to the dung heap of your family. I've been busy gettin' settled'r I'd'a been in here afore now to clear out this rat's nest."

Shirt Lady wept and pleaded.

The parson frowned.

Brewster pushed and goaded.

Grant's fists clenched.

He saw Hannah and knew he'd ruined this play that had meant so much to her. He'd somehow allowed this scene and shamed his children, undone all the hard work that had allowed them to be accepted in the school.

"You will do right by this girl, Grant." The parson had always been a supporter of Grant's. Now he looked so disappointed. Grant felt his will being crushed. The guilt and the trapped-rat feeling choked off any more self-defense."

"Many of us in town saw you courting her." Harold looked between the crying woman and Grant. "You can't walk away from this responsibility."

Mabel nodded.

Charlie slipped up to Grant's right side. "He's not going to marry you," Charlie shouted in his childlike voice, high enough to carry over the madness.

"You stay out of this, boy." Festus Brewster put his hands on Charlie, and Grant saw red.

Charlie was tough, a fighter, but he had taken on too big a target with the likes of Festus Brewster.

Festus was diverted from hassling Grant. He looked down at Charlie with a sneer on his whiskered face. "You're another one'a them orphans. Stay out'a this. I don't need to hear nothin' from the trash they sweep up off'a the alleys in the city and dump on us."

"You get away from Pa, and you. . ." Charlie jabbed this woman who had turned herself into Grant's noose.

Grant noticed the little cry-baby, frowning in anger, in contrast to the tears that kept falling. He had the first inkling that, whatever her motives for crying and shouting lies, Shirt Lady wasn't all *that* upset. Just determined.

His humiliation faded, and his head worked for about two seconds before Festus grabbed Charlie by the front of his shirt and lifted him off the ground to eye level. With a vicious shake, Festus said, "I told you to stay out'a this."

"Get your hands off him." Grant caught Festus by the wrist. The night, so hopeful, so full of the Lord and the joy of the season of resurrection, was ruined and Grant was in the center of the whole mess. Everything was ruined for his children, for all of the other pupils and parents, and for Hannah. It was supposed to be a night of joy; instead it was going to be a brawl. The match was lit by Shirt Lady's accusations, the crisis deepened by Festus, but the situation was pushed into a free-for-all by Grant-the-orphan, the one who brought all of these unwanted children into their midst. Because Grant wasn't going to stand by and watch Charlie take a beating at Brewster's hands.

Just as Festus appeared ready to toss Charlie to the floor and turn on Grant, Charlie reached into his pocket and pulled out a sheet of paper. "This is a marriage license. The lady who threw herself at Pa is married. Her husband has been hiding out in her house all this time."

The whole crowd froze. Eyes blinking, the parson reached between Charlie and Brewster's burly stomach and took the paper.

Shirt Lady grabbed at the document.

The parson evaded her and stepped out of her reach. Then he looked at her, fire and brimstone in his eyes. "What is the meaning of this?"

She let go of Grant's neck to wrestle the parson for the paper, but the parson blocked her. "I don't know where the boy got that."

Grant saw the cold, calculating look harden her features. He saw something close to pure evil as she dove for that paper.

Grant stopped her.

Charlie spoke into the stunned silence. "I deliver parcels all over town. The day Pa came to tell Prudence he couldn't go riding with her, after she tricked him into asking her, I looked in her window after Pa told her he wasn't interested in seeing her ever. I saw her with a man. A man standing with his gun drawn, held backward like he was going to hit someone with it.

"You, Pa, if you'd have gone inside. While you were talking to Miss Cartwright, I sneaked inside and hunted around. It didn't take long to find that paper. I knew she was up to something, with all her lies and the way she chased after you. So I kept it."

The parson held up the document for all to see. "That's what this says. She's married. It's dated ten years ago."

Hannah spoke up. "I saw a man in her room the first night I was here. The night of the blizzard. Then again one other time. I didn't know her well enough to wonder who was there, and then I forgot all about it."

Grant looked up to see Hannah pushing her way through the crowd, closer to him.

"And then, when I was delivering to the sheriff's office, I found this." Charlie held up a wanted poster with Prudence's picture and a man's, wanted for pulling cons up and down the Mississippi River.

Prudence slid quickly sideways and reached for the doorknob.

Grant slammed a flat hand against the door to keep it closed. The sheriff fought his way from the back of the crowd and grabbed Shirt Lady's arm. "Let's go across to the jail and talk about this." He looked down at Charlie and studied the wanted poster. "There's a good reward for these two. It looks like that's yours if we can round her husband up."

Charlie said, "Give it to Pa."

"No," Prudence screamed. "It wasn't me. It was my husband, Horace. He's hiding in my shop right now. I'll help you catch him." Prudence's voice rose until it was a wonder she didn't shatter the schoolhouse windows. "He forced me to do this. He beats me. I didn't want to hurt anybody."

Joshua looked more closely at the wanted poster, and his eyes sharpened as he rubbed his head. The stitches were gone, but he'd carry the mark all his days. "That's him. I remember now. That's the man who hit me with his gun butt and knocked me off that cliff."

"We'll want your testimony if it comes to a trial, Josh." The sheriff tucked the poster in his shirt pocket.

"If?" Grant asked. "Why do you say if?"

"These two are wanted for a whole slew of crimes, and they've hurt some powerful people with their cons. That's why the reward is so high. They'll probably want to take them to trial in Mississippi. Here we can charge them with assault and attempted murder, but the charges back East would lock them up for the rest of their lives. I'd as soon see them found guilty back there and be done with them."

The sheriff pulled a clean handkerchief from his pocket and stuffed it in Prudence's mouth. "We want to keep her quiet so we can snag her husband."

"I'll help you bring him in, Ned." Harold went out. Several other men followed.

The door closed.

Parson Babbitt came to Grant's side. "I'm sorry I doubted you, Grant. I know you well enough that I should have taken your side from the first second. It's just"—the parson shook his head—"I've never seen a woman do something like that before. I can't fathom that kind of public humiliation, and to force a marriage."

"But why?" Gladys asked. "Why would she want Grant so bad?"

"Oil." Charlie held up one more piece of paper. Grant really should scold the boy for all his sneaking around.

"What about oil?" the parson asked.

"I found this paper right by the marriage license. Her husband's been digging at the spring. Buckets of oil are worth money if you ship it out of LaMont. He wanted to own Pa's land. She'd have married Pa. Then she'd be part owner."

"B—but how would her being part owner do her husband any good?" Grant was still too befuddled to make sense out of any of this.

"She wouldn't be *part* owner if you were dead, Pa." Charlie scooted closer to Grant. It chilled Grant to realize the vicious plans Prudence and her husband had in store for him. But that chill was swept away as Grant realized his most recent problem child had finally truly joined the family.

Grant rested his hand on the young shoulders. All of the boy's wiliness had paid off for Grant. All the sneaking and lying and stealing had saved the day. Grant knew he had to have a serious talk with the boy.

But maybe not tonight.

Brewster grabbed Charlie by the front of his shirt and lifted him off his feet. "I want you and all of yours out of this school."

Grant's stomach sank, and his eyes flickered to Hannah's face. He was still going to ruin this night she and his children had worked so hard on. But he couldn't let Brewster hurt Charlie. He reached for Brewster.

"You let Charlie go!" The tiny voice brought dead silence to the room.

Grant, along with everyone else, turned toward that voice.

Hannah gasped. "Libby!"

Everyone in town knew about the little girl who never spoke. She charged straight up to Brewster and stood side-by-side with Charlie, her little fists clenched, her jaw tight and angry. Her tiny anger even stopped Brewster in mid-rant.

Grant couldn't hold back a smile as he reached down and picked Libby up. "You spoke. Libby, honey—" Grant wanted to laugh and dance and spin the little girl around, but he didn't want to scare her back into her shell of silence.

Charlie looked up at the little sister he'd ridden into town with. "Hey, Lib. You've got a pretty voice."

"Thanks, Charlie." Libby's sweet smile bloomed.

Hannah came to Grant's side and grabbed Libby out of his arms. "Oh, Libby, honey, honey, you talked!" She looked to be planning on the dance Grant had thought better of. He smiled as Hannah gave Libby a kiss on the cheek.

Grant saw the love and joy shining in Hannah's eyes.

When Hannah glanced at him, her cheeks flushed a bit and she whispered, "Libby is my little sister."

"Your sister?" Grant tried to add and subtract all that Hannah was telling him. "That's why you tried to mess things up at the train station? You wanted her to come with you?"

"Not really. I mean, we had a plan that she'd just duck away from the train and get herself left behind. Then the two of us would hide. We knew no one would let me keep her if we asked permission, but we pulled the same trick in Omaha and it worked. Of course we were supposed to be in a big anonymous city. Not tiny Sour Springs."

Hannah caught Grant's arm, her touch gentle, her eyes warm. "We never dreamed anyone would adopt a little girl with a limp. When you took her, I could only think of Parrish, my adoptive father, and how cruel he was, how he made us work in the carpet mill then took all our money and barely fed us. I didn't know a man could ever be so kind."

Hannah's hand settled on Libby's back. "And now she finally feels safe. Safe enough to speak. Safe enough to fight a bully to protect her big brother."

Grant took Libby back and was honored that Hannah let him have his daughter.

Libby twisted in Grant's arms, glared at Brewster, and jabbed a finger right at his nose. "I'm not going to let you hurt my brother."

"We're not going to let it happen either, little gal."

Grant looked past Libby and saw the parson, determined and focused right on Brewster.

The parson, a man of peace, took hold of the town bully. All of a sudden ten sets of hands were laid firmly on the bully's arms and shoulders.

Will, Ian, Joshua, Doc Morgan, Zeb, Quincy, more and more people throwing into this fight on Grant's side. He'd learned to expect the worst from this town, but now they were standing with him.

Festus's hands were wrenched loose from Charlie's shirt without any blows being landed. Charlie slipped away and the crowd closed around Festus.

The parson spoke for all of them. "God says to turn the other cheek, but tonight I think He's on our side. He doesn't expect good people to quietly stand by while a bully abuses a child. We won't let you hurt one of God's precious children."

Festus wrenched against the hands restraining him.

"And they're all his children, Festus," Quincy Harrison added. "Wherever they were born and however they came to be in our lives."

"Harrison, you've always been on my side." Festus raised his glowering eyebrows at Quincy.

"And I've always been wrong," Quincy replied. "I've seen the error of my ways, and I'll not side with you while you harm these youngsters. I'll not stand by while you hurt this fine young boy or Grant or anyone else in this town."

When Festus looked around and saw everyone in the town siding against him he quit struggling.

"Caring for children is a sacred trust." The parson took his hands off Brewster and pushed Grant aside so he faced the man. Grant, holding Libby tight, gave way.

"God's given that trust to you, Mr. Brewster. He's given you children who can grow up hating like you do or loving as God wants them to." The parson quoted: " 'But whoso shall offend one of these little ones which believe in me, it were better for him that a millstone were hanged about his neck, and that he were drowned in the depth of the sea.' "

They were familiar words. The parson's voice was as clear as a night sky. As pure as God's Son and His sacrifice of love.

"You will behave decently tonight or you will be thrown out. Your choice, Brewster."

Festus didn't answer.

"And from this day on," the parson added, "if you harm Grant or one of his children or anyone else, you will answer to the whole town."

The parson's voice lost its edge and became softer, kinder. "Festus, please, if you only knew how much God loved you, all the turmoil would be gone from your life. God wants to fill you with His peace."

"Peace?" A look of longing shone on Festus's face so intense and personal that Grant felt he should look away.

"Yes. Do you stay in peace or leave this building?"

Grant saw the war inside Brewster and prayed. It was the first time in Grant's life that he'd ever been able to pray for Festus.

Finally, into the endless quiet, speaking barely above a whisper, Festus said, "I. . .I'd like to stay."

The parson laid his hand on Festus's head like a baptism. "Good. I'm glad. And later I'll walk home with you and your family. You've got some decisions to make about your life."

"Can we have the pageant now?" Libby spoke into the silence, and the exasperation in her voice broke everyone into laughter.

Into the chaos Hannah spoke, "Let's get on with it."

Everyone filed into the schoolroom and settled into chairs. Grant felt the presence of the Holy Ghost in that room on that warm spring night.

The children lined up. All of them recited the old familiar story of Jesus' crucifixion and resurrection. It sounded fresh coming from childish lips.

The highlight of the night came near the end.

It was impossible that Hannah had planned for Libby to have a speaking role. But now, from the place she'd stood in the front row, singing along, Libby stepped forward. Reading from a slate, Hannah must have quickly written up for her, Libby's voice rang out. " 'Go ye therefore, and teach all nations, baptizing them in the name of the Father, and of the Son, and of the Holy Ghost. Teaching them to observe all things whatsoever I have commanded you: and, lo, I am with you always, even unto the end of the world. Amen.' "

Grant prayed that he lived up to the Great Commission. He prayed that, in his own small corner of the world, he did teach. He did baptize. He did spread the word, at least to his own children, that God was with them.

The whole building finished the program with a quiet verse of "Just as I Am." As the song faded, the parson said a quiet closing prayer.

When Grant saw Festus Brewster bow his head, Grant realized he couldn't hold on to the foolish promise he'd made to himself to avoid Hannah. She deserved to be thanked for all her work and the new sense of closeness and community she'd brought to Sour Springs.

Grant went over and took her hand. "The pageant went perfectly."

TWENTY-NINE

The pageant was a disaster." Hannah smiled despite the fact that she was dead serious. "What are you talking about?"

"No, it wasn't," Grant objected.

"We had six little singers who kept running down to sit with their parents. I could barely hear the students saying their parts over the din. Gordy tripped over his robe, landed on Emory, and the two rolled down the risers punching each other. Benny and Libby got into a tug-of-war over the cross and ended up in a slap fight, and—"

Marilyn rushed up, interrupting Hannah. Grant's daughter's face blazed so pink Hannah could see the blush in the part of her white-blond hair. "I can't believe I pushed that big paper stone, and it started rolling and knocked into Megan holding her baby. If Ian hadn't moved so fast, I could have hurt them both."

Hannah patted her shoulder. "It's a good lesson to learn."

"Why's that?" Grant asked.

Hannah grimaced. "I have plans for a Christmas program next winter, and I considered asking Megan if we could use her baby."

Marilyn gasped in horror and covered her face with her hands. "No, the poor little thing will never survive!"

"I'm sure Benny wouldn't stage a tug-of-war over a real baby like he did with the cross." Hannah had a brief vision of Benny and Libby doing just that and shuddered. "We'll think of something."

"Those were all little things," Grant said. "The pageant was perfect."

Hannah shook her head.

"I'm never going to convince Wilbur to marry me now," Marilyn said. "He'll be scared to death of what might happen to our children."

A young man Hannah thought had better be Wilbur came up behind Marilyn and hooked his arm around her slender waist. "You're not getting out of marrying me," he said, talking into the back of her neck. "I think you're gonna be about the finest mother who ever lived." He dragged a giggling Marilyn away.

"I'd better get Marilyn through her books quick." Hannah turned and smiled at Grant. "I've heard Wilbur's clearing land for his house."

Grant stepped just a bit closer to Hannah. "I want you to know—"

Megan came up beside them. "Thanks so much, Miss Cartwright." She put her arm around Grant. "Didn't know if I'd make it here or not, Pa. Ian kicked up a fuss, but I wouldn't hear of missing it. You know how Ian is."

"I know." Grant nodded. "It won't be long now."

"Till you're a grandpa again." Megan started laughing and several others around her joined in. Even Hannah had to laugh at Grant, so young, being a grandpa.

Grant crossed his arms and furrowed his brow. "This'n'll be my tenth grandchild. I'm used to it."

The whole crowd laughed again.

Gladys had helped arrange for cookies and cider, and the parson said a heartfelt prayer.

The party began winding down and the crowd headed for home.

As they stepped outside, Will held his lantern up to light the way to the hitching post.

Hannah watched them all leave then closed up the schoolhouse, her heart singing with the success of the Easter pageant, despite the fiasco with that horrible Prudence. Her heart still glowed with the kind words and the many thanks.

With a smile, she walked through the quiet night. Her pleasure faded as she let herself into her lonely room. Tomorrow was Easter, a day that was the foundation of her faith. But it would just be another lonely day for Hannah.

Of course Parrish had never made the day memorable. Once she'd escaped Parrish and lived in one hideaway or another with her collection of brothers and sisters, she'd spent Easter focusing on the holiness of the day, but she'd rarely gone to church or had the means to prepare a special meal. At least tomorrow she'd attend services.

She realized as she prepared for bed that she didn't even have any food in her room. The diner and mercantile were closed tomorrow because of the holiday, so she couldn't buy any. The pageant and the Brewsters had claimed all her attention for so long that she'd neglected almost everything else. With a sigh, Hannah realized she'd have to go without food on Easter. Well, she'd done without food before. It wouldn't kill her.

The night had cooled and the diner's heat had burned away and faded. So she'd be cold as well as hungry. After all she'd survived in her life, she didn't mind her little room and an occasional day of cold and hunger. She did mind the loneliness though. She'd never been alone on Easter before.

Self-pity grew and she indulged herself in it as the loneliness overwhelmed her. She wept into her pillow even as she knew she was being selfish.

Libby was safe at the Rocking C.

She prayed for her big sister, Grace, and wondered if she'd ever know what happened to her. After the foolish tears were spent, she settled into her cold little bed.

As Hannah walked out of church the next morning, Charlie rushed up beside her. "Miss Cartwright, have you made plans for today?"

Hannah smiled down at him. "No, I haven't."

"We'd like you to come out and celebrate Easter with us at the Rocking C. Joshua bagged himself a huge turkey, and the girls have been baking since dawn. A lot of Pa's grown children are coming and bringing food along. We're going to have more food than even all of us can eat. We'd like it very much if you could come."

"Well, I don't know." Of course the answer was no, but Charlie looked so hopeful. Hannah decided she'd find Grant to turn down the invitation rather than disappoint Charlie.

The crowd was thinning fast, everyone hurrying home to their Easter dinners. Grant was nowhere in sight. She didn't see his wagon either, or any other of his children.

"Do you know the way through the pass?"

"I know the way."

"Then I'll head back. Put your riding skirt on, and I'll tell Zeb to have any horse but Rufus saddled up for you and waiting out front of the diner."

Hannah nodded but didn't answer his question. There was no possible way she could spend the day with Grant.

Charlie headed toward the livery that would, Hannah realized, be closed today. Charlie would figure that out soon enough.

Hannah hurried around the church, searching for Grant to tell him she couldn't come. His wagon was nowhere to be found. She hurried toward the livery, but Charlie had vanished and the building was locked up tight.

Not sure what to do, she walked home to find a quiet, gentle-looking mare standing, bridled and saddled, right outside her door. "Charlie!" Hannah's voice seemed to echo down the deserted Sour Springs street. Charlie didn't answer. With a shake of her head, she admitted she was thrilled to not spend the day alone and rushed inside and ran upstairs to change into her riding skirt.

The horse behaved perfectly and the high trail was clear and dry.

When she rode up to the Rocking C, she pulled the reins so abruptly the horse backed up a few paces. Where had Grant's little cabin gone?

A sprawling log ranch house stood where the humble home had been. So completely had it been transformed, Hannah could barely remember the other house. The center jutted out nearly twenty feet farther than it had. There were impressive additions on each side and the roof was higher. It wasn't just bigger, someone had taken the time to make it beautiful. A neat porch with dozens of slender support spindles graced the front. There were shutters on each window, and the land around the house had been leveled with well-rocked paths leading to the barn. It looked like someone had worked himself near to death to make it so lovely.

And the children were all outside. Hannah remembered that Grant had said the children spent all their time outside, and from the looks of things, it was the absolute truth. Libby ran along, keeping up with Benny, her limp a distant memory. They chased after Charlie, whose sullen scowl was long gone. Joshua rode his horse toward the corral. The two older girls sat on the porch steps visiting.

Benny yelled, "Miss Cartwright's here."

Joshua tipped his hat at Hannah. "Happy Easter, Miss Cartwright!"

Hannah noticed that Joshua carried himself with the same assurance as Grant.

Charlie came over and held her horse. "Glad you could make it, Miss Cartwright."

"Hannah!" Libby came running toward her, and Hannah swept her little sister up in her arms and had to swallow back tears at the sound of her voice.

Marilyn and Sadie got up and walked toward her with all the poise of women. The air fairly rang with "Miss Cartwright" and "Happy Easter," shouted by six happy children.

Hannah remembered last Easter, Libby and her alone in a cold, dilapidated shed with only stale bread to eat. The change from last year to this was nothing short of miraculous. She couldn't remember another time in her life when she'd been welcomed into a family like this.

Regaining her composure, she thanked Charlie for his help with the horse and headed for the house carrying Libby.

"Are you going to help us cook, Miss Cartwright?" There was no missing the fear in Sadie's voice.

Hannah couldn't help but laugh. "No, your meal is safe."

Hannah would have said for sure that a black person couldn't blush, but Sadie proved her wrong. Then all the children started laughing and the awkward moment passed.

The children thronged around her. Even Joshua hurried out of the barn to join them. Hannah and the children headed for the greatly enlarged house, not a cabin at all anymore. "Do all of you have your own rooms now?"

"Some of us still have to share." Joshua fell into step beside Sadie. "Pa turned the back room into an entryway like it was supposed to be, although he made it way bigger and stuck two more bedrooms on the back. He tore out the wall to the old bedrooms to make the kitchen bigger and pushed the front wall out a whole bunch. Then he added two bedrooms on one side, plus the loft is three times as wide as it was and twice as high. So we have five bedrooms counting the loft."

Hannah noticed Sadie steal a glance at Joshua. Had Grant noticed the attachment between these two?

"I have my own room," Benny bragged. "I have the loft to myself, and it's huge cuz Pa made the kitchen huger'n ever."

Hannah's eyebrows arched. "It sounds like he's been busy." He'd never come again after he'd built the risers, until last night. She'd noticed because she'd been wondering if he might steal another kiss. Not that she wanted one, but a girl could wonder. . .couldn't she?

"We all helped." Benny rammed his shoulder into Charlie, and Charlie smiled and slung his arm around his little brother's neck. The two looked like they'd become best friends in the months since Hannah had found Benny bleeding from Charlie's assault.

"Marilyn and I have been sharing a room so we decided to stay together," Sadie said.

"Especially since I'm getting married soon," Marilyn added with a shy smile.

"You're planning to finish school first, aren't you?" Hannah asked with a stern frown.

Marilyn nodded. "With spring work, Wilbur might be awhile finishing the cabin. I'll be through all my books by the end of this term."

Hannah studied the girl. Marilyn was telling the truth, but Hannah had seen a determined light in Wilbur's eyes last night. Hannah decided to push Marilyn through her books fast.

"And I've already filed a homestead claim." Joshua shook his head at the new house. "We've got this great big house after all these years. Pa'll rattle around in it with the two of us gone." He glanced at Sadie again and the two smiled at each other.

Hannah subtracted another child from the house very soon because Sadie wanted to be with Joshua, and though she was young, she was a mature young woman who knew her own mind. That left Grant with three children in this sprawling home.

"I've got the biggest room." Benny puffed out his chest.

Sadie sniffed and gave her little brother a gentle shove. "You might have the biggest room, but ours is the warmest cuz it's closer to the fireplace. And it's the prettiest. It doesn't matter how crowded it is when we sleep. We never go inside 'cept for bedtime and meals anyway. I think Pa's gonna need more kids. It's gonna be lonely with only four of us, plus Pa."

"Only four children. . .what a tiny family." Joshua shook his head and smiled down at Sadie. "I want lots more kids than that."

Sadie shoved him sideways, and he pretended to stagger and nearly fall.

The whole group started laughing.

"It's a good thing he made the kitchen huge because Will's family is coming today and a bunch of our other brothers and sisters," Benny added. "We have the biggest and bestest family get-togethers of anyone."

"Ian and Megan can't come," Sadie reminded them. "Ian's too nervous."

They all laughed over that. High holiday spirits nearly burst out of them as they dragged Hannah toward their new home.

Then Grant rode into the yard.

Hannah only had to look at him for a second to see he had no idea she was coming for dinner.

She turned a dismayed look on Charlie.

He smiled at her and held the door open to the ranch house. He leaned close enough to her to whisper, "Trust me."

Although it made absolutely no sense, Hannah did.

THIRTY

G rant turned away from the celebration in front of him the minute
Hannah went in the house surrounded by his children. Riding his
horse into the barn, he got down, his movements uncoordinated. He
pulled the leather off his horse with unsteady hands and gave it an extra
bit of grain to avoid going inside for a little longer.

"What is she doing here?" He asked the question directly to God.

With no excuse not to go in, Grant turned toward the house and
came to a dead stop, afraid of what he'd say if he had so much as a second
alone with her. And he knew what he'd promised God and the desperate
need of all the orphaned children in the world.

"God, why did You let her come here?" Grant heard no thunderous
voice. No finger of fire carved answers like commandments on stone. No
burning bush spoke to him. No still, small voice whispered to his heart.

He was so alone in his barn, with his family all surrounding Hannah
in his house, that his ears almost echoed with the aloneness. Grant knew
that somehow the answer to all his aloneness was in that house and in
that woman.

Grant, alone in the empty barn, asked, "What about my promise,
God? What about all the children who need me?" Grant ran his hands
over his face, trying to wash away the temptation to be selfish away. "I
had a good reason for that promise. There are still orphans suffering.

"I can't give as much to a child if I have a wife to consider and children of my own." Something bloomed in Grant's heart as he thought about having children of his own, maybe a son with speckled eyes. Maybe a daughter with Hannah's brown curls.

He needed to trust God with his loneliness. He needed to trust Hannah with his love. A weight lifted, and Grant looked up to heaven to thank God.

When he lowered his eyes, he saw Hannah coming into the barn. Looking a bit fearful, she said, "Dinner is almost ready. Will's here and several other families are coming down the trail." Hannah's lips trembled. "You know it will be the first Easter dinner of my life?"

Her expression turned so vulnerable Grant couldn't stay away. Walking toward Hannah, he walked toward his future. She kept moving in his direction just as steady and solid as the mountain behind his home.

They met, and Grant reached out to grasp her hands. "You can be with me for every holiday from now on, Hannah. You can be a mother to all these children. They've already claimed you anyway."

Grant lifted her left hand and kissed it. "I love you. I think I fell in love with you when you crawled under my kitchen table chasing potatoes."

Hannah smiled warm enough to bring summer to Texas. "And I've loved you ever since you spent an afternoon fixing up Libby's shoe so she could walk without a limp. Even when it went against every hard-learned lesson of my life, I still loved you."

"Will you marry me, Hannah? Will you join our family and make our house a home?"

Hannah hesitated, and Grant's heart dived hard enough it'd break if it hit bottom.

"I have a lot to learn about how to be a woman. My upbringing didn't teach me a lot of what I need to know."

Grant's heart didn't crash after all. He smiled and then he laughed. "You'll learn." He wrapped his arms around her waist and lifted her off the floor. He swung her around joyfully, and she squeaked a little and laughed with him.

"Between Sadie and Marilyn and me, we'll teach you all you need to know." Grant lowered her to her feet and kissed her. Not the stolen kiss of those brief times at the schoolhouse, but the honorable kiss of the only man who would ever be given leave to kiss her.

He lifted his head, his heart thundering. "Shall we go in and tell the children?"

"Yes, I can't wait."

They turned to leave the barn. She'd never change her mind if it meant disappointing them. He slipped his arm around her waist and urged her along.

Hannah started moving, such a perfect fit in his arms that Grant decided he was never going to let her go, not even for one more day.

Hannah moved closer to him as if she was cold. She leaned against his shoulder. He thought his shoulder was the perfect size and plenty strong. She could lean on him for the rest of her life.

"You know, you're younger than quite a few of my children."

Hannah's brow furrowed. Then she shrugged and smiled. "Considering Ian's age, you're almost younger than a few of your children. That's a tricky thing to explain."

The wonder of her, alive and loving in his arms, was nearly too sweet for him to bear. They opened the ranch house door, and Grant saw a couple dozen sets of shining eyes staring straight at them, Will and his family, and several others.

"I asked Hannah to marry me. She said yes."

The children exploded with noise and hugs.

In the midst of the chaos, Hannah pulled Libby into her arms in a way that let Grant know how much she'd missed her little sister. His heart overflowed just watching them be truly reunited.

He looked past his present brood of children and saw wagons and horses hitched here and there. The rest of his family had arrived. His family finally had a ma. The dinner was forgotten for a long time as they celebrated this special day.

After they ate, the whole family hitched up the wagon and went to town for a wedding. Grant pulled his wagon up beside the church, Hannah at his side, the wagon box full of children.

He looked behind him and saw what amounted to a parade, following him down Sour Springs Main Street. Doors started opening as curious townsfolk noticed the commotion.

Putting on the brake, Grant scrambled to beat his sons to Hannah's side and help her down. Joshua slapped him on the back. Ian came out of his house behind the blacksmith shop with his hand resting on Megan's back and his daughter hanging from his hand. Gordy saw Benny and Libby and dashed toward the crowd.

Will laughed and shouted, "Everybody's invited to a wedding!"

Grant lowered Hannah to the ground, her face shining with excitement. Something caught in Grant's throat to think this beautiful, smart, feisty, loving woman was excited. Excited to marry *him* of all people.

Suddenly he knew everything in his life had been preparing him to love this woman the way she needed to be loved, and her life had been a preparation to be his perfect match. He could thank God for the things he'd been through, even thank Him for the things many hurting children were going through. Ian being sent out here when he was so old. . .because Megan was here. Josh and Sadie. . .the streets had prepared them for each other. And Marilyn and Wilbur. Somehow Wilbur, from a strong family with two great parents, had grown up to have that perfect place in his heart for Marilyn with her broken past.

He could breathe more deeply, thank God more fully. His eyes open, his head unbowed, Grant could still pray his thanks with every step.

A hard slap on his back made him realize he'd been holding Hannah, her toes still dangling off the ground, smiling like a maniac as he watched her and prayed.

"Put her down." Will came up beside him. "And if you'd like to have a little talk about the facts of married life, I'll be right here to help you. . .Pa."

The whole crowd erupted into laughter. Grant gave Will a sheepish grin and didn't admit he had a few questions. He reluctantly put Hannah on the ground and slid his arm around her while he gave his irreverent son a shove.

The parson came out of his home, which was next door to the church, and quickly caught on to the celebration. His wife was a few steps behind him.

Walking arm-in-arm with Hannah, Grant approached him. "Can we tear you away from your Easter dinner to perform a wedding ceremony?"

The parson smiled. "I'd be proud to, Grant."

As they headed in, Sheriff Ned came up beside Charlie. Grant noticed and stopped to listen.

"We picked up Horace with no trouble. And by the time those two got done accusing each other of being the real bad guy, we had confessions for a lifetime of criminal activity. You've earned that reward, boy. The U.S. Marshal will be bringing five hundred dollars for each of them two crooks within a week."

"A–a thousand dollars?" Charlie's face went pale, and then he turned to Grant. "It's for the family, Pa."

"No, boy, that money's yours. You earned it." Grant still needed to scold Charlie about his sneaking ways. Thinking of a life tied to Shirt Lady made it real hard for Grant to get too upset. But God wouldn't approve of such underhanded means, no matter that it had turned out for good.

Charlie shook his head. "I don't need that kinda money. You'll put it in the bank for us, won't you, Sheriff? In Pa's account?"

The sheriff nodded.

"We'll settle this later," Grant said, mussing Charlie's hair. He needed to pray about whether it was right to give a young boy so much money. . . especially as a reward for being a sneak thief.

There wasn't much ceremony to the wedding. Grant refused to turn loose of Hannah long enough to let her walk down the aisle. The only delay was in having the guests troop in, which took awhile considering the whole town was idle and available due to it being Easter Sunday.

Grant held both her hands, and she held on just as tight, while the parson had them swear vows before God. Never in history, at least Grant couldn't imagine it, had vows been given with such sincerity.

Grant barely had time to kiss the bride before his whole family surrounded them to offer congratulations.

The townsfolk all brought out their leftovers from Easter dinner and turned the wedding into a party that lasted until the sun set. Grant's grown-up children were the last to leave the reception.

Grant turned to his new wife. "Let's stop at your room and get your things, Hannah."

Hannah smiled. "I'll be glad to see the last of that place."

Grant followed her upstairs with all of the children coming behind to help carry things.

Except there were no things, or almost none.

"Charlie said this was small." Grant was appalled at the size of the room. His head came to the peak of the roof, which slanted sharply. "And where are your things?"

Hannah blushed and pointed to a small pile of clothes that tucked easily into her satchel. She also produced proudly two dollars and fifteen cents.

"I've been saving my wages."

Grant turned to the children who were pushing their way inside. "Go on back down kids. There isn't room for all of us in here." The understatement of a lifetime.

They all seemed to need peeks. Then they grabbed the few bits of Hannah's possessions, ran into each other coming and going, but finally were all gone.

"You've been living here for three months?" Grant ran his hand up and down Hannah's arm.

With a reluctant nod, Hannah said, "It's awful, isn't it? Let's get out of here and go live in the mansion you built."

Grant kissed the pretty smile right off Hannah's face, caught her hand, and they left behind the teacher's quarters for good. He headed home with his wife. Newlyweds who already had six kids.

After a festive evening meal, Grant wanted to suggest the children all head for bed. It was a little early, but he had a powerful yen for some quiet time with Hannah. A pang of guilt hit him for wanting his children to go away. Truth to tell, he wasn't sure just what the point was of quiet time with Hannah.

From the looks of Megan, Ian had figured out what to do with a wife. Grant would die before he'd ask his son's advice.

Of course he lived on a ranch. He had a fair notion.

Marilyn left for a ride with Wilbur.

Hannah took the last coffee cups into the kitchen to wash. Grant looked after her, confused and fascinated.

He rose from his chair and opened his mouth to shoo the children off to bed just as his front door slammed open and a wild-eyed woman rushed in.

Grant backed away. The woman looked unhinged and that was a fact.

"Hannah?" She shouted so loud Grant was tempted to cover his ears. "I heard Hannah was here."

Before anyone could answer, an explosion of noise and shoving came through the open door. Five boys arguing at the top of their lungs clogged in the door, battling to get through first.

"Climbing out of that canyon is stupid an' if you do stupid things, you're stupid, an' that's that."

The boys came in two sizes. Medium and large. One of the medium ones ripped his hat off his head and whacked one of the larger ones in the face. They had to be brothers—no brood could look this much alike and not be.

"Hannah, where are you?" The blond-haired madwoman ran into a side bedroom.

Grant hoped this wasn't another one like Shirt Lady. He stayed well away from her.

"Don't you be calling Ma stupid." Blinded, the bigger boy fell over the younger, and both landed on the floor so hard the lantern sitting in the center of the table rattled.

The wrestling boys shouted. The larger one roared through his fingers as he rubbed his stinging face. "That ain't right to insult her like that, Mark."

"But it *is* stupid." The smaller boy jumped out of the fight, threw his coat toward a pair of antlers on the wall, missed, and hit another boy in the face with the garment.

"Hannah! Hannah, are you here?" The crazed woman dashed back into the room shouting, ignoring the chaos in her wake.

"Don't call me stupid, stupid." Mark was knocked sideways by a smaller child yet. Grant hadn't noticed him at first. Three sizes. Small, medium, and large. The toddler jumped on Mark's back, screaming until Grant thought his ears might bleed.

The toddler grabbed Mark around the neck and pretended his feet had spurs and Mark was a stubborn horse. The little boy screamed for Mark to "Giddyup."

"Hannah!" The female voice cut through the chorus of shouting boys.

A giant replica of all of them came into the house last. "Man oh man, was it ever stupid to come all this way, Grace."

"Grace?" Hannah came dashing in from the kitchen then froze for just a second until Grace, ignoring the riot that came in the door after her, and the terrible insults being hurled right and left, turned and looked at her.

"Hannah?" With a little scream, Grace threw her arms wide. "Oh, Hannah." Grace ran toward Hannah, and Hannah ran toward Grace.

They caught each other and swung each other around in a circle, laughing and crying at the same time. Grant had heard enough about

Hannah's childhood now to know who Grace was. But he'd never expected her to come with a crowd attached.

Joshua quickly snatched the lantern off the table and left the room with it and another breakable lamp. Sadie backed Benny and Libby into a corner to guard them, and Joshua came back and stood beside her. Benny looked between them, thrilled to see the newcomers.

Charlie scaled the ladder to the loft with a third lantern so it was out of reach but the room didn't fall into complete darkness. He left it well back from the side of the attic, swung his legs over the edge, and began climbing down into the fray.

Grant was tempted to yell for Charlie to stay up there where it was safe and send the rest of the family up, too.

Mark began bucking and hurled his younger brother on a flying trip toward the ceiling.

Their father snagged Matthew in midair. Settling his son on his hip, the adult man turned to Grant and offered his hand. "We found someone in town to direct us out here. We just came in on the train. My wife was bound to visit her sister. I'm Daniel Reeves and these are my boys." Daniel seemed to yell every word, far too loud to be explained away by the riot. He swept his arm at the chaos and didn't bother trying to point out who was who.

Grant appreciated that. "I'm Grant Cooper." They shook hands.

"Grace has kinda made a habit of escaping from me this winter. Every time I relax and quit watching her like a hawk, I'll be switched if she doesn't disappear."

Grant did his best to listen to Daniel over the crying women and the screaming boys.

"My contrary wife made me bring her here." Daniel smiled and blushed just a little. "Women are the almightiest hardest critters to figure out, Grant. I can't get mine to be submissive worth a lick. I've got it underlined in the Bible and everything. But she's just plain stubborn."

Grant had been raising girls for nine years. He could probably give

Daniel a little advice. It would start with, "Don't call her stupid. . .or stubborn. . .or a critter."

Then he looked at the six children Daniel had managed to father and wondered if Daniel had some advice that could make the coming night go more smoothly for Grant. Grant had no idea how to ask. "Uh. . . Daniel, did you hear Hannah and I got married today?"

The crying women had turned on Sadie and Libby and were chattering like a flock of chickens.

Hannah pulled Sadie close and introduced her as "my daughter."

Grace began crying as if her heart was breaking.

"What is that infernal woman crying about now?" Daniel pretended to drop Matthew and the boy screamed and laughed. Daniel flipped him upside down, dangling him by one ankle for a couple of seconds while the boy shrieked and swung his fists at his pa's knee. Then Daniel swooshed his son around by the leg, flipped him right side up, and tossed him head first over Daniel's shoulder. The little boy clung like a burr and swung himself around and ended up riding piggyback on his pa.

"Too many menfolk." Grant had seen it all before and accepted it. "Women like to talk to other women from time to time."

Daniel nodded earnestly, soaking in every word Grant said, even though his son was strangling him and yelling for a horsie ride. "She's expecting another young'un, too. Probably die from this one." He looked over at Grace. "I am surely gonna miss that woman."

"Ma's gonna die!" Matthew shouted right into Daniel's ear.

Grace whirled around and fairly screamed. "*I am not going to die*, Daniel Reeves. You quit saying that. If I hear you say that one more time, I swear this is going to be the first baby ever born where we lose a father."

Hannah looked wide-eyed at Daniel. With a glance at Grant, Hannah pulled Grace back into the little circle of women.

Two of the medium-sized boys—they had to be triplets because there were three that were a matched set—rolled under the table wrestling and tipped it over.

Daniel shouted, "You boys get outside!"

Shouting with joy, his boys vanished, along with Benny, leaving the door wide open. Grant, his ears ringing, prayed for his son to survive this visit.

After a moment's hesitation while he looked between the women and the open door, Charlie grabbed his coat and went out after the others. Grant hoped living most of his life on the mean streets made him tough enough to survive the Reeves boys.

The Reeves stayed the night. Grant had no choice but to spend his wedding night with the menfolk in the barn, and Grace slept with Hannah. Grant's children skipped school the next day, and by nightfall, the Reeves family still showed no signs of leaving. Of course the train wouldn't come through for a week, so there was no escaping the Reeves until then.

Grant was ready to start building on to his house, maybe a big playroom with no breakables. Something with a lock on it, so Grant could shoo them in there and pen them up.

By midweek, Grant worked up the nerve to ask Daniel, in carefully discreet terms, about being married. Near as Grant could tell, Daniel thought women were a dangerous temptation from the devil, died at the drop of a hat, and a man with any sense at all would move himself permanently into the barn.

Terrified by Daniel's dire predictions, Grant didn't ask questions after that.

Grant barely kept from tearing his hair out while he waited for the visit to end. The only thing that saved him from a bald head was the joy he saw on Hannah's face—on the few occasions he saw her face since he was living full-time in the bachelor quarters in the barn now—as she talked nonstop with Grace.

Grant did his best not to shout for joy when Daniel declared it to be time to go home. Grace, relaxed and happy, went along with her family without protest.

After the Reeves tornado spun itself back toward west Texas, and Grant repaired the furniture, their home went back to normal.

THIRTY ONE

P eace and quiet at last." Grant sank into his rocking chair, enjoying the relative silence of his household with only eight people in it.

"It just seems quiet without the Reeves." Hannah glanced away from the room and smiled at Grant. "We've still got six children making noise."

Libby looked up from where she sat at the table listening to Marilyn read.

"I think you and Ma had better only have babies one at a time, Pa." Josh pulled his harmonica out of his pocket.

Laughing, Hannah shook her head. "Are you really going to call me Ma, Josh? I'm pretty sure you're older than I am."

Grant settled more firmly in his rocking chair. "I like the sound of Ma. I think you kids had oughta all call her that."

"But she's my sister, Pa." Libby screwed up her face and pouted. "Do I have to call her Ma, too? That's kind of confusing."

Sadie and Joshua started to laugh.

"Well, you could call her Hannah for your sister"—Marilyn pushed the book aside—"Miss Cartwright for your teacher, Ma because she's married to your pa. . . She's right. It is confusing."

"Well, we'll keep it simple and you can call me Ma." Hannah sat struggling over the knitting lesson Sadie and Marilyn had assigned her.

Grant did his best not to laugh at the mass of knots.

"But I declare if Will and Ian start calling me Ma, I don't know if I'll put up with it."

"They can call you Grandma instead." Libby nodded innocently. The whole room erupted into laughter.

Grant jumped to his feet and scooped his little daughter into his arms. Once she'd started talking, the little girl seemed to be catching up for years of silence. "I never get tired of hearing you talk." He danced her around the room, whirling and hoisting her toward the ceiling.

"Say something else, honey," Grant cajoled as he tossed her in the air. "C'mon, let me hear that pretty voice."

Libby giggled. "I love you, Pa."

Grant stopped in midstep. He pulled Libby into a bear hug. "Thank you, sweetheart. The day God brought you and Charlie and your meddling big sister into my life is one of the very best days of my life. And you did that without saying a word."

"I'm not a meddler, Grant Cooper. You take that back." Hannah came and stood in front of him, her hands on her hips, doing her very best to look fierce when the sparkle in her eye told him she was fighting not to laugh.

"I know a way to make Pa behave, Ma." Libby giggled as if saying the word *Ma* was hilarious.

"How's that?"

"Pa's ticklish."

Hannah's eyes zeroed in on him. Benny roared like a Comanche warrior, a six-year-old Comanche warrior. They ended up in a pile on the floor, tickling and laughing and being the biggest, happiest family ever sheltered by a Texas mountain.

And later, when the house was quiet and Grant finally had her alone, he found out Hannah was ticklish, too.

ABOUT THE AUTHOR

MARY CONNEALY is the author of the Lassoed in Texas series which includes *Petticoat Ranch* and *Calico Canyon*. Also coming soon are *Of Mice. . .and Murder*, book one of a three-book series with Heartsong Presents Mysteries, and *Buffalo Gal*, book one of a three-book series for Heartsong Presents. Her novel *Golden Days* is part of the *Alaska Brides* anthology. You can find out more about Mary's upcoming books at www.maryconnealy.com.

Mary lives on a Nebraska farm with her husband, Ivan, and has four grown daughters: Joslyn (married to Matt), Wendy, Shelly (married to Aaron), and Katy.